FOR THE LOVE OF SARA

C.K. LEE

Published by Dolman Scott in 2021

Cover design by Evie Mai Barker

ISBN

978-1-8384967-2-2 – PoD

978-1-8384967-3-9 – iBooks

978-1-8384967-4-6 – Kindle

Dolman Scott Ltd

www.dolmanscott.co.uk

So let us vow a friendship beyond friendship and meet again beyond the stars.

Li Po

PROLOGUE

The pain was no longer intense. A heavy boot crashed into the side of his face and he could hear bone splinter. It echoed around the empty chamber of his head. His head was swollen like a ripe melon, one eye was completely closed. Through the half closed slit of the other eye he could make out the shape of the attacker.

They had flipped her onto her front and splayed her legs into a wishbone. The larger of the two men was kneeling on her arms, pressing her head onto the cold tiles of the church floor. His spade-like hands were tearing at her buttocks. The other man was crazed with excitement. Saliva dripped from the side of his mouth. He shifted on his knees to get a better position between her thighs. Her sobs were quiet now, more like a child's whimper. Then she screamed a scream so loud as to wake every tormented soul in Hell as her attacker forced the full length of his organ into her. That's when Grant blacked out.

CHAPTER 1

A thin chink of sunlight broke through the heavy drape curtain making a triangle of light on the nude on the wall. It was only a print, but a limited edition print. Grant had often wondered who she was. It's how he imagined Helen of Troy might have looked. But why were all Greek goddesses portrayed as tall and willowy with long golden tresses when all the Greek women he had met were small, dark and invariably had a moustache? He smiled and thought about getting up.

It was 5.36 according to the radio alarm perched on a shelf under the picture. The plane was not due to take off until ten and all the packing had been done. Jill had seen to that. In her own inimitable way everything had been packed the night before, only the toilet bags to be included. Toilet bags, what an unfortunate term, sanitary bags? No, that was even worse.

He wondered if any of the children were up. The youngest two had still been awake when he and Jill had eventually gone to bed. They were so excited. It was to be their first time on a plane. Emma and Tim, the elder two, were old hands at flying.

"Don't worry, Ben," Tim had chided his younger brother. "If we do crash, you probably won't feel a thing."

There was no sound from the bedroom next door, so he guessed the children must still be asleep. He propped himself up on one elbow and looked down in to the face of his wife. She was beginning to show her age, but was still an attractive woman. The four children had taken their toll on her 41 year-old body. Her breasts were now spread to either side of her chest. Her nipples were flat, like huge pimpled saucers. There were crow's feet around the corner of her eyes, those oh so blue, blue eyes. The skin, once rosy pink was now tightly drawn over her high cheekbones and had a slightly yellow hue.

Their lovemaking the night before had not been earth shattering. Sex had become more of a routine for her, but remained a hungry need for Grant. Even when they had married twenty years ago it was never that good. He had never found the right button to turn her on. It didn't seem to bother her, but it bothered Grant. Maybe if she had made love to someone else? But she never had. They met as teenagers and married four years later, their virginity a wedding gift to each other.

Maybe she should have had someone else. Maybe she will meet someone on this holiday – drink too much sangria and cop off with a couple of waiters. His hand wandered to his groin. Thinking of her with other men had always given him an erection. He was just about to take one of her exposed nipples in his mouth when he heard the bedroom door open. He pulled the duvet over her just as Ben poked his head around the door.

"Is it time to get up yet?" he asked.

Jill opened her eyes.

"What time is it?" She yawned and stretched leaving the duvet in danger of falling. She snuggled it close.

"Is anyone else up?"

"No only me," said Ben. "Here mum, I had a dream last night and in it the plane did crash and it did hurt, not like Tim said."

"And where did they bury the survivors?" Grant joked.

"Don't be silly dad, they don't bury survivors. I'm getting up," and with that he disappeared round the door.

"That's funny," said Grant, putting his hand under the duvet, around his wife's waist. I was about to do the same thing just before he came in." Jill removed his hand, not amused. "I think you need a shower," she said clutching the duvet tightly, "preferably a cold one."

CHAPTER 2

In Yorkshire the sun was peeping above Boulsworth Hill, 1700ft up in the Pennines. Sara blinked as her mother pulled the curtains apart, flooding the room with light. The walls were covered in posters. James Dean looked down on her. How often had she imagined his strong arms around her. How often had he whisked her away from the village on the back of his Harley-Davidson. How many times had she wished there were boys in the village like James Dean, not just the spotty yobs who hung around her.

She had only had one boyfriend, Jeff, who worked at the stables where she kept her pony. Sara was crazy about horses and rode as often as she could. Jeff and his family were new to the village. They had moved from Hong Kong where his father had been in banking. Jeff told fascinating stories about life in the former colony. He was like a breath of fresh air from Wadsworth Moor in an environment in which Sara was becoming increasingly bored. None of the village lads had been further than Bradford, let alone Beijing. The other thing Sara liked about Jeff was that he never tried anything on with her when they were alone. The village boys were always trying to grope her. She had once been foolish enough to let Adam Cochrane, the local gang leader, kiss her. The next day it was all around the village that she was "easy".

She visited the stables every day, mucking out in exchange for free board and keep for the pony her father had brought her – the day he had died.

It was to have been the happiest day of her life. She had nagged her parents to buy her the 14-year-old black and tan pony. The riding school no longer wanted it. She was convinced they were going to sell it to the slaughter house over at Harrowgate. It wouldn't have been the first time that old horses from the stables had been picked up by the knacker's van. Sara couldn't bear the thought of Scout sharing the same fate. With love and attention he would be good for a few years yet, besides, Sara had been riding him for six years. Her mother had said she couldn't have her own horse, but she had managed to sweet-talk her father. She could always get around him. When he dropped her off at the stables on the morning of her fifteenth birthday and told her Scout was officially hers, she thought he was the most marvellous man in the world.

She had stayed at the stables to groom him. On the drive home, her father's car was struck by an articulated lorry. He was dead on arrival at Bradford General Hospital. Multiple head injuries they said. Just as well he had been killed outright. If he had survived the crash he would have been a vegetable.

Far from being in a dream-like haze, Sara could remember every detail of that dreadful day. She remembered getting a lift home from Susie, one of the stable hands. She remembered the police cars outside the home and the look on the face of Mrs Jenkins their next door neighbour, how she looked away as Sara got out of the car. At first she thought they might have been burgled. There had been several break-ins around the village. Many people thought Adam Cochrane was behind them.

"You stay away from that lad," her father had told her.

It was not until she saw the look on the policewoman's face as she entered the hall. Then she heard her mother's sobs coming from the front room. Then everything went into slow motion. Her mother looked up. Her voice seemed slurred.

"Sara, its Daddy, he's dead." It was five words that collapsed her world. Then everything speeded up. She rushed at her mother, fists clenched and pounded at her.

"He's not dead, he's not," she screamed, sobbing, angry, frustrated. It was her uncle Alan who moved in to grip her arms and pull her away.

"Get off me," she hissed. "Don't touch me. Don't ever touch me." And with that she turned and with tears staining her face ran upstairs to her bedroom, slamming the door behind her.

Alan put a comforting arm around his sister-in-law. "She'll come round, Liz. She's in shock. I guess we all are."

In her room, Sara sat huddled up in a ball. Through eyes blurred with tears, she looked at the small photograph she kept on her bedside table, a picture of her father as a child. People always said how much alike they looked. If it hadn't been for Scout, he would still be alive. It was only because he had taken her to see that stupid pony he was dead. It was Scout's fault. I hate him, I hate him. She sobbed again. It wasn't the pony's fault, it was her fault. If she hadn't kept nagging him to buy Scout, he would be alive now. If only she hadn't gone to the stables. It was her fault. Then the sobs came again.

It was some time later that she fell asleep, curled in a ball, her long blonde hair matted to her tear-soaked cheek. She was on the back of Adam Cochrane's motor bike outside the phone box on the village green. Jeff was standing nearby eating Chinese take-away out of an aluminium carton using chopsticks. Adam was grinning.

"Hold on tight," Adam told her.

She gripped him tightly around his waist. He revved the bike. Now it was her father standing there eating Chinese.

"You stay away from that lad," he warned her again, but it was too late. Adam throttled the accelerator and let out the clutch. The powerful bike reared up and Sara had to cling on as they roared away. She tried to look round Adam's shoulder, but the wind in her face was too strong so she snuggled close to his back and watched the hedgerows speed past. A mixture of fear and excitement made her stomach tingle. The bike showed no sign of slowing. Adam ignored the give way sign at the crossroads and made a mad whoop as they sped across. Then the bike slowed enough for Sara to look over Adam's shoulder. They were in Featherbed Lane leading to the stables. In the middle of the road ahead, Sara saw her father sitting astride Scout. Adam accelerated towards them. She could see the look of terror in the pony's eye as the machine bore down on them.

"No, stop," she screamed.

She was shaken awake by her mother.

"Sara, Sara, it's all right. You are having a bad dream. Wake up." Her mother cradled her in her arms.

"Everything will be all right, I promise."

She heard the words, but didn't believe them. Nothing would ever be right again.

She remembered every detail of the funeral. Her mother wore a black crocheted dress which Sara thought was too short. Crocus and daffodils decorated the lush green carpet of the cemetery lawn. Yellow roses adorned the coffin. She remembered how pale the mourners looked – many of them strangers to her. She remembered how cold it seemed inside the church as the congregation sang All Things Bright and Beautiful. A shaft of sunlight came through the stained glass windows and shone directly onto the coffin. She remembered the whispered words of the relatives back at the house for the wake, the egg and cress bridge rolls, the candlesticks and condolences.

When everyone had left, Sara went to her bedroom and sobbed. She wanted her mother to come and comfort her, to share in this terrible grief, but she didn't come and Sara cried alone.

It had been six months since the accident. Accident, what bloody accident? It was no accident. God had made it happen. It was his fault.

The insurance money on the life assurance had come through and her mother had decided they needed a holiday and that they should go to Spain.

"It will be nice, just the two of us," Sara had told her mother.

"Well there won't just be two of us, Sara, "said her mother, "your uncle Alan will be joining us."

Alan was her father's older brother. A thick set man in his late forties, he had been a frequent visitor to the house both before and after her father's death. He was a sombre man, unlike his late brother. Sara could not remember seeing him smile or hearing him laugh.

"He's taking care of things for us," her mother said. "He's only thinking of us. He's very fond of you, Sara." And Sara knew just how fond of her he was.

She stretched and pulled down the duvet using her feet, scrunching up her toes, working the cover down until it was a bundle at the bottom of her bed. She lay there in her Marks and Sparks pyjamas before swinging her legs over the side of the bed. She looked at herself in the pine framed mirror opposite the bed. Her hair had grown again. She had it cut short after the funeral because she couldn't bear the thought of her father not brushing it for her the way he had done every night before she went to bed. She ran her hands over her bosom and felt her nipples stiffen slightly. A picture of Jeff flashed into her mind.

Her hands settled on her waist and she closed her eyes imaging they were Jeff's hands.

"Come on Dolly Daydream."

She opened her eyes with a start as her mother brushed past to make the bed.

"Alan's picking us up in an hour, and you're nowhere near packed."

Alan? Alan? Whatever happened to Uncle Alan?

CHAPTER 3

The holiday was going well. The hotel and apartments were excellent and the location ideal for the children – near the beach with no busy roads to cross. Within minutes of arriving all four children were in the swimming pool leaving Grant and Jill to unpack.

Grant was a partner in a successful London advertising agency. He worked hard and this was his first holiday in three years and, how he needed it. Two weeks away from clients, the office and commuting with only sun, sea, sand and sex to look forward to.

Their apartment was small for a family of six; two double bedrooms, a living room and kitchen combined and a bathroom with no window, just an extractor fan that must have exceeded every EU noise regulation. The patio was spacious and overlooked the larger of two swimming pools. Grant had already rearranged the furniture in the apartment. The pine dining table and chairs were relocated to the patio meaning that meals would be al fresco, creating more space inside which would be much needed when it came to making up the bed settee.

It had been left to the children to sort out the sleeping arrangements. Nobody wanted to sleep with Sally because she snored. In the end, Tim drew the short straw. Emma would have preferred a bedroom to herself, but that was Emma all over. Perhaps you have to make allowances for teenaged girls. It is a funny age for young ladies, as Grant was about to find out.

Grant felt the early effects of the Spanish sun on his pale English skin as he stepped under the shower. A tingling sensation swept his body as the powerful jet of water crashed over him. The children had already changed and gone down to the hotel leaving Jill and Grant alone. He emerged naked from the bathroom, dripping puddles onto the marble floor. He was a powerfully built man, over six feet tall and weighed fourteen stones. Jill was in her dressing gown, a light-weight chocolate coloured wrap-around she had bought especially for the holiday. Underneath Grant could see the lace of her white brassiere. He walked across to her and slid his hands around her waist, then up to cup her breasts. She straightened up and stiffened recoiling from his advance. He persisted and nuzzled her neck, his hands kneading her breasts, needing her breasts.

"Not now, Grant, the children might come back," she said struggling free from his grasp. "Besides, you're soaking wet."

He let go and went to the bedroom to get dressed.

"Ah well," he thought to himself. "Maybe it's going to be sun, sea sand and no sex."

When he emerged from the bedroom he heard the shower running. Jill was in the bathroom. Normally he would have been tempted to join her, but in view of her earlier reticence, he didn't bother.

"I'll see you down there," he called out. "Don't forget to bring the key."

He descended two flights of stairs and walked past the swimming pool which was now empty. A row of sun loungers stood sentinel over the liquid blue waters. In the sandpit next to the diving pool a handful of children still played, oblivious to the drop in temperature.

The thirty or so white metal tables outside the hotel bar were mostly empty. Inside, children engaged in musical games organised by the children's club entertainer Yolande, a plump Spanish girl employed by the hotel for the season.

Grant walked through the lobby and had to swerve to avoid a stampede of children playing chase – Ben and Sally among them. He walked through the carved oak double doors into the bar. He ordered a large beer and took it through the sliding glass doors onto the patio.

The air was cool against his skin. He wore a plum coloured short sleeved silk shirt over a pair of C&A white casual cotton trousers. On his feet he wore a pair of red Pringle golfing socks and Reebok trainers.

He looked around at his fellow holidaymakers. He noticed a pretty dark haired woman wearing a tight low cut red chiffon dress sitting at a table near the end of the bar. She looked Spanish, not just because of her olive skin, but there was something about her eyes. She caught his gaze and he immediately turned away. When he looked back she had been joined by a swarthy looking companion.

He sipped his beer and was looking across to the apartments trying to make out which one was theirs when he saw Jill. She was wearing a plain blue cotton dress with a white jacket over the top matched by white sandals. She spotted him on the patio and came across to join him. She smiled, none of the frostiness from before.

"What would you like to drink?" Grant asked his wife.

"White wine will be fine," she replied, "or something with lemonade. Have you seen the children?"

"All except Emma," he replied, leaving his chair. "But she's here somewhere."

Grant got a white wine and another beer for himself and went back outside. The evening had taken on a degree of stillness. Crickets sang in the hedgerows surrounding the diving pool. They sipped their drinks and Jill shuddered slightly.

"Do you want to go inside?" asked Grant. "It's a bit chilly."

"I wouldn't mind," replied his wife. "Bingo is about to start."

It was Grant's turn to shudder.

Bingo came and went. Jill didn't win and Grant didn't play. Emma re-appeared. She had made friends with a group of youngsters led by a boy who looked about eighteen.

"Is it all right if I go up to the twins' room?" she asked breathlessly having run across the dancefloor.

"Who are the twins and where is their room?" asked Grant.

"They are here with their nan and grandad staying in the hotel, but they have got to be in bed by eleven," said Emma.

"If it's okay with mum, it's okay with me," said Grant. "Just be careful."

The disco was in full swing and the lambada was playing. A snake of youngsters crossed the dancefloor with Emma second in the line. With hands held high above their heads like olive pickers, they gyrated across the floor.

"I bet he fancies himself," said Grant pointing out the big lad in the front. He was the leader and wherever he went, they all followed – except one. She was a tall girl with long blonde hair. She wore blue trousers and a plain white t-shirt. Her movements were different to the rest. She seemed uncoordinated, awkward even.

It was the first time he had seen her. It was not to be the last.

CHAPTER 4

It was too hot in the disco and besides, Craig was getting on Sara's nerves. Why the others looked up to him she didn't know, maybe because he was older than the rest. She left the dance floor and went into the lobby to the video games machine. It was one of the early Space Invaders. They had one just like it in the fish and chip shop in the village. Sara reached into her pocket and pulled out a coin. She put it into the machine and pressed Player One. She was up to 27,000 before she lost her first life and that was only because Craig had jogged her arm as he had come past with the Conga chain. Her concentration went and she lost her second life with only the addition of 3000 points. Her last was wiped out by a bomb. 39,000. Way below her best.

She walked over to the hotel reception desk and looked through the postcards. She wanted to send one to Jeff, but they were all too boring – the market at Ciudadela, a donkey on a beach, a plate of lobster soup, oh yeah, he'd really think I was a dork if I sent him that, she thought.

She walked out of the front reception into the street. Next door to the hotel was a car hire agency where "Uncle" Alan had hired a car that afternoon. He had taken her mother out for dinner. Sara had pretended to feel unwell to avoid going. The truth was she felt she would be in the way. They had been spending a lot of time together since her father's death.

She walked down the side of the hotel smelling the sweet hibiscus and oleander bushes. She walked over to the diving pool and sat on the springboard gazing down into the dark depths of the deep end. It was hypnotic staring at water. She suddenly shivered and her arms and neck became covered in goose pimples. It was getting cold. She decided not to wait up for her mother, but have an early night instead.

It was gone one o'clock when she heard the key in the door. They were back. She heard giggling. It was her mother and she sounded tiddly. Sara propped herself up on one elbow craning her neck to listen.

"Shush," she heard her mother whisper. "Stop it, you'll wake Sara. Let me check that she is asleep."

She heard Alan grumble something then heard the extractor fan in the bathroom. She dived back under the covers and shut her eyes as her mother opened the bedroom door. She couldn't see her, but she felt her come across to the single bed where Sara slept. She wished they were not sharing a room. She wanted to be on her own, needed her privacy.

Her mother moved to the other bed and sat down heavily. She took off her blouse and tossed it on the floor. Next she stood up and fumbled with the zip of her skirt. It must have caught the lining and got stuck. She obviously tugged it too hard and Sara heard a rip, followed by a curse. The skirt fell to the floor and her mother stepped out of it. She stood with her back to Sara in just her black bra and panties. Then she went across to the chair in the corner and reached for her dressing gown. She put it on and did up the sash as she went out of the bedroom and back into the lounge. The voices were muffled. Sara pulled back the covers and hopped out of bed, crossing to the door. She put her ear to it, but all she could hear was her own heartbeat. She twisted the doorknob and opened the door the merest fraction. The lounge was in darkness but a chink of light through the balcony curtains gave enough light for Sara to see the room was deserted. The door to Alan's bedroom was slightly ajar, although there was no light on. Her heart was beating even faster now and she thought about going back to the bedroom, but she couldn't. She had to know if anything was going on. She owed it to her father to find out.

She was just feet away from the door, trembling in her short cotton nightie. Just as she was about to push open the door a voice called:

"Sara, what are you doing?"

It was her mother coming out of the bathroom.

"Don't go in there, dear. Alan is probably sleeping. I think he's had a little too much to drink. Sara, are you ok?"

"Erh, yes, I guess so," said Sara. "I guess I'm just a bit disorientated, being in a new place. You know?"

Her mother led her back to their bedroom and closed the door behind them. Sara climbed in to bed and her mother bent down and kissed her gently on the forehead. Then she climbed into her own bed.

"Goodnight, Sara," she whispered.

"Goodnight mother," she replied, then added; "you did love daddy, didn't you?"

Her mother sat up. "Of course I did darling. Now get to sleep." She couldn't see her daughter's face in the shadows. She couldn't see the single tear that trickled down her cheek and onto the pillow.

CHAPTER 5

The sun streamed in through the patio doors. Grant opened his eyes and blinked in the bright sunlight. Jill was still asleep next to him. She lay face down, the white bra cutting in to her freckled back. She hadn't bothered taking it off the night before – and neither had he.

He got out of bed and walked out onto the patio. The tiles were already hot. He was still naked, but the balcony was high enough to hide his modesty from any neighbours. It was just before six and not a soul was about. The pool below looked cold but inviting so he decided to go for an early morning swim to wake his body up.

He tiptoed into the bedroom where Tim and Sally were fast asleep, and rummaged through the wardrobe for a pair of swimming trunks. He slipped them on, found a towel and stopped only for a swig of mineral water before making his way downstairs.

The first decision of the day was which pool to use. The one nearest the apartment was large but shallow, whereas the diving pool near the hotel was smaller, deeper and therefor probably colder. He chose the latter. Dropping his towel by the side, he plunged headfirst into the deep end. The cold water was a shock to the system and he hit the surface gasping for air.

"What's it like?" asked a female voice coming from behind. He swivelled to see where it was coming from. She was sitting on the spring board, her knees pulled up to her chest. She wore a plain black swimsuit with a Speedo logo on the hip. Her legs were very long and very white, her arms freckled. At first he didn't recognise her as the girl from the disco.

"It's cold, but once you're in...."

"It's not too bad," she laughed at finishing his sentence.

"Is it deep?" she added.

Grant put his hands above his head and submerged so he was standing on the bottom before pushing back up to the surface.

"OK," she said, and slipped off the board into the water like a seal. Grant waited for her to reappear, but she didn't. He turned in the water to look around the pool. Nothing. Before his mind even began to think she might be drowning, the water directly in front of him erupted and she surfaced and burst out laughing.

"You are right, it is cold," she gasped. "It's a good job you're not a brass monkey." Then she sprinted off to the other end doing a racing crawl, tumble-turned and disappeared again. He turned trying to track her position under water. She was an excellent swimmer for sure. He floated on his back and looked up at the clear blue sky. Again she burst to the surface next to him, half submerging him with the wake.

"Hi, I'm Sara. You must be Grant, Emma's dad. I saw you in the disco last night, eyeing up that Spanish woman."

"I'll have you know I am a happily married man," he said, trying to sound affronted.

She laughed again and swam across on her back to the side of the pool, when there, she levered herself out of the pool leaving a trail of water behind her. She walked over to the springboard where she had left her towel, picked it up and wrapped it around her shoulders. She headed back past the sand pits to the apartments. He watched her go. She stopped and looked back over her shoulder.

"See you later," she called, walking off.

What a precocious young lady, thought Grant.

CHAPTER 6

He swam fifty lengths of the pool before getting out to dry himself. By the time he got back to the apartment Jill was up and dressed in pink shorts and a pink and white striped t-shirt. The children were still asleep.

"Enjoy your swim?" asked Jill, milking two mugs for their tea.

"A bit cold, but yes, it was nice once you get in." He thought of how Sara had finished that sentence for him. He was going to tell Jill about seeing her in the pool, but didn't. Then he wondered why not.

"Can you pop to the shops to get some milk for breakfast if the children want cereal," asked his wife. "We only have enough for our tea."

"Sure," said Grant. "I'll check out that car hire place next to the hotel and see what vehicles they have available."

The supermarket was almost empty. Grant bought a large container of milk, a loaf of bread and some butter and a box of cornflakes. The car hire shop was closed, but it had a large selection of cars on offer according to the photos in the window. He would return later when they opened.

By the time he got back to the apartment the children were up. Emma and Tim had gone down for a swim. Sally and Ben were playing cards.

"Did you check out the cars?" asked Jill.

"I did," he said. "They have a six seater 4x4 that would do us if it's available."

Luckily it was, and within the hour Grant had collected the keys and parked it at the rear of the apartments. The children were so excited.

"Can we go to the beach?" pleaded Sally. "I want to go in the sea."

"Me too," echoed Ben. "Can we go out on a boat?"

Before leaving the apartment he picked up his wallet from the bedside table and asked Jill to put it in her shoulder bag. The pockets in his shorts were too shallow. There was no safe and he didn't want to leave any cash in the apartment as the wallet contained all of their spending money – 1500euros.

They were all in high spirits when they set off. Grant swung the vehicle out of the slip road and headed for the old part of town. It was going to be a good day.

The land looked parched with only small oasis of vegetation in the small gardens of some of the houses which lined the road. Cascades of bougainvillea created colourful waterfalls on the whitewashed walls of the red-roofed villas. Soon after entering the old town, Ben spotted a bakery.

"Let's stop and get some cakes," he shouted. "I'm starving."

"You're always starving," chided Emma.

"We could get some for later," said Jill. "Pull over."

Grant signalled and pulled into the car park of a small plaza near the shop.

"I'll go, you lot stay in the car," ordered Jill, got out the car and walked across to the bakery.

Grant kept the engine running and tried to tune the radio which was still refusing to work. Five minutes later, Jill returned empty-handed.

"No cakes," she said, "only bread."

"Not to worry," said Grant. "I have to stop for petrol, so I'll see if there are any in the garage."

"At least we can get sweets," said Ben. "They must have chocolate."

After travelling a few miles, Grant spotted a Mobile sign. There were no cars waiting to fill up, so Grant hopped out and put 50litres of fuel in the tank.

Finished, he went to the passenger side.

"Can I have the wallet, Jill?" Grant asked. Jill reached for her bag on the floor, picked it up and put it on her lap and rummaged through it. Grant held out his hand in anticipation. She looked again, plucking out an assortment of female bric-a-brac.

"It's not here," she said alarmed.

"Grant, it's not here," she said now panicking.

"It must be in there, we haven't gone anywhere," said Grant.

Jill tipped the remaining contents of the bag onto the driver's seat. It was futile. The wallet wasn't there.

"OK, don't panic," said Grant. "Look under your seat, maybe it's slipped out of your bag."

Jill got out of the car, crouched down and looked under the seat. Nothing.

Tears now welled up in her eyes.

"It's gone," she cried. "We've lost all our money. Why didn't we bring travellers cheques? I told you we should take travellers cheques."

It was at that point the petrol station attendant came across from the office and said something in Spanish which Grant didn't understand. Jill was now bawling and that had started Ben and Sally off too.

"No money. Stolen, all gone."

The Spaniard looked bewildered.

"What are we going to do?" sobbed Jill. "We can't even pay for the petrol."

"Yes we can," said Grant. "I still have my American Express card." He reached into the back pocket of his shorts and brought out a thin card holder. He brought out the gold Amex card.

"American Express no good," said the attendant, pointing to a sign on the door of the garage shop.

"No accept."

Grant thought quickly. He took off his watch and showed it to the attendant.

"Look. Rolex," he said. "You keep watch until I come back with money. OK?"

The man shrugged his shoulders and took the watch,

Grant stuffed the contents on the seat back into his wife's bag. He got in the car, throttled the accelerator and headed back the way they had come.

"Where are we going?" asked Jill.

"Back to that damned bakery," fumed Grant.

"But I didn't buy anything," said Jill, still anguished.

"No, but I bet that's where you either dropped it, or had it pinched from your bag. It's probably a waste of time, but we have got to try."

It was. The two elderly assistants in the shop spoke little English.

"Come on, let's go," said Grant furiously. "We have to find a police station and report it."

Nobody in the car spoke as they searched for a police station. They found it in the main square in the old quarter of the town, a crumbling sandstone building with huge front doors and narrow windows.

Grant parked the car and told the family to stay inside. He had to report the loss if he was to have any chance of claiming on the insurance. As soon as he entered the building he noticed the drop in temperature and wished then he had kept his shirt on. He had left it in the car, so was only dressed in shorts and trainers. Two armed police brushed past him as he walked along the tiled corridor to reception. Inside he heard animated voices. As he entered, the moustached police officer behind the desk took one look at him at shouted "Out!" Thinking he had walked in on some private conversation and that he was meant to wait outside the room he turned and went back out.

The conversation inside reception again became animated and a few seconds later the elderly bespectacled gent who had been the object of the policeman's anger shuffled past Grant in the corridor. Grant went back in.

"Out!" the policeman shouted again. Grant ignored the order and went to the counter.

"I have come to report the theft of my wallet," he began to say.

"Out!" shouted the officer again. "You offend our king coming in to a government building improperly dressed."

It wasn't the first time he had been reprimanded for not wearing a shirt in a public place. He had once been unceremoniously ejected from Chartres cathedral for the same reason, and another time he was marshalled off Wentworth golf course. He wasn't even playing, just spectating.

"I'm sorry," he began to apologise.

"Go away," ordered the policeman and turned his back.

Dumbfounded, Grant turned and left and went back to the car.

"What's up?" asked Jill.

"They won't talk to me because I'm not wearing a shirt," he fumed. He grabbed his shirt from the seat and headed back in to the police station. The same officer was talking to a colleague. He looked at Grant, then turned away and continued the conversation. Eventually he came over to the counter.

"Where did you leave your wallet senor?" he asked.

"I didn't leave it anywhere," Grant said indignantly. "It was stolen from my wife by one of your countrymen." Now he was getting annoyed.

"So you saw who took it?" pressed the policeman.

"Not exactly," Grant stuttered. "It was taken from her bag in a bakery. It had 1500 euros in it."

There was no flicker of sympathy.

"And where is this bakery?" asked the officer.

"Plaza de Torres," he said, "less than an hour ago."

The official went across to a filing cabinet and took out a buff coloured form. He brought it back to the counter and rubber stamped it.

"Fill this in and bring the top copy back to me. You keep a copy for your insurance."

"So you don't think there's much chance of finding the money?" asked Grant.

"Not with 150 euros in it," said the policeman.

"Not 150 euros," corrected Grant, "1500 euros."

The policeman's jaw dropped. "I am sorry senor," he said. "I misunderstood. That is a great deal of money to lose."

Grant accepted the apology.

"I'm sorry about earlier," he said, "about the shirt. I didn't think."

The officer nodded.

"I'll drop the form in later," said Grant, and went back to the car.

"Will we get it back on the insurance?" asked Jill.

"Not all of it," said Grant. "There is an excess on the policy."

On the opposite side of the street was a bank with an ATM. He crossed over and withdrew the 500 euro limit on his card.

"What do we do now dad? "asked Emma.

"Go back to the garage and get my watch," said Grant, "Before they sell it."

It had not been such a good day after all.

Sara was not having such a good day either. Her mother and Alan had taken her to one of the small beaches by the hotel and she was bored.

"Why don't you play with some of the children you met at the hotel?" her mother asked.

"Maybe," Sara replied. She wriggled closer into the hot sand and rested her head on her hands and looked idly across to a young couple about 20 feet away. She was topless and had small breasts with conical shaped dark brown nipples.

I have bigger boobs than that, thought Sara. The couple must have been in their late teens, early twenties. He was slim, almost thin, with short fair hair. He wore a small gold cross and chain around his neck that glinted when it caught the sun. Sara's eyes became transfixed on the cross and her mind darted back to the gold cross on her father's coffin. She blinked. Her gaze followed the line of his body over the hairless contours of his chest past his flat abdomen to the slight bulge in his light blue swimming trunks. Her thoughts raced back to Adam Cochrane sitting astride his motorbike in his tight leather trousers. The young couple broke off their embrace.

"Sara, Alan and I are going back to the hotel. Do you want to come with us, or stay here a little longer?" asked her mother.

"I'll stay," said the teenager. "You go back and I'll catch you later."

They got up and Liz brushed the sand from her beige cotton shorts. Alan put on the straw Panama hat she had bought for him at the hotel shop and the two of them headed off. Sara watched them until they disappeared, then sat up and looked around.

There was nobody from the hotel on the beach. She wondered what Emma's dad would be doing now and if he would be in the pool the next morning for another early swim.

She brushed the sand from her legs. One of them still had a small nick on it from her mother's razor. She had borrowed it when she showered after getting back to the room from the pool. She had also shaved under her arms, unlike one Spanish woman lying on the beach in front of her, arms above her head and hairy armpits of full view. Ugh, what a turn off, thought Sara.

Leaving her towel she walked down to the water's edge and waded straight in. The cold Mediterranean waters caressed her thighs, and then she dived forward under the brine. She was amazed by the number of fish, most of them grey with yellow bands, all moving in unison. The seabed sloped sharply away and the water looked a darker blue as she swam towards the bottom.

She saw what looked like an old stump sticking out of the seabed. Around it swam five long grey fish with pointed snouts. She swam towards them and they darted away. She examined the stump and found a large rusty iron ring attached to it with a section of rope. Her lungs were telling her she needed more oxygen. She kicked upwards leaving swirls of sand around the stump and broke the surface some 20feet above. She drew in the life giving air and turned to float on her back, gazing up at the crystal blue sky. A jet passed overhead and she wondered where it was going.

By the time the family had got back to the apartment, Jill had developed a blinding headache, either too much sun, or PMT. Either way she didn't feel like dinner and was glad when Grant offered to take the children to one of the nearby restaurants.

Showered and changed into a green silk shirt and sand coloured slacks, Grant splashed a palm-full of his favourite Jean Paul Gaultier aftershave on his face. He looked at himself in the mirror. Just one day in the sun and he already looked like a lobster. Lobster, now there's a thought. I wonder if they will have any on the menu.

They left Jill lying on the settee and headed off in search of dinner.

"Will we have enough for dinner now that mum's lost all our money?" asked Sally.

Grant smiled. "I think so sweetheart."

They found a restaurant and the children plonked themselves down at a table. A waiter in a smart white tunic and black trousers came over with an armful of menus. The girls had omelettes, Tim had the roast chicken and Ben had squid, everything with chips. There was lobster on the menu, but when Grant saw the price of it, he had second thoughts, remembering the 1500 euros they had already lost. He had a steak instead.

As they waited for the food, Ben said he needed the toilet. Sally said she wanted to go too, and Tim offered to take them. The food arrived just as the children returned. It was an okay sort of meal, nothing special. Grant had a beer and the children all had cokes. They all wanted ice cream for desert, three different flavours served in long glasses topped with strawberry and chocolate sauce.

Grant got up and went to the loo. As he crossed the restaurant he noticed three people sitting at a table in the corner, a man and woman and what could have been their daughter. It was the girl from the swimming pool, or was it? She had her back to him, but he thought he recognised the blonde hair. When he came out he looked across again, but this time the girl had gone. As he headed back to his own seat he saw her standing there, talking to Emma.

"Hello stranger," said Grant as he approached. "Sara, isn't it?"

"That's right," she laughed.

"This is my dad," said Emma.

"I know," said Sara "We have already met."

"Is it alright if we go back to the hotel with Sara?" asked Emma.

"Sure," said Grant. "Catch you later."

"Can we go as well?" asked Sally.

"You can all go," said her dad, "but all stick together." And off they went

Grant ordered a large Carlos One brandy. He looked across to the table in the corner. The woman was not particularly attractive. Grant thought she must be about the same age as him, perhaps a little older. He couldn't quite make out the face of the man with her, the face of the man he was later going to try and kill.

When he entered the foyer he saw Sara playing the video games machine. She was on her own. He quietly walked up behind her so he wouldn't spoil her concentration.

"Shit, now look what you've made me do." She didn't turn around even though she was addressing Grant.

"I have one life left and I need 25,000 points to be top scorer. What was wrong with your wife tonight?"

She said it all so matter-of-factly it took Grant by surprise,

"Erh, she wasn't feeling well," he said peering over her shoulder at the screen. "A headache, I think."

"Time of the month, eh," she said, still zapping aliens, "poor old Grant, on holiday too."

That was enough for Grant. She had gone too far. He turned and headed back towards the bar when she called him back.

"I'm sorry," she said loudly, loudly enough for the hotel receptionist to look up from the magazine she was reading.

"My mouth just runs away with itself sometimes. I didn't mean anything." She left the machine and walked over to him and put her hand on his arm,

"I shouldn't have spoken like that," she said. "I really am very sorry."

Grant looked into her emerald green eyes and smiled.

"It's OK, maybe I'm a bit touchy," he said.

"So no hard feelings?" asked the teen.

"No," said Grant.

"Well in that case," said Sara, "come on, you can buy me a drink."

They found a table near the patio doors, away from the dance floor. As Sara sat down Grant couldn't help noticing her long legs as she crossed them. She was wearing a short blue denim dress.

"I suppose you want a large vodka and coke?" joked Grant.

"No. I prefer tequila," she laughed. "But a coke will do for now."

He made his way to the bar. It was at times like these he was grateful for his height. It meant he usually got served straight away. Sure enough the barman came across and Grant ordered a coke for Sara and a Carlos One for himself. As he weaved his way across the dance floor he saw Sara had been joined by Emma.

"Hi dad," she greeted him. "Sara and I are going back to play cards at her place if that's okay?"

"Fine," said Grant, handing Sara her drink. "Just don't be back too late."

Shortly after Tim, Ben and Sally came back.

"We're ready for bed," said Sally. "We're knackered."

"I beg your pardon, young lady," said Grant admonishing his eight year-old, "I am tired out," he corrected her.

"You're tired too, dad? That's what I said, we're all knackered."

When they got back to the apartment Jill was fast asleep in Emma's bed.

"Shush, don't wake her up," said Grant. "You three go to bed and Em can sleep on the put-you-up with me."

"She won't like losing her bed for the night," warned Tim.

"Well, she'll just have to put up with the put-you-up," joked Ben.

Emma came back shortly after eleven o'clock.

"Where's mum?" she asked Grant who was sitting out on the patio.

"I'm afraid she's fast asleep in your bed. You're lumbered with me tonight."

"No way," she said playfully picking up a cushion making to club her dad around the head.

"If you snore I will push you out onto the patio."

When the two of them snuggled down on the settee bed Grant said to Emma; "Did you have a good time at Sara's?"

"She's OK," said Emma. "She's cool."

"Is she here with her mum and dad?"

Emma snuggled up to her dad.

"Well, she's here with her mum, but that's not her dad. I think he's her uncle. Night dad."

She kissed his cheek and turned over to snuggle down.

"And no snoring".

Within minutes of his head hitting the pillow, Grant was asleep, probably helped by the Spanish brandy. A few hundred yards away, Sara was still wide awake. She lay in bed waiting for her mother and Uncle Alan to come home. When they did return, some two hours later, Sara was fast asleep, which was just as well for had she glanced across at her mother's bed, she would have seen that it was empty.

CHAPTER 7

Grant woke up alone in the bed and wondered what had happened to Emma. There was no sign of her. He checked the bathroom. No. He opened the bedroom door and saw Tim and Sally fast asleep. He closed the door and looked in the second bedroom. Jill was in one bed and Emma and Ben in the other. He checked his watch. It was 6.30. He went to the bathroom and the extractor fan roared into life when he switched on the light so he turned it off immediately. But with the door closed and no light in the bathroom he couldn't see where to pee. He solved the problem by putting the waste bin against the door to keep it slightly open. He stood there urinating, looking at himself in the mirror above the wash basin at the side of the loo. He wondered if she would be in the pool.

He found his gold coloured trunks and slipped them on, putting his boxers in the black plastic sack Jill had earmarked for dirty washing. He grabbed his American Express beach towel and headed for the pool.

He passed the larger pool and headed for the smaller one. He had half hoped she would be there, but she wasn't. He placed his towel and apartment key on the diving board and dived in. The water seemed colder than the previous day. On his back, he looked up at the balconies of the hotel, but couldn't see anyone. He could smell the aromas of breakfasts cooking in the hotel kitchen. He swam a couple of lengths and promised himself a cooked breakfast when he got back to the apartment. Then something hit him on the chest, something sharp. He floundered momentarily. It was his apartment key, now on its way to the bottom of the pool. He recognised the impish laughter. He could hear her, but couldn't see her.

"Sara?" he called. "Where are you?"

She stepped out from behind the hedge which bordered the pool and screened it from the service road by the hotel. She was wearing the same black swimming costume. She ran around the pool and climbed on the diving board from where she had taken the key.

"Morning," she giggled. "Do you want your key back?"

"I wouldn't mind," said Grant, "but I can get it." Even as he surfaced dived and swam down towards the bottom he saw the young girl cutting through the water like a dart. Her dive from the board had given her greater impetus. She kicked hard and they both reached the key at the same time. Grant reached for it and so did Sara. Her hand clasped it first, his hand clasped hers. They looked at each other, their faces only inches apart. Grant was running out of breath, his cheeks already puffed. Sara giggled and a stream of bubbles escaped from her mouth and blazed a trail upwards. She put both her hands on his shoulders and pushed him down and herself up. Grant kicked off from the slippery bottom of the pool and propelled himself to the surface. Sara was waiting holding the key aloft like a trophy.

"If you want it, you'll have to get it." And with that she tossed it back into the pool. Grant dived again. Sara dived after him. Side by side they raced towards the key which glistened near to the grid in the middle of the pool floor. Again she reached it first, a split second before him. He tried to pull it out of her hand, but she clenched it too tight. As he caught her wrist with one hand, she put her other hand on his shoulder and pressed her lips to his. Before Grant realised what was happening she broke off the embrace and shot to the surface. Grant followed. By the time he had got his breath back, Sara had hauled herself out of the water and ran around to the diving board where she dropped the key on his towel before running back towards the apartment.

Grant was stupefied. He watched her run off. She turned, waved then ran on. He couldn't believe what had just happened.

Then he told himself it was too ridiculous to be true. She was a very dangerous young lady and if he didn't put a stop to this right now, he would be in serious trouble.

He climbed out of the pool and sat on the side, his legs dangling in the water. Something would have to be said. A voice inside his head said; "For Christ's sake man, you're nearly 40 and she's young enough to be your daughter!"

He got to his feet and wrapped his towel around his shoulders and walked back towards the apartment. Nothing like this had ever happened before. What the hell was he going to do?

On the walk back he met Jill and suddenly felt terribly guilty, like a naughty schoolboy who'd been caught out. He smiled sheepishly.

"Have a good swim?" she asked.

"Yes, great," he replied. "The young girl from the disco made a pass at me in the pool. She kissed me underwater then ran off." The words were forming in his head, but not being spoken out loud.

"I'm off to the shop," she said leaning forward to kiss his cheek. "I'm sorry about last night. I think I was still upset about losing the money."

"Don't worry, it was an accident, everything will be fine." As the words left his lips he unconsciously looked up. Standing on the balcony of one apartment was Sara looking down, smiling.

Grant was back in the pool lying on the floor eight feet under. Sara was writhing on top of him. Her long blonde hair swirled around her head like a golden halo. He held her gently around the waist sliding his hands up and around her firm young breasts. She giggled and gurgled. Grant's thumbs found her nipples which stood out like wheel nuts. His hands moved back to her waist, then lower. He expected her buttocks to be soft and yielding, but they were hard and scaly. He moved his hand to seek out her femininity, but something was wrong. Instead of finding her sex her flesh was cold and rough. He pushed her away and she laughed again sending a crescendo of bubbles towards the surface. As her body propelled away from him her hair cascaded towards him covering her face. Through blurred vision he could now make out her true form her beautiful face and hair, her long neck, soft breasts, slim waist and ... her hips disappeared not into slender legs, but into an aquamarine tail with brilliant blue and green scales. Her hips undulated and circled him like a porpoise.

"Dad, can we go and play," shouted Ben. And in an instant Grant was back in the apartment.

"Blimey dad, you were miles away," added his son. "We're all going down to the pool."

"Huh, okay," said Grant, and wondered what on earth was happening to him.

The family spent the day on the long beach at San Bou. Grant spent two hours carving a two-seater sports car out of wet sand for Ben and Sally. Emma spent most of the day catching rays – solar, not fish. The boys went off exploring the rocks and Jill read several chapters of the Maeve Binchy novel she had bought at the airport. Grant spent most of the day wondering was Sara was doing.

She was twenty miles away around the coast on the back of a pedalo. Her mother and Uncle Alan were providing the pedal power. She sat in the back, wondering what Grant was doing.

Grant took Jill and the children to a small fish restaurant where they dined on shell-fish, loads of garlic bread, which all the children loved, and lashings of albarino, Grant's favourite white wine from Galicia.

They didn't get back to the apartment until gone eleven. Despite that, the children asked to go to the hotel disco, but Grant and Jill said they should all turn in for the night, besides, Jill had a bit of a twinkle in her eye and Grant felt as randy as hell. Must be the sea food working, he thought, they say it's an aphrodisiac. Then another thought flashed into his head – I wonder if Sara likes lobster? Why couldn't he get her out of his head?

The children went off to bed and Jill made two cups of coffee which she took out onto the patio. After going in to kiss the children goodnight, Grant joined her.

"Fancy a night cap?" he asked Jill reaching for the bottle of duty-free Bacardi.

"Just a small one," she replied. "To tell you the truth, I still feel a bit tiddly from dinner."

"It's good to see you look so relaxed," he said.

They sat and chatted while they drank their coffee and rum. Jill went back into the lounge and pulled out the sofa bed. Grant looked at her bent over as she spread the sheets. He could make out the outline of her white panties under her long white skirt. He got up from his chair and moved quickly and silently behind her and placed his hands either side of her hips pulling her bottom into his crutch. She gave a little gasp of surprise.

"Wait until I have made the bed," she protested.

"Fuck the bed," said Grant curtly, and moved his hands to the hem of her skirt and drew it up over her hips. With thumbs either side of her panties he yanked them down to her knees.

"Grant, wait a minute," she pleaded. But Grant was in too much of a hurry. There was no time for foreplay, no time for loving. He wanted her sex now. He yanked at the belt of his shorts and undid the belt with his left hand his right pressing on his wife's back, keeping her bent over.

His shorts slipped to the floor and he kicked them away. He reached inside his pants and yanked out his stiff penis and testicles. Roughly he parted the cheeks of her buttocks and thrust his hips forward entering her to the hilt. She gave out a loud gasp.

"Grant, you're hurting me," she said hoarsely. But he ignored her protests and thrust harder, his pace becoming frenzied. He reached underneath her chest and grabbed her right breast as it hung loosely inside her T-shirt. He pinched the nipple, pulling it roughly.

"Grant, stop it, you're hurting me. Don't be so rough." She tried to straighten up but Grant pushed her back down as he felt his climax building to an unbearable crescendo, his sperm screaming for release. Then he erupted into her as spasms of ecstasy ripped through him. He gave a grunt, reached down and withdrew his semi-rigid organ. Jill collapsed forward onto the unmade bed, face down with her legs curled up. Grant said nothing. He walked to the bathroom, his penis pointing the way.

He flicked on the light and the fan came on. The door swung shut. He collapsed against the wall, thoroughly drained. His forehead rested against the mirror and he looked at his squashed image. His breathing was still heavy and laboured, his breath forming a misty cloud on the glass. He looked into his own eyes and saw a callous bastard staring back – mocking him

"Well done son, fucking good job." He stood over the toilet and waited to pee. When he finished he wiped himself with some toilet paper, dropped it in the pan and flushed. He turned on the cold tap and, cupping his hands, threw some of the salty water over his face. He looked at the now dripping face in the mirror then turned away in disgust. When he went back into the lounge she was still lying there, but had pulled a sheet over herself. Grant slid in beside her and stared up at the ceiling. He turned on his side facing her back and put his arm over her. She shrugged and elbowed him away.

"I'm so sorry," he said feebly. "I don't know what came over me." She made no reply. He turned the other way, closed his eyes and promised himself to dream about mermaids, but he never did. He never dreamt at all that night.

CHAPTER 8

He woke early and thought about going for his early morning swim, but then thought better of it. She might be there. As crazy as it was, he was frightened of seeing her.

When Jill got up she made no mention of the previous night's events. She showered and dressed while Grant made tea and set the table on the patio for breakfast. It was as he was munching through a plate of cornflakes and reading a guide book when there was a knock on the door. It was barely eight o'clock.

He padded across the tiled floor to open the door. He just knew it was going to be Sara standing there demanding to know why he hadn't gone for a swim. Instead it was the twins from the hotel, a couple of fair-haired 13 year-olds, identical in every way, even down to the braces on their teeth.

"Hello is Emma coming out for a swim?" asked one.

"We arranged it last night," said the other.

"I don't think she's even awake," replied Grant. "Hang on, I'll go and check." He peeped in to the bedroom. Emma was dead to the world. He went back to the twins. "I'm sorry, she's still asleep," he said. "I will tell her you called."

"Tell her we'll be in the big pool," said one, then turning in unison, as if they were Siamese twins, they marched off.

"Who was at the door?" asked Jill emerging from the bathroom.

"Just some friends of Emma," said Grant going back to the patio to finish his coffee.

"What did they want?" asked Jill, drying her hair with a towel.

"Apparently they had arranged to go for an early swim," said Grant, "but she's still asleep."

He picked up the guide book. "There's an interesting monastery up in the mountains that might be worth a look," said Grant. "What do you think?"

Just then the bedroom door opened as Emma appeared.

"What time is it?" she yawned.

"Just gone eight," said her dad. "The twins knocked for you."

"Oh no, I forgot. We were supposed to be going swimming."

"They said they'd be in the big pool," said Grant. "You've only just missed them."

"Mum, where are my swimming things?" she asked.

"On the patio where you left them," said Jill.

The teenager scooped up the striped swimsuit and a towel.

"You haven't had any breakfast yet," said Jill.

"That's OK said the teenager. "Dad always says you shouldn't swim on a full stomach, right dad? I'll have some when I get back. Bye."

Minutes later Grant watched her skipping across to the pool. She knew he would be watching her because she turned, waved and ran off.

She came back just before ten. The other children were all up except Sally who was still snoring. Grant was reading a Shaun Hutson paperback he had bought at the airport.

"Dad," said Emma.

"Yes love," he said not looking up, engrossed in a particularly gory piece of prose.

"Dad, would it be okay if Sara came out with us today?" His concentration was immediately broken at the mention of her name. He looked up. There standing behind his daughter was Sara dressed in a bright pink and green one piece swimming costume with a towel wrapped around her head like a turban. She didn't speak, just fixed him with those dazzling green eyes.

"Her mum's not feeling too good and they can't go out so I thought she could come with us. She can, can't she?"

"Of course she can," interjected Jill before Grant had a chance to reply.

"We're doing a bit of site seeing then going to a beach. She's welcomed to join us, isn't she Grant?"

"Well, I suppose so," stuttered Grant, "if it's okay with her mum and dad."

"I haven't got a dad," Sara said sharply. "He's dead."

"Oh, I'm sorry," said Grant apologetically. "I didn't know."

"Why would you," said Sara. "I'll just tell mum."

There were three rows of seats in the car. Emma and Sara sat in the middle row, three other children sat in the back. Sara sat behind Grant which made him feel distinctly uneasy.

They took the road to Ciudadela then the main drag to Mahon. Monte Toro is twenty kilometres from the capital, near the old market town of Mercadel. They could make out the monastery roofline bristling with aerials and radar dishes. The four kilometre climb by road to the top makes it the highest point on Menorca. From the car park at the summit, visitors can see the entire coastline, to Cala Fornells in the north. The air was much cooler and the corridors of the old building felt chilly. The younger children ran off to explore, but Emma and Sara stayed with Grant and Jill.

"What happened to your father, Sara?" asked Jill.

"Jill," interrupted Grant. "He was killed in a car crash last year," said Sara.

Grant looked at her and thought how terribly lonely and vulnerable she looked. Gone was the precocious teenager and in her place was a frightened child. Grant put his arm around her and gently squeezed her shoulder. She looked up into his confused brown eyes. Their gaze was locked for a second, which seemed like eternity and in that moment in time, time itself stood still. He didn't know what to say so he said nothing. Instead he released her and they walked on, making their way up the white cobbled stones.

Emma and Sara went to the gift shop while Grant and Jill went inside the chapel. Jill lit a candle and sat on a pew facing the altar. Emma came in and sat next to them.

"Where's Sara?" asked Jill in a hushed voice.

"She won't come in," replied Emma.

"What do you mean she won't come in?" Jill repeated.

"She says she hates churches and will never go in one. She's a bit weird."

"Never mind, Emma," said Grant, hugging his daughter, "each to their own."

They left the chapel and found Sara sitting by the well, drinking cool fresh water from the spout. She wore grey leggings which ended just below the knee and a baggy white Greenpeace T-shirt with a picture of a whale on the front. On her feet she had a pair of Reebok trainers – no socks.

"Is it safe to drink the water?" asked Emma. "The monks have been drinking it for centuries and they're all right," said Sara.

They found the other children playing a game of chase around the huge statute of Christ built to commemorate the Civil War. They stopped at a café and ate Menorquina ice cream.

"Where to now?" asked Tim.

"I know a nice beach," said Sara. "It's just north of here. We went the other day and hired a pedalo."

"Pedalos are for kids," chirped Ben, "have they got any jet skis?"

Grant handed Sara a map and she pointed out the location. The spot in question was on the north coast at Cala Tirane. Access was on an unmade road past barren fields enclosed by dry stone walls which had been battered over the years by the Tramontane – a vicious northerly wind which had torn away the topsoil of the former olive groves.

There were very few cars in the make-shift car park. The children scrambled out of the car and headed for the water. Jill and Grant unloaded the bags containing a picnic Jill had prepared.

Sara had been right about the pedalos. A sun-baked old Spaniard sat on a rickety deck-chair jealously guarding three gaily painted pedalos drawn up on the beach near his feet. Tim and Sally didn't fancy it, so Emma and Sara sat in the front with Grant and Ben in the back, but Ben was insistent that he wanted to have a go at pedalling.

"That's okay Ben," said Sara, "You swap with me and I'll go in the back with your dad."

They exchanged places. Grant was enjoying the sea air as they set off, what he was not enjoying was the close proximity of Sara who now had her left leg pressed against his right thigh. There wasn't much room in the back so nowhere to shift position. Grant tried to ignore it. He told himself that maybe it was his imagination, but after that sub-aquatic kiss, well…

"Head towards those rocks," instructed Sara leaning forward between Emma and Ben. As she bent forward her left breast rested on the back of Grant's hand which, in turn rested on his thigh. He could feel the heat of her body burning his knuckles. He daren't move it. She sat back and the problem was resolved.

"I saw some caves out by the point," said Sara. "It's a great place to swim, loads of fish around the rocks."

"The current looks a bit tricky," said Grant. There was a clear channel of water flowing swiftly out to sea, like a rip.

"No it's not too bad," Sara lied, "I have swum there before."

Ben and Emma stopped pedalling and allowed the craft to drift towards the rocks.

"Look, I can see the caves," said Ben excitedly. "Can we get out and have a look?"

"If we can find a mooring," said Grant. "Pedal towards that flat rock over there."

Grant struggled to get the craft sufficiently out of the water so as not to float away. It was heavier than he had first thought. He finally managed it and sat exhausted on the rock beside it.

Ben was already clambering towards the cave with the two girls in hot pursuit.

Grant stood up to follow.

"It comes to a dead end," shouted Ben. "No pirate treasure here."

"Maybe if we go to the other side of the point," said Emma.

"Yes, but we might not find anywhere for the boat," said Grant.

"I'll swim round and take a look," said Sara.

"I'm not sure that's a good idea," said Grant. "Perhaps we should go back."

"Come on, don't be a spoilsport," laughed Sara and with that she plunged into the water. Grant waited for her to break surface, but there was no sign of her.

"Where is she dad?" asked Ben. Grant began to panic. He knew she was a good swimmer, but…

"There she is," said Emma, pointing to her friend, now about thirty yards away.

"Look she's waving," said Ben, waving back. "What's she saying?"

They couldn't make it out, but then she disappeared under the water again.

Alarm bells gave a deafening ring in Grant's head.

"She's in trouble," he said. "I'm going after her. You two stay here." He launched himself into the water heading towards the spot he had last seen her. He could feel the current pulling him out towards the open channel. He saw her surface again, still thirty yards away being dragged out further. He swam faster and faster breathing only every ten strokes. He felt a surge of strength despite the burning in his chest. The current was running at its strongest now taking them both around the headland. Sara saw Grant coming towards her as she clung to the last reserves of her strength. Then it gave out and she slipped beneath the waves.

Grant dived and kicked hard. He kicked again towards her lifeless body as it floated five feet under the water. His arms clawed the water away as he propelled himself towards her limp form. Then he was upon her. His hands grabbed either side of her rib cage and he pulled her up towards the surface. He gasped for air as he came up. His left hand cupped her under the chin while he clawed at the water kicking towards the rocks. He couldn't tell if she was breathing, but he knew her only chance was if he could get her back to the rocks. He kicked until his legs felt like lead weights and for a moment thought neither of them was going to make it, but then the heel of his foot hit a rock. He scrambled up and pulled her from the water. She wasn't breathing. He arched her head backwards, clearing her airways, then, kneeling over her put a finger in her mouth to make sure she had not swallowed any seaweed. It was clear. Pinching her nose and holding her chin back he placed his mouth over hers and breathed hard. Her body contracted in a spasm and she wrenched spewing a mixture of seawater and puke over Grant. She coughed and spewed again.

"God I thought you were dead," he gasped. "I thought you had drowned."

She stopped coughing and pushed herself up to a sitting position. She looked like a drowned kitten.

"Nearly had it that time," she said, "but still, I knew you'd save me."

It was then the truth dawned on him.

"What! You did this on purpose. Are you mad? Are you completely bloody mad? We could have both drowned!"

His anger boiled over like a rolling broth.

"Is this some silly bloody game, Sara? Is that what it is? Well I'll tell you now young lady, stop fucking with my life."

That was it. He'd said his piece. He'd got it all out and he felt purged.

She sat there not saying a word, looking at him forlornly, not capable of understanding his wrath, wondering what she had done that was so terribly wrong. All she wanted was his attention, his affection. All she wanted was for him to care for her a little, love her a little. A tear rolled down her cheek and she sniffled. He knelt down beside her and put his hand on her shoulder.

"Are you okay?" he said, his voice now tender. She flung herself to him and hugged him, her golden brown arms wrapped around his back.

"I thought I'd lost you," he whispered.

For the first time since her father had died she felt safe, but these were not the arms of her father, she knew that.

"Come on, we must get back to the children," he said quietly. "They'll be worried sick. Can you walk or do you need me to carry you."

"You Tarzan, me Jane," she coughed, wiping the tears from her eyes. "No, I'm okay. I just need a drink. I've got this horrible taste in my mouth."

He pulled her to her feet. The climb back was tricky, but they were soon reunited with Emma and Ben.

"Are you okay, Sara?" Emma asked her friend. "You look awful."

"I swallowed a load of water and your dad had to save me."

"Did he give you the kiss of life?" asked Ben dramatically. "You know, like on Baywatch?"

"He sure did," said Sara. "I was about to join the mermaids."

Grant's dream flashed into his mind, had it been some weird premonition.

"Come on, we've got to get the pedalo back or Pedro will charge us a fortune."

"He shouldn't be called Pedro, his name should be Pedalo," joked Ben and they all laughed.

When they got back to the beach Ben was out of the boat running to be the first to tell the others of the rescue. By the time the others had got back to Jill, Ben had told everyone the story.

"You poor thing," said Jill motherly. "Do you think you should see a doctor?"

Sara knelt down on the picnic blanket. "No I'll be fine, I just need a drink." Jill handed her a can of coke which she swigged.

"How did it happen, Grant?" asked Jill in a tone of admonishment. "I thought you were supposed to be looking after them."

"She got caught in a rip tide off the point," said Grant.

Sara took the can away and wiped her lips.

"He saved my life," she said looking at Jill. "It was my own silly fault."

She turned to Grant and looked into his eyes.

"I'm sorry," she said, then burst into tears. Jill moved forward and put her arms around her.

"There, there, love, you're okay now."

The tears continued to flow, her eyes puffed up, her cheeks turned red.

"Please don't tell my mum, she'll go mad. Please don't tell her."

"Okay," comforted Jill. Sally handed Sara a handkerchief to dry her eyes.

"You should have seen dad," said Ben wanting to tell the story again. "He dived in and saved her, just like Baywatch."

"Okay, okay, that's enough," said Grant. "The sooner we forget about this the better."

The rest of the day was spent sunbathing. Sara didn't go in the water again, neither did Grant. Jill had a game of volleyball with the children, but Grant and Sara just sat and watched, neither saying a word.

When they arrived back Grant wondered if he should say something to Sara's mum, but decided against it. Grant parked the car and the children got out. Sara was last.

"Thank you for taking me out today," she said turning to Jill. "I'm sorry I caused so much trouble."

Jill touched her arm in a motherly gesture. "Don't be silly, it was just an accident."

Sara turned to Grant who was biting the inside of his lip wondering whether or not it had been.

"Are you all going to the disco tonight?" asked Sara.

"Not tonight," answered Grant.

"Are you going for an early morning swim tomorrow?" she persisted.

"I think I've done enough swimming to last a fortnight," he said.

Her shoulders slumped. "Well, I'll see you around them," she said and walked slowly back towards the apartment.

"You were a bit abrupt with her," said Jill returning from the back of the car where she had been unloading their things.

"I don't know about her," he said taking two bags from his wife. "I just think she's trouble."

When Sara got back to her apartment it was empty. There was a note from her mother on the table.

"Dear Sara, we didn't know what time you would be back so Alan and I have gone out for dinner. There's some money on your bedside table for a pizza or something. Don't wait up. Mum."

Sara didn't want to eat. She went straight to bed.

CHAPTER 9

The rest of the holiday seemed to fly by. During the day they went site seeing. The island was covered in talayots – megalithic rock mounds that date back to the second millennium BC. The children climbed the taulas – huge T-shaped stone slabs and played inside the navetas, stone slab constructions which look like inverted loaf tins.

They visited the early morning fish market at the Plaza Espana in Mahon reached from a twisting flight of steps from the quay. They shopped in the municipal market housed in the cloisters of the Carmelite church behind the Plaza Carmen, and they visited the ice cream factory in Alayor.

During the evenings the children disappeared off to the hotel while Jill and Grant played cards on their patio. Grant saw Sara around the hotel, often on the space invader machine, but apart from a polite hello, had no further contact with her. He took his swim later in the morning with the rest of the family.

"It's our last night tonight dad," said Emma. "Are we doing anything special?"

"I think it will be good in the disco tonight," said Jill applying some mascara. "There are a lot of people going home tomorrow and I think they are having a party night."

"Way to go, man," shouted Ben. "I'm a party animal, dude."

Sally laughed. She was already, dressed in a pink and green jumpsuit with matching hair ribbons.

"That's settled then," said Grant picking up his Rolex watch from the table. Party time it is then."

Dinner was 'scrum' according to Ben, burgers and salad. Grant thought Jill looked particularly nice in a plain white dress cut just above the knee. It showed off her deep tan to perfection. They finished their meal with ice creams served with lighted sparklers. Aware of having to drive back to the hotel, Grant limited himself to two glasses of wine. Jill finished the bottle and giggled all the way back. When they got to the disco, the bar was already heaving and they had to settle for a table by the patio. It suited Grant as it was a hot and humid night. Jill insisted on a large cuba libre despite Grant's warning that she had already drunk a lot of wine. The children ordered cokes, but had disappeared into the melee by the time Grant got back from the bar.

"Come on let's dance," said Jill pulling her husband to his feet. "It's the Lambada." She pushed her hips against him, threw her head back and laughed out loud.

"Come on Grant," said Jill thrusting her knee between his legs, "You're not partying."

The fact was Grant was becoming embarrassed by his wife's antics.

"Maybe we should sit this one out," he said trying to steer her away from the dancefloor. But she was having none of it. Jill wanted to party. He managed to manoeuvre her back to the table and sat her in her chair.

"Is mum okay?" Emma had appeared from nowhere.

"She's fine," slurred Jill, "let's party."

"Let's get her back to the apartment," said Grant putting his arm around her waist and pulling her to her feet.

"Shush, not in front of the children," giggled Jill.

"You stay here with your brothers and sister," said Grant to Emma. "I'll take mum back."

He reached in to his pocket and pulled out a 50 euro note and gave it to his daughter. "That's for drinks, I will not be long."

"Grant, make love to me," said Jill in a voice loud enough for people at the neighbouring tables to hear.

"Sure babe, let's just get you home first, eh?"

A nearby table of young lads gave a loud cheer as Grant struggled past supporting his amorous wife.

"Lucky bugger," he heard one say

Twice on the way back to the apartment Jill nearly had both of them in the large swimming pool when she staggered heavily sideways. He somehow managed to get her up the stairs and into the apartment and propped her up against the wall while he fumbled for the key. He took it out and fitted it into the latch just as Jill emptied the contents of her stomach over his back. He felt a warm stickiness penetrate the silk of his shirt and smelled the undeniable odour of fish as she wretched again.

"Ah shit," he gasped. "What a bloody mess."

It was too, down the wall and running into a pancake on the tiled floor.

He turned the key and opened the door and carried her across to the bathroom. He pulled the light switch and the extractor fan roared into life. For the first time he was grateful for it to dissipate the smell.

He unzipped the dress which earlier had looked so elegant and now looked so …stained. He pulled it from her shoulders like undressing a rag doll. The dress dropped to the floor. He reached into the shower and turned on the taps. It sprayed him with cold water. He waited while it ran warm. He removed her white lace bra, knelt down and removed her panties, momentarily glancing at the thick patch of curly pubic hair.

"Come on girl, get under the shower and let's clean you up," said Grant. "You'll feel better after a shower."

He left her while he cleaned up the sick. Grant returned to the shower, turned it off and wrapped a large towel around his wife.

"Can I get you anything?" he asked.

"Just a new head," she replied.

He took her into one of the bedrooms and helped her into Emma's bed and put the covers over her.

"I'm sorry Grant," she said wearily, "never again." Her words trailed off as she slipped into a deep sleep.

Grant went back to the bathroom, stripped and showered. He dried himself and put on a generous amount of Jean Paul to mask any lingering smells of vomit. He put on a pair of light green trousers and a yellow shirt. A quick inspection in the mirror and he headed back to the hotel.

The disco was in full swing. Most of the tables were empty because everyone was on the dance floor. He made his way to the bar and ordered a San Miguel. As he waited for the drink to be poured he flinched as a hand snaked around his waist. It was Sara.

"I'll pay for that," she said now moving to his side. "It's the least a girl can do for her knight in shining armour."

Grant looked at her and smiled. "I'm afraid my armour's a bit rusty. And I will be expelled from the Round Table if I let a fair maiden buy me a drink."

"I had you down for the Rotary rather than the Round Table," joked Sara.

In fact he was a member of both.

"So what would this fair maiden like to drink?" said Grant carrying on the joke, "and don't ask for anything stronger than a shandy."

"A coke will be fine," she replied.

"Anything in it, ice or lemon?" asked Grant.

"Tia Maria would be nice," she laughed.

Grant was taking a sip of beer and gulped. Some of the beer went down the wrong way and he coughed and spluttered. Sara hit him hard on the back.

"Do you need the kiss of life?" she teased, her face full of mischief.

Grant caught his breath and composed himself. "Aren't you a bit young for Tia Maria and coke?" he asked.

"I won't be getting drunk, if that's what you're worried about," said Sara, then added; "How is Jill? Sleeping it off?"

"She's a bit under the weather," said Grant defensively.

"Rat-arsed more like," said Sara.

"And does your mother know you drink Tia Maria and Coke?" asked Grant.

"Course she does," lied Sara, "as long as I stick to just the one."

"And how many have you had tonight?" Grant asked.

"None yet," she lied again. In fact she had drunk three.

"And a Tia Maria for the coke," Grant said to the barman.

"Where shall we sit," asked Sara, "on the patio?"

Grant followed her out. They sat down at a table. Grant forced himself to look into the young girl's face and not at the vast expanse of thigh showing below her tight black mini-dress. She crossed her legs and the dress rode higher.

"So have you enjoyed your holiday Sara?" asked Grant, sipping his beer.

"Why have you been avoiding me?" she asked.

The directness of her question stunned Grant into silence. At business meetings when he was pitching for a new account he was never caught off guard.

"Well?" she said leaning forward. "You have been avoiding me, haven't you?"

He looked up at her, magnetised by those soft green eyes.

"Look, this is ridiculous," he said almost in a whisper. "To start with..."

"You're old enough to be my father," Sara again finished his sentence for him.

"But you are not my father and I am not your daughter and if I'm not mistaken, what you feel for me is nothing fatherly."

He went to speak, but she put a finger to his lips.

"Let me finish, then you can say whatever you want. Tell me to get lost if that's what you want. I fell in love with you the first night I saw you. I know you are married and I know there is a big age difference between us and I know you don't think I know my own mind, but you are wrong. It's not a schoolgirl crush. I love you and I want to be with you. I think about you all the time when I'm not with you. I cry myself to sleep thinking about you making love to your wife."

Grant continued to stare down at the floor.

"After my father died I thought my world had come to an end. I was so wretched I didn't want to go on living because I could see no future. Meeting you has changed all that. When I am with you I feel so alive again."

She paused and took his hands in hers. He looked up into her face, into her moist eyes. He swallowed hard trying to remove the lump that had been swelling in his throat.

"Sara," he began to say.

"Hi, dad!" said Emma "hi, Sara." Sara was still conscious of the fact her hands were still clasped over Grants and quickly moved them away.

"It's no good trying to drag him up on the dance floor," Emma giggled. "He's far too old to boogie."

"Oh, I don't know," said Sara taking his hands once more. "I think there's a bit more life left in the old dog yet. What do you say? Will you dance with me?"

She pulled him to his feet and led him onto the dance floor.

"What time do we have to be back at the apartment?" asked Emma.

"Midnight," said Grant, as she became lost in the crowd.

The music changed tempo and Tina Turner gave way to Chris de Burgh. Sara wrapped her arms around Grant and pulled him close to her. His hands rested lightly on her back. She swayed like a piece of seaweed being washed by the surf. Grant could feel the heat from her groin pressed against him.

"I'm very flattered," said Grant trying to hold his body away from her, "but you will go home tomorrow and forget about me. I bet there are dozens of boys your own age back home waiting for you."

"Hundreds!" she said snuggling into his shoulder. "But that's just it, they are all boys, out for what they can get."

They continued dancing.

"The thing is," Grant said philosophically, "losing your father when you did, you just see me as a substitute, a kind of surrogate dad."

She stopped dancing and pulled away glaring at him.

"Well that's funny," she said. "So how comes I never wanted to fuck my dad?"

She turned and ran off the dance floor. Other couples who had been dancing nearby momentarily stopped and muttered something.

Grant called after her, but she was through the patio doors and running as fast as her tight dress would allow her.

Grant followed her, not running, but walking at a fast pace. When he got to the patio he saw her running out of the hotel gardens down the path towards the beach. He broke into a jog and caught up with her as the path deteriorated into scrub and sand. He caught her by the shoulder, but she shrugged him off.

"Leave me alone," she sobbed. "Go back to your precious wife and kids."

He caught her by the shoulders again. This time she made no move to pull away. He turned her around and she put her head on his chest. He held her gently until her sobs subsided. She raised her head and looked up. Her mascara had run giving her panda eyes. He gently supported her chin with his hand. His face lowered towards her. He could feel her hot breath as she reached up to greet him. Then his lips brushed hers in a gossamer embrace. The touch was electrifying. It lit a spark of dark urgency which dwelled within them both. Hungrily their lips crushed together as Grant pulled her to him. Her mouth opened and Grant searched for her sweet tongue with his. She responded in the same manner and the two of them stood there locked in a forbidden embrace completely unaware of the shadowy figure on the path. Her own eyes moistened with tears in the moonlight. Emma turned and ran back to the hotel.

They walked hand in hand along the beach at the water's edge, star-crossed lovers wishing they had the world to themselves. They didn't speak. There seemed no need for words. They walked until they reached the rocks at the side of the bay. Sara found a flat rock and sat down. Grant sat behind her and put his arms around her. She pulled her legs up to her chest as they watched the waves break on the beach.

"Will you make love to me?" asked Sara.

"I already have," replied Grant, "over and over in my mind, a hundred times!"

She laughed, nervously.

"And was I any good?"

"You were a mermaid," he said.

She turned and looked at him quizzically. He kissed her forehead.

"Make love to me now," she said softly.

Grant took a deep breath and exhaled.

"No," he said. "May God forgive me, but I think I love you too much." He enveloped her with his strong tanned arms and kissed the hair on the top of her head.

"It's time you went home."

"Where do we go from here?" asked Sara getting to her feet.

"I don't know," sighed Grant. "I honestly don't know."

They joined hands and walked back the way they had come.

"Will I see you tomorrow?" asked Sara. "Can we have one last swim together?"

She reached up and kissed him briefly on the lips.

"Okay," said Grant, "one last swim."

She turned and ran off towards the apartments. Grant headed back to the hotel where he rounded up Tim, Ben and Sally. "Where's Emma?" asked Grant.

"She's in reception," said Tim. "She's in a right mood."

"Well go and find her," added Grant. "I don't want her being her on her own."

"No," said a voice in his head. "You never know what might happen to her."

When they all got back to the apartment Jill was still fast asleep in Emma's bed.

"Looks like you're lumbered with me again, Em," joked Grant.

"I'd rather share with Sally," said Emma coldly.

"Can't stand the snoring, eh," said Grant

"Something like that," she replied. "Goodnight," and brushed past him into the other bedroom.

"I told you she had the ump," said Tim.

"Probably time of the month," said Ben. Grant did a double take.

"You know," added Ben. "End of the holiday."

CHAPTER 10

A sharp knock on the apartment door woke Grant with a start. He looked at his watch. It was 8am. Before he could even get out of bed there was another knock, this time louder.

"Okay, I'm coming," he shouted as he climbed out of the bed settee and reached for a pair of shorts on the nearby chair. Slipping them on he zipped them up and opened the door to find himself staring into the face of the police chief he had seen some thirteen days ago.

"Buenos dias senor Campbell," he said. "May I come in?" Before waiting for an answer he brushed past Grant. It was then Grant noticed two uniformed armed officers waiting outside the door.

"Have you found my wallet?" Grant asked, "Is that why you've come? I must say I never really expected..."

"No senor. It is not about your wallet. I am afraid it is much more serious."

"Grant, what is it?" asked Jill appearing from the bedroom with a sheet wrapped round her. "What are the police doing here?"

"We are investigating the disappearance of one of the guests," explained the policeman. "A 15 year-old English girl named Sara Mattherson."

Grant swallowed hard. Fifteen! Christ! He hadn't realised she was only 15. His head began to swim and his mouth dried completely.

"We understand she was seen leaving the hotel discotheque with a man fitting your description. What have you to say?"

Grant was speechless. His mind was racing.

"Grant?" said Jill inquiringly. "Is that young Sara he's talking about, Emma's friend?"

Grant had to sit down before he fell down.

"Missing? What do you mean missing? She can't be."

"She did not return to her apartment last night, senor. I ask you again what do you know of this?"

Grant looked bewilderingly at his wife.

"Know? I know nothing about it. I saw her in the disco last night, but that's all."

"We have witnesses who claim you were dancing intimately with her on the dance floor and then you had a row and she ran outside very upset. At least five people saw you follow her. It was you, was it not, senor."

Grant began to panic. He realised how bad all this was beginning to look.

"She was upset," he said defensively. "I was just trying to comfort her."

"Is that why you were plying her with alcoholic drinks from the bar?" said the inspector.

"Grant?" said Jill not believing what she was hearing. "Grant, tell him this isn't true. It can't be true."

Grant said nothing.

"Where were you last night, senora?" the inspector asked Jill.

"I was here, I had an early night. I wasn't feeling well."

"Perhaps you had too much of our Spanish sun," he said, "or, perhaps too much sangria? Isn't it true senora that you were, as you British say, worse the wear for drink and that senor Campbell had to carry you from the hotel to stop you making a scene?"

"Don't be so damn rude," barked Jill. Grant was surprised by her reaction.

"I apologise," said the inspector, "but we are very concerned for the whereabouts of this child and we think your husband can help us, either here or down at own offices."

"Like I said," began Grant. "I saw her in the disco. I came back here with my children around midnight."

"And you did not leave the apartment again last night? You did not arrange a rendezvous with the girl – on the beach, perhaps?"

"No! No,"" protested Grant. "I was here all night."

The inspector rocked backwards and forwards on his toes.

"So you were not with her on the beach last night?" asked the policeman.

"Well, yes, but earlier, only briefly. Look, she was upset and ran off so I ran after her."

"And why was she upset?" persisted the inspector.

Jill was now glaring at her husband.

"I think she had a bit of a crush on me," said Grant sheepishly. "She lost her father recently and I think she sees me as a sort of father figure."

"It's a monstrous suggestion that my husband would have anything to do with this girl's disappearance," said Jill defiantly. "He saved her from drowning when we took her out last week."

As soon as the words left her lips the inspector pounced.

"So you have taken this girl out before last night?"

"Well, yes," said Grant. "She made friends with our children and they invited her to spend the day with us."

"And what of this rescue your wife speaks about?" asked the inspector.

Grant briefly explained the circumstances.

"And you told the girl's mother about this?" the officer asked curiously.

Grant fumbled for words. "Well, no. She asked us not to say anything."

"And why was that?"

Grant was cornered. Jill came to his rescue. "Because she said her mother would be upset. She's just lost her husband. The thought of losing her daughter as well might drive her to a nervous breakdown."

But still the inspector persisted with his questioning.

"So you know Senora Mattherson well?"

"No, we've never met the woman," answered Jill.

"But she allows her daughter out with perfect strangers? Now why is that?"

"Perhaps you'd better ask Mrs Mattherson," said Jill. "And I think if you persist in this offensive line of questioning then we will have to call the British Consulate."

Grant couldn't believe his ears. This mild mannered woman he had married had turned into a Rottweiler.

"I apologise again if my questions upset you," he said. "Perhaps it would be better if you stayed in the hotel complex today in case we have any further," he gave another pregnant pause "information for you."

"But we are flying home to the UK this afternoon," protested Grant.

"I think not, senor," said the inspector. "You will not be leaving this island until this matter has been resolved."

There was a knock at the door.

"May I?" asked the inspector reaching for the door handle. He opened the door and standing outside stood a man in his early fifties dressed in a light brown suit, open neck shirt and wearing a trilby hat.

He spoke rapidly in Spanish to the inspector. Whatever he said agitated the policeman.

For a fleeting second Grant thought he had come to say they had found Sara's body raped and mutilated in the dunes on the beach, he would be arrested and spend the rest of his life in a Spanish jail for a crime he did not commit.

The inspector turned.

"It would appear the girl has returned safe and well. Apparently she has been at an all-night disco in Mahon. She has made a statement which supports what you have told us. I am sorry you have been troubled." He turned to leave.

"So is that it?" stormed Jill.

"You come in here accusing my husband of abducting a young girl. You accuse me of being a drunk and you say sorry if you have been troubled."

Grant wanted the floor to open and swallow her up.

"There is still the matter of your husband buying the young lady alcoholic drinks, which is against the law. However, I understand she looks appreciably older than her years, so I am prepared to overlook this." He turned and left the apartment.

Jill had tears streaming down her face. He sat beside her and put his arm around her.

"It's all right, they have gone. It's over, just a misunderstanding."

She glared at him. "Is it?" she asked. "I bloody well hope it is." She looked at Grant and wondered if she could ever trust him again or if she would ever know the truth.

Baggage packed, the six of them waited outside the hotel for the transfer to the airport. Emma popped back into the foyer to spend her last few coins on the games machine. Just as she was going to put a coin in she felt a tap on the shoulder. It was Sara.

"Hi Em, she said solemnly. "I'm glad I caught you before you left. You haven't given me your address so I can write to you."

"To me, or my dad?" she said harshly.

"Em, what do you mean?" Sara said innocently.

"You know what I mean," said Emma. "I saw you two kissing on the beach last night. How could you?"

"You silly thing," said Sara jokingly. "That was just a dare. The twins bet me 10 euros I wouldn't give your dad a big sloppy kiss. I did it for a laugh. He was ever so embarrassed. You should have seen his face."

The relief swept over Emma.

"So it was just a joke?"

"Of course, silly," said Sara hugging her friend. "You can't possibly think I fancy him, do you?"

Emma laughed. "Course not," she said. The idea was preposterous.

"So are you going to give me your address? Look, write it on one of these postcards," and she took a card off the nearby rack on the reception counter.

"But what about your address?" asked Emma,

"I know," said Sara, and she tore the card in half.

"There," she said. "It will be like in the movies. You have one half and I will have the other. The two halves will be reunited when we meet up again."

The girls wrote their addresses on the cards and swapped.

"Right, I've got to go," said Sara. "I still have my packing to do. Give my love to your mum and dad and your sister and brothers."

CHAPTER 11

Grant stood at the bar at Langan's Brasserie in Stratton Street, one of London's most celebrated restaurants. Grant was sipping a glass of Bollinger – his favourite tipple. It was only a five minute cab ride from Grant's office in Covent Garden. He had arranged to meet an American friend for lunch. When the two of them got together it was usually at Langan's. This time was Grant's turn to pay.

The restaurant was busy. Grant had booked a downstairs table for I o'clock and had arrived twenty minutes early. There was a sprinkling of celebrities, and part owner Michael Caine was at his usual table behind the front door by the window. He was chatting to Michael Douglas who was in the UK filming. They were accompanied at the table by a fat bald-headed Jewish man – probably a producer Grant thought – and a gorgeous blonde who looked unmistakably like the actress Sharon Stone. Grant loved the atmosphere at Langan's. The food wasn't bad either.

It was gone one when Tom arrived looking immaculate in a Gieves and Hawkes suit, Coles hand-made shirt, Balenciaga silk tie and Gucci shoes. Although he had lived in London for two years, he hadn't lost his deep Californian tan. It was little wonder women found him so attractive.

"Hi bud," he said approaching Grant with an open hand. "How's it going? Was the holiday good?" He put his crocodile skin Louis Vuitton briefcase on the floor against the bar and smoothed back his light brown hair.

"Don't ask," replied Grant. "Apart from the fact Jill lost 1500 euros on the first day and I nearly got arrested for abducting a 15 year-old schoolgirl, it was great."

Tom laughed.

"Boy, I thought I was the one supposed to be leading an exciting life. What are you drinking?"

"I'm on Bollinger. I'll get a bottle."

"Are we celebrating something?" asked Tom.

"Just life getting back to normal, that's all."

"So are you going to tell your old buddy all about it," asked Tom sipping his newly poured glass of champagne.

"Well, it's difficult to know where to begin. This girl who was staying at our resort developed a crush on me. I thought she was about 17 or 18, but I was a couple of years out. She was only a year older than Emma."

"Sounds innocent enough," interrupted Tom.

"I know this sounds ridiculous, but I was really attracted to her," said Grant.

"Did you screw her?" Tom asked matter-of-factly.

"Of course I didn't screw her," said Grant indignantly. "She's a 15 year old schoolgirl."

Tom's eyes were scanning the restaurant. "Isn't that Sharon Stone?" asked Tom having spotted his fellow American.

"Some of these chicks start really young. You remember my friend Marty who you met at my place in San Francisco? "

"Marty with the Ferrari cabriolet?" added Grant.

"Yeah that's the guy," said Tom. "So two months ago he meets this chick at one of our Indian Princesses pageants, a kind of fathers and daughters club. Now he's left his wife and he's moved in with her. She's 16. He's been married 18 years. These things happen."

"Well nothing serious happened," Grant continued. "Except she did kiss me once underwater and we had a snog on the beach the last night of the holiday. Oh, and I saved her life when she nearly drowned, which I think she may have done on purpose. She's had a profound effect on me and I don't know how to deal with it."

"Sorry," said Tom, "so how did the cops get involved?"

The head waiter came over and told Grant the table was ready. Grant asked for the bottle of Bollinger to be brought over and they took their seats.

"I'm sure that's Sharon Stone," said Tom eyeing the film star. "I saw her in Carmel last year."

"So the night before we are due to fly home she comes on to me in the disco."

"Who, Sharon Stone?" quipped Tom.

"Look," said Grant, "if you're just going to make fun of this ...."

"Sorry," said Tom, "I'm listening."

"So she comes on to me in the disco," repeated Grant, "and I give her the old 'you just see me as a father figure because your dad's just died' and she turns around and says 'so how comes I never wanted to fuck my father?'"

"Shit," said Tom now engrossed in his friend's confession,

"Well, she starts crying and runs off. I run after her and catch up with her on the beach. She's all upset and we end up kissing."

"So the cops arrest you for a kiss?" Tom said quizzically.

"Not quite," Grant continued. "Nothing else happens. She goes off and I take the children back to the apartment. The next morning there's a knock on the door. It's the police saying the girl is missing and I'm the prime suspect."

"Shit again," said Tom.

"Anyway it all works out because the girl shows up. Turns out she's been at an all-night disco."

"So you're in the clear?" asked Tom.

"Well I am with the police, but I don't know if I am with Jill. She's been very icy since we got back."

"Forget it, man," said Tom picking up the menu. "It will all be forgotten in a few weeks."

Grant bit the inside of his lip, a nervous habit he had developed as a child.

"That's just it," he said. "I don't think I can forget it – or her. The fact is Tom I think I love her."

His friend lowered the menu and gave him a disconcerting look.

"What you need is to get laid to get it out of your system, get her out of your system."

That was Tom's answer to everything. Business good, go and get laid, business bad, go and get laid. Problems at home go and fuck yourself senseless.

"I've joined a club since you've been away," said Tom, "There are some mighty fine looking women," adding, "none of them a day under 30. What do you say? Tell Jill you're staying at my place."

"I don't know," said Grant hesitantly. "I don't know if I am in the mood for socialising and it will go down like a lead balloon at home."

"Well it's your call," said his friend. "I'm meeting a guy coming in from the States at Café Pacifico. We're going to do some jugs of margaritas and have something to eat then hit the club around eleven, eleven thirty. If you fancy it, you're welcome to join us. Right, what shall we eat?"

They finished the meal around 2.30 and Grant was back in his office by quarter to three. He and his partner were preparing to re-pitch their biggest single account – American Express. Internal changes at Amex had meant they had brought in a new American supremo from New York, a tough lady from the Bronx who had a xenophobic dislike of Englishman. Grant had done most of the work on the proposal and two executives in the agency, Andy Crane and Kim Mellor were running through the AV presentation for Grant. But he couldn't concentrate. His mind was still back on the beach in Menorca.

"I'm not happy with the ending," said his partner John. "What do you think Grant?"

The mention of his name brought him back to the meeting.

"Huh, sorry John, what was that?"

"Can you excuse us for a few minutes," said John to Andy and Kim. "I need the room."

Kim scooped up a folder full of paper work and Andy opened the boardroom door before the pair of them left. Everyone in the office knew they were having an affair despite the fact that Andy, who was twenty-six and had been with the company for four years, was married. What was more important to Grant and John was the two of them worked better together than they did apart. Kim was a very attractive blonde with a great figure and legs up to her armpits. Clients loved her. Men thought they had a chance of bedding her, but none managed it, she only had eyes for Andy.

"Grant, what the hell is the matter with you?" asked John. "Ever since you came back from holiday you've been moping around like a wet weekend. We have two weeks to get this presentation right. You know as well as I do what it would mean if we lost the account."

Grant was playing with his Mont Blanc fountain pen, turning it over and over in his hand.

"I'm sorry John," he apologised. "I can't get my head in gear."

"Is it Jill?" asked his partner "is there something wrong with one of the kids?"

His concern was genuine, although he was Grant's partner theirs was a business relationship rather than a close friendship. He hadn't told John about Sara. He didn't want him to think he had a pervert for a partner.

"No, Jill and the kids are fine," he said. "It's just me. I'll work it out."

"Well it is eight o'clock and we're not going to get anything else done tonight, so let's call it a day."

Grant looked at the old British Rail station clock on the boardroom wall. It had been a gift from John when Grant had landed the Network South East account two years ago.

"Good idea," said Grant. "I'll just give Jill a ring. I promised Tom I'd meet up with him later. I'll see you tomorrow."

He dialled the home number from the office and Ben answered.

"Hi dad, where are you?"

"Still at the office," said Grant. "Is mum there?"

"Sure, I'll go and get her."

Jill came on the phone. "Are you still at the office?"

"Yeah, still here," said Grant. "We're working on the Amex pitch and it looks like it's going to be a late one so I thought I'd stay over at Toms."

There was silence.

"You don't mind, do you?" He waited for a response. He knew she did mind. She thought Tom was a bad influence.

"No I don't mind," she said. "Your mother called and wants you to ring her."

"Do you know what it's about," asked Grant.

"Nothing important," she replied, "something about some investments."

"The kids all okay?" asked Grant.

"They're fine," said Jill. "Emma got a letter from that girl Sara."

"What did she want?" asked Grant, caught off guard by the mention of her name.

"I don't think she wants anything," said Jill. "I think it was just chit-chat. What time will you be home tomorrow?"

How did Sara know their address, Grant hadn't given it to her. What did she want? Why was she writing?

"Grant, are you still there?" asked Jill.

"Erh, sorry love, someone just came into the office. I'll try and get in early. See you tomorrow." He put the phone down. He thought he had seen the last of Sara, but he hadn't.

Café Pacifico is a Mexican restaurant around the corner from Grant's office in Covent Garden. When he arrived he saw Tom sitting at a window table with a tall thin man casually dressed.

The girl on reception greeted Grant like a family friend. He was a regular customer.

"Grant, my boy, you made it," said Tom seeing his friend approach the table. "I'd like you to meet Larry, Larry Finnegan."

"That's a good old Anglo-American name," joked Grant extending his hand in friendship.

"Pleased to meet you Grant," said the tall American. "My grandparents came from County Cork."

"Whereabouts in the States are you from?" Grant asked.

"Mississippi," he replied.

"I've been telling Larry about your little Lolita," said Tom. "He's of the same opinion as me. You need to get laid tonight."

A broad grin broke over Larry's face. "I'm for that," he said.

They left the bar after having shared a couple of jugs of margaritas and some steak and prawn fajitas. They got a cab to Tom's club in Mayfair. Grant went to pay the driver, but Larry got there first and peeled off a note from a large wad of money held together with a gold clip.

One of the two large Mafia-looking doormen outside the club recognised Tom.

"Good evening Mr Cody, welcome back."

"Good evening Bernard," replied Tom. "Is there any fresh tail in tonight?"

"It's a bit quiet at the moment," replied the doorman, "but it's early. Are these two gentlemen members?"

He knew they were not. He may only have been a doorman, but he had a knack for remembering names and faces. He had spent ten years in the police force, a career cut short when he was discovered taking back-handers from clubs like the one he now guarded.

"No, they are my guests," said Tom "I will sign them in."

The reception area had a white marbled floor and lots of potted palms. Tom handed his briefcase to the pretty black receptionist. Grant had left his case back at the office.

"This way guys," said Tom leading them through an archway and down a flight of plush carpeted stairs to the club below.

There was a long bar with a small dance floor at one end and about a dozen tables at the other. Half way along there was another area off the bar set aside for diners. Grant estimated there were no more than thirty people in the club, only eight in the dining area.

"What do you two want to drink?" asked Larry.

"We'll go back to Bollinger," said Tom, "okay with you, Grant?"

"Sure."

While Larry was waiting to get served, an attractive dark-haired girl came over to Tom and whispered something in his ear. She was small, a little over 5ft. She had a very pretty face curtained by straight dark hair. She reminded Grant of Liz Taylor in Cleopatra. She wore a micro short gold mini skirt and black sequinned top, no bra as her breasts jiggled free inside.

Whatever she said made Tom laugh. She gave Tom an affectionate peck on the cheek and walked away.

"Who was that?" asked Grant.

"Her name's Jo," said Tom "gives fantastic blow-jobs. I met her in here last week. She stayed the night at my place. She's one foxy lady."

Larry returned from the bar with a bottle of Bollinger and three glasses.

Most of their fellow clubbers were in their mid-thirties, Grant thought probably married or divorced. Tom noticed two women sitting further along the bar. One was a very elegant blonde in her late forties. She wore a bright pink two piece suit. The skirt was short and showed plenty of well-tanned leg. Around her neck was a thick gold rope necklace which matched the bracelet on her left hand. On her right wrist she had a gold Rolex and an assortment of rings on her fingers including a wedding, engagement and eternity ring.

"Classy lady," said Tom. "That's what you need to straighten yourself out."

Grant looked at her. She was attractive without being beautiful. The woman with her was a complete contrast, dark and much bigger build. She wore a low cut blouse which showed lots of cleavage.

"Not my type," said Grant sipping his champagne.

"What do you do for a living, Larry?" asked Grant.

"I work for the government," he replied.

"Doing what?" pressed Grant.

"If I told you that I'd have to kill you," he laughed. "No I'm a pilot. I fly military aircraft."

Tom had wandered off towards the two women at the bar. After a couple of minutes he returned, with the two women in tow.

"Boys, I'd like you to meet Barbara and Tatiana." The women smiled and they all clumsily shook hands, getting in the way of each other. Barbara, the blonde, laughed. Grant noticed her perfect teeth, brilliant white and perfectly set.

"Tom tells me you're a pilot, Larry," said Tatiana. "Do you fly commercially?"

"No military," said Larry.

"What about you, Grant," asked Barbara, "what do you do?" Her voice was low, almost husky, sexy, very refined.

"I look after these two guys," said Grant. "I make sure they don't get into any trouble."

"So you're a kind of minder?" she said, now intrigued.

Grant had often been mistaken for being a policeman.

"Let's just say I look out for them," he said enjoying the charade.

"And who looks after you?" she asked provocatively.

"I look after myself," said Grant. "Come on, let's dance." He put his glass down on the bar, took her hand and led her to the dancefloor which was deserted.

A slow Diana Ross record was playing. He put his arms around her and held her close. She was shorter than him and had to reach up to put her hands around his neck.

"Are you always this domineering?" she asked as she moved her nails over his neck.

"No," he said, then he pushed her away slightly which made her look up. He crushed his lips to hers and their heads did a separate dance to their bodies. Her mouth opened and her tongue snaked into his mouth darting back and forth. They stayed locked in a passionate embrace, his hands holding her tightly, crushing the breath from her. She removed her hands from his neck and replaced them under his jacket. He could feel her long nails carving pictures into his back. The record finished and they broke the embrace.

"Your friend told me you said I wasn't your type," she said looking up at him.

"I guess I was wrong," said Grant and this time brushed her lips lightly with his, making her quiver.

Tina Turner's Simply the Best came on next and the two of them stayed locked together on the dancefloor oblivious to the emptiness around them. They danced and kissed unaware of the floor filling up around them. When they eventually left the floor they joined Tom and Tatiana.

"Well you two seem to be getting on like a house on fire," said Tatiana to her friend.

Barbara put her hand on Grant's shoulder.

"I've got to go to the little girls' room," she said. "Tanya, are you coming?"

The two women went off.

"So how's it going?" asked Tom. "She looks a lively lady, great legs."

"Yeah it's all good," said Grant. "Where's Larry?"

"Oh he had to split," said Tom, "his girlfriend is coming in from the States tomorrow and he's got to pick her up early from the airport."

The girls returned from the cloakroom.

"Shall we finish up here and go back to my place?" suggested Tom, "There's some champagne in the fridge."

"That's the only thing you'll ever find in Tom's fridge," added Grant.

They walked to Tom's flat. It was two minutes from the club, almost opposite Albert Mossiman's famous Belgravia restaurant. It was a company flat paid for by the Bank of America where Tom was a European vice-president. It had two bedrooms, a huge lounge, separate dining room complete with a 12-seater marble table and plush chairs. The kitchen included every modern convenience. Everything was white except the pink granite working surfaces. What Grant liked most about the flat was the two patios. One led off from the lounge and linked with the other one which came off from the kitchen. The one off the lounge had a large stone fountain with underwater lighting. The one off from the kitchen had a brick built barbecue, large wooden table and eight chairs. The master bedroom had a super king sized bed covered in yellow silk sheets and matching duvet. It was a bachelor's paradise.

Tom turned off the security system behind the door while Grant ushered the women inside. Grant had stayed in the flat many times when his friend had been away on business and meetings kept him late in London.

"Very nice," said Tatiana approvingly.

"Come through," said Grant as if he owned the place.

"Tom, get the girls some champagne."

"Actually I would prefer coffee," said Barbara slipping off her short mink jacket.

"Champagne is fine for me," said her friend settling into the large four-seater settee.

"I don't think I have any milk," shouted Tom from the kitchen. "Will you take it black?"

"Black will be fine," said Barbara moving across to the patio doors.

Grant unlocked them. The cool air was refreshing. He reached for the light switch concealed behind the curtains and flicked it on. The fountain lit up and seconds later the figurine in the centre was sprayed by dozens of jets of water from around the circumference of the rim.

"That's pretty," said Barbara moving back into Grant so she was pressing against him. He put his arms around her waist and kissed her ear lobe.

"Can't you two at least wait until the coffee," laughed Tatiana. "Honestly Barbara you're like a bitch on heat."

Tom came back into the room with a bottle of Krug and three crystal flutes.

"Coffee's on," he said to Barbara. "Does anyone mind if I switch on the TV?"

He picked up the remote and pointed it towards the Bang and Olufsen set. An old Phil Silvers show was on so Tom flicked through the channels and settled on a satellite sports programme. He turned off the sound.

Grant opened the champagne and poured three glasses handing one to Tom who had joined Tatiana on the settee. Barbara sat on the arm of an armchair.

"Did Grant tell you how we met at the Le Mans motor race?" Tom asked Barbara.

"No he didn't," she replied. "In fact he hasn't told me very much about himself at all."

Grant sat in the armchair and she slipped onto his lap.

"It was the first time I had been to Europe.." Tom began the story which Grant had heard a hundred times before.

"A pal of mine in San Francisco had given me the address of an auberge he was supposed to be staying at near the circuit, but I lost the fucking piece of paper. All I could remember was that it was near a place that sounded like a girl's name, Lucy Pringle or something like that. Anyway, I'm in this taxi for three hours and he's taking me to every fucking boarding house in France.

"Well, its one o'clock in the morning when I knock at this place thinking I am going to find old Charlie. The rest of the group he is staying with are all members of the Aston Martin Owners Club, so when I see all these classy motors outside this place I know I've hit pay dirt.

"I knock on the door and Grant is standing there, glass of Armagnac in his hand. I say is this where Charlie Robbins is staying, and Grant says you must be the American. They knew I was coming but had given up on me."

"And we have been giving up on him ever since," laughed Grant.

"I'll go and see if the coffee is ready," said Barbara getting off Grant's lap and straightening her skirt.

"I'll come and give you a hand," said Grant and followed her out to the kitchen.

"Where are the cups?" she asked looking at the array of cupboards.

"In the end one," said Grant. She reached up and opened the cupboard. Inside was a complete dinner service of white Wedgewood. As she reached up for the crockery Grant slid his hands under her arms and onto her breasts. They were soft and yielding. She gasped, but made no attempt to stop him. Through the thin material of her silk blouse Grant felt her nipples stiffen. He pinched them lightly between forefingers and thumbs. She breathed heavily.

"Oh God that feels good," she said turning to face him. His lips met hers in the same urgency as on the dance floor. She bit his lower lip making him flinch. She knew she had hurt him and pulled away.

"I'm sorry, so sorry," she said and immediately smothered his lips with butterfly kisses. Grant's hand was squeezing her buttocks. He bent lower and felt for the hem of her skirt. He found it and pulled it up moving his hand up her thigh. Her tights felt like snakeskin. His hand roamed over her thighs and settled in the warmth between her legs. She moved them apart to allow him better access and he pressed hard against her sex with the tips of his fingers.

"Stop or you'll make me come," she panted. He removed his hands and put them back on her waist. He kissed her fully on the lips then broke the embrace.

"I think I'd better have a coffee too," he said and returned to the lounge.

There was no sign of Tom and Tatiana. They had gone to the master bedroom and taken the champagne with them. Grant didn't mind. He had drank enough already, maybe too much. Barbara came out of the kitchen carrying two cups of coffee.

"Where have they gone, or need I ask?"

"I hope you don't think I make a habit of this," said Grant defensively. "I think you should know I am married with four kids."

"I already guessed that," said Barbara, "the best ones always are."

"Does that bother you?" asked Grant.

She put the coffee down on the table. "Should it?" she said. "We're just having a bit of fun, aren't we?"

Grant took another look at her. She was much more attractive than he had first thought. The only blemish on her skin was a small scar above her right eyebrow, the result of a car accident when she was younger.

"Well I'm certainly having fun," said Grant. "I just don't want anyone getting hurt."

"Don't worry about me, I'm a big girl," she said crossing to Grant. He cupped her breasts again. "Not that big," he smiled "just about the perfect size."

She reached up and kissed his lips.

"Do you really want that coffee," she asked provocatively.

"Not really," said Grant. He reached down and scooped her up in his arms and made towards the spare bedroom.

"What about the TV?" she asked noticing a tennis match was on.

"I've seen it before," he said. "Federer wins in straight sets."

He carried her into the bedroom and laid her gently on the bed. He stepped back and kicked off his shoes. She leaned back on her elbows and watched him undress. He wasn't too muscular, but had a good physique. He crawled on the bed to where she was waiting for him. He undid the three pearl buttons on the front of her blouse and the matching ones on the cuffs of her sleeves, then easing it from the waistband of her skirt pulled it over her head. Underneath she wore a white silk camisole. Grant noticed the label on the back – La Perla – Princess Diana's favourite lingerie brand. She lay back fully on the bed and Grant unzipped the skirt from the side and unfastened two buttons at the waistband. She raised her hips to allow Grant to pull the garment free. The camisole was buttoned under the crutch. She eased her legs apart allowing Grant access to undo them. Neither of them spoke. Undone she sat up again allowing Grant to remove the silky garment. Now he had sight of her naked breasts. Her nipples were small and dark, now fully erect and half an inch long. He nuzzled the right one in his mouth and snaked his tongue across it. She moaned and arched her back forcing her breast deeper into his mouth.

Grant's hands found the top of her tights and he eased them down over her neatly trimmed pubic mound. He slid off the foot of the bed and removed them leaving her totally naked. Kneeling on the floor he grabbed her legs and pulled her down the bed towards him. He pushed her thighs upwards and apart revealing her moist open sex. He traced a pattern with his tongue down her right thigh stopping short of her vagina. He traced a similar path down the other thigh. She squirmed and gasped for breath. She pressed her heels into the softness of the mattress as Grant's tongue found the hard bud of her femininity. He flicked it with his tongue his hands exploring her breasts. He heard her breathing become more laboured as she built to a shuddering climax which wracked her body. She moaned out loud as the orgasm gripped her, then Grant felt her relax. He moved up her body planting delicate kisses on her abdomen, her chest, each breast, her neck and shoulders. Finally he kissed her lips and she could taste herself on him.

He lay on the bed beside her and she reached down for him, but found a limp penis.

"What's the matter baby?" she said huskily, "too tired?"

Grant sat up and she rested her hand on his back.

"I'm sorry," he said, "maybe too many margaritas."

"You sure it's not a guilty conscience?" she asked, "You are not thinking of your wife are you?"

"No, I'm not," said Grant staring at the blank wall opposite the bed. "I'm not thinking about my wife."

And he wasn't, he was thinking about Sara.

CHAPTER 12

Anthony Dark tapped the end of his 22-carat gold Schafer pen on the exquisite walnut table four times in sharp succession.

"Ladies and gentlemen can I please call the meeting to order."

The chattering around the table subsided and a cloak of silence fell on the room. The man at the head of the table rose to his feet and leaned forward resting his outstretched fingers on the polished surface. He was a thin man with angular features. His black wavy hair, black bushy eyebrows and long pointed nose gave him a rat-like appearance. He looked like he needed a shave.

"May I first start by welcoming Mrs Mattherson here today and say how very saddened we all are by the death of her husband. Michael was..." he paused and looked directly at the woman sitting at the opposite end of the table, "..not only well respected by everyone in this room, but much loved as well. His business acumen made this company what it is today. Without his guidance, without his foresight Mattherson's Industries would not be such a growing industrial force as it is today.

"We meet today to elect a new chairman. Michael will be a hard act to follow and I am sure nobody will envy the task of his successor. In accordance with Article 17, members of the executive committee have met and put forward proposals contained in the reports before you." There followed a rustling of papers as the board members picked up copies of the documents in front of them.

"To save time," Dark continued," it is proposed that Michael's brother, Alan, our current managing director be elected chairman with full executive powers."

There was a mumbling around the table as people turned to each other in whispered agreement.

"Not only am I sure this is what Michael would have wanted, but I am equally sure that he is the right man for the job. I have also been authorised to tell you that his nomination for chairman also has the full support of his widow."

The woman at the end of the table kept her gaze fixed firmly on the bowl of flowers on display.

"If we could vote then," said Dark. "All those in favour raise their right hand." Three people on the left hand side of the table immediately raised their hand prompting two people opposite to do the same then another and another until only one hand remained down. Dark looked at the young man in the dark grey chalk stripe suit who, in turn, was looking scornfully at the widow.

"It would be nice to have a unanimous decision," Dark said addressing George Travers. "I am sure the new chairman would like the full support of the board."

"I am afraid I cannot support the nomination," he said getting to his feet. "You will have my resignation by the end of the day." He pushed the mahogany chair away from himself and walked across to the double doors of the boardroom. Before opening them he turned and looked at the widow again. She looked up briefly burnt by the heat of his glare then she looked back at the table. He opened the doors and walked out. In the outer office Alan Mattherson stood leaning against the Adams fireplace.

"Going somewhere George?" he smirked. The young man stared at him

"Don't think this is over you bastard," he hissed.

Alan Mattherson took a cigarette from the silver box on the mantelpiece and reached into his waistcoat pocket for his Dunhill lighter.

"But it is over – for you," he said quietly, lighting his cigarette. "If you take my advice you'll take a long holiday somewhere. The air around here doesn't seem to agree with you. It would be such a shame if anything happened to you or that lovely young wife of yours. Paula isn't it?"

The young man's temper flared and he rushed across to the chairman elect and grabbed the lapels of his Amani suit forcing him back against the fireplace with brute force knocking the cigarette from his fingers. Their faces were close enough for the young man to smell the stale breath of his boss.

"If you ever come near my family I'll kill you." He spat the words out. He let go of the now crumpled suit and left the office.

Alan Mattherson was smoothing his suit and trying to regain his composure when the boardroom doors opened again and Dark walked out.

"Mr Chairman," he said, "your board awaits you."

Alan Mattherson entered the room to a round of applause as all the members stood up.

"Please," he said, "please be seated. Thank you for putting your faith in me. You can imagine this is a very emotional time for me. With your indulgence I suggest we adjourn the meeting to a later date. Thank you once again."

The meeting broke up and everyone filed away. On their way out they shook hands with the new chairman and patted him cordially on the back. The only other woman on the board, Freda Strong, who was personnel director, kissed him lightly on the cheek.

When they had all gone, the new chairman moved across to the doors and locked them. He turned around and leaned back heavily looking up at the crystal chandelier which hung from the ceiling. His sister-in-law was still sitting at the end of the table. She shifted in her seat and crossed her legs. The lime green skirt rode a few inches above the knee. He crossed the room and stood behind her resting his hands on her shoulders.

"We did it," he said squeezing the loose flesh through the lace blouse. She leaned her head back and her long brown hair cascaded over the back of the chair.

"You did it," she said, "I knew you could."

He bent down and kissed her on the mouth. His hand went to her bare knee and moved swiftly up her thighs and between her legs.

She gasped and broke the kiss.

"Any regrets?" he asked and kissed her again, his fingers digging into her. She pulled her head away and shifted in the chair allowing him better access.

"No regrets," she said breathing heavily now.

"Not even about Michael?" he panted, his hand working furiously between her legs.

"You had to do it," she said her breaths now coming in short gasps. "He was too weak, and in....uh..uh..oh God, in the waaaay!"

He withdrew his hand and rubbed the stickiness with his thumb against his forefinger.

"I think we might have a problem with George," she said readjusting her skirt. "He could be trouble."

Alan moved around and perched on the table.

"Do you think he knows something?" he asked.

"What, about us?" asked Liz.

"About any of it?" he replied.

"He can't," she said, "he knew Michael was against the deal with the Chinese, but he can't prove anything. The police were convinced it was an accident. The coroner's verdict was accidental death. The insurance people are happy and nobody will ever know he altered his will."

He stroked the side of her face with the back of his hand.

"Nobody will ever know he left everything to his darling daughter when he found out his wife was screwing his own brother."

She rubbed her face against his hand. "Wasn't it a co-incidence the only two witnesses to the new will met with untimely deaths before the old will was read. You were a great executor. Michael made the mistake of showing me the new will when he demanded a divorce. No witnesses, no loose ends."

"Nevertheless," said Alan, "we had better keep an eye on George, he's very bright."

"I know," said Liz, "that's why Michael brought him in to the firm, but don't worry, I can handle him."

He looked into her eyes and felt a stirring in his loins.

"You would like to handle him, I suppose," he teased. She reached across and started to undo the belt on his trousers "only if you want me to Mr Chairman!"

CHAPTER 13

The bucket of the mechanical digger thudded into the soft earth and clawed up another huge clump of soil. Inside the cab the operator manipulated the controls with the aplomb of a concert pianist making the machine dance to his tune. The arm of the digger swung around and the contents of the bucket were dropped into a waiting skip.

The swimming pool was Grant's birthday present to himself. It had caused an argument with Jill. She didn't want it and said it would be a five minute wonder which wouldn't be used. Grant thought differently. It would save him going to his gym every time he wanted to swim and besides, it would be great for the children and good for parties, the first of which was going to be for his fortieth birthday. He wanted it to be a night to remember. He wasn't going to be disappointed.

"Dad," said Emma reaching across the back of the armchair and putting her arms around his head resting them on his chest. He put the book down he was reading. It was a Ludlum one of Grant's favourite authors.

"Dad," she said again nuzzling his hair with her chin. "Did mum tell you I got a letter from Sara?"

Grant grunted. "How is she?"

"Oh she's fine," said his daughter. "She says she's coming to London and might look us up."

Grant sat upright in his chair and took Emma's hands away from his chest.

"When?" he asked.

"Well that's just it," she said, "she will be here the weekend of your party."

"And?" said Grant.

"And I wondered if it would be okay if she came to the party?"

Grant twisted his nose to one side.

"I don't know honey. There are a lot of people coming?"

"I know," said Emma, "a lot of boring old people, all people from your work."

"Hey, not so much of the old," reprimanded Grant. "Have you told mum you want her to come?"

She hesitated.

"She won't mind if you don't, and you would like to see her, wouldn't you?"

You don't know just how much said a little voice in his head, then out loud; "Yes, it would be nice to see her again."

"So shall I talk to mum?" pressed Emma, now excited at the prospect of seeing her friend again.

"We'll see," said Grant, "let's just wait and see."

That night when they went to bed Jill was in the bathroom cleaning her teeth.

"I understand Em's asked you if that girl from holiday can come to your party," she called out.

She came into the bedroom wiping her mouth on a towel.

"What do you think?" asked Grant.

Jill put the towel on a chair. "It's your party, do you want her there?"

"I'm not bothered one way or the other," he lied. "I suppose she will be company for Emma."

Jill pulled the duvet back and climbed into bed and picked up a book from the bedside table.

"Right then, I'll add her to the list," she said and opened the book to start reading. Grant looked at the nude print on the wall. Every ounce of common sense in his body told him it was a mistake to have Sara stay at the house, but something else told him 'we all make mistakes.'

The pool was finished two days ahead of schedule and exceeded Grant's wildest expectations. It was open air, but surrounded by a series of Roman arches. It was 40feet long and 15feet wide and eight feet deep at the deep end. It was tiled with blue mosaics. The shallow end had steps leading down into the pool. A York stone patio surrounded it and to the side was a timber chalet changing room.

"So who's going to be first in?" Grant asked the children.

"I'm the youngest," said Sally.

"I think it should be dad," said Tim. "It is his pool."

"I think we should all hold hands and jump in together," suggested Grant and that's what they did. They all went in except Jill. She watched from the side.

They had races and played volleyball. Ben turned blue trying to swim two lengths under water and Tim was told off by Jill for squirting Sally in the face with the water cannon. When they were drying themselves in the changing room Emma said to Grant: "Dad, Sara telephoned today and said she will be arriving by train tomorrow at half past eleven. Can you pick her up?"

Grant rubbed the towel across his back.

"I thought she wasn't coming until Saturday," he said.

"Well so did I," replied Emma, "she says there has been a change of plan. It doesn't matter, does it?"

"No," said Grant drying his hair, "you can come with me."

"Well, that's just it, I can't," she explained. "I have an interview for that Saturday job at eleven, so I will not be finished in time."

"Okay," said Grant, "which station is she coming in to?"

"Kings Cross," Emma replied "the 8.40 from Bradford."

"Okay," said Grant. He then turned to his other three children.

"Come on you lot, race you back to the house."

CHAPTER 14

Sara was grooming her pony at the stables when a red MGB roadster pulled up in the approach road. She turned and looked at the young driver behind the wheel. He was good looking, about thirty with thick wavy blonde hair which peeped out from under his flat cap. He wore a brown tweed jacket and beige coloured cavalry twill trousers. Sara thought he had just climbed out of the pages of Country Life.

He got out of the car and walked across the gravel road. It scrunched under his brown leather brogue shoes. Sara went back to grooming Scout.

"Sara?" he called. "Sara Mattherson?"

"Who wants to know?" Sara said cautiously.

"My name's George Travers," he said. "I worked for your father."

Sara reached out and shook his hand after putting the brush down on a nearby bench. Scout nodded his head as if to welcome the stranger.

"What can I do for you Mr Travers?"

"I was commercial director of your father's company up until the time of his...." He hesitated.

"Accident" said Sara helping him out of his embarrassment.

"Well that's just it," he began to say, "I don't think...."

"Why George," cried a woman's voice. "George Travers, I thought that was you." It was Sara's mother.

"George, I didn't have a chance to talk to you earlier."

She turned to Sara.

"Darling," she said "why don't you let Scout out into the paddock while George and I have a little chat?"

Sara looked at George who shrugged his shoulders. She led the horse away. Liz Mattherson took George by the arm and led him back to his car.

"What did you want with my daughter?" she asked.

"We were talking about horses," said George.

"You didn't come all the way out here to talk about horses," she said disbelievingly.

"I'm thinking of buying a horse for Paula," he lied, "for her birthday."

"I didn't know she rode," probed Liz.

"Well, she doesn't, but she's thinking of taking lessons."

They had arrived back at the MGB.

"I would be very careful if I were you, George," she said pleasantly. "Riding can be very dangerous, especially for novices. I'd hate to think of her heading for a fall."

He got in the car.

"I wouldn't try to see Sara again, if I were you. She's so young and impressionable and, after all, you are a married man. The police might think you are grooming her."

He started the car, pressed the accelerator and let out the clutch. The back wheels spun spraying up loose gravel. He watched her in his rear view mirror, arms folded across her chest. He knew she was involved in Michael's death, but how could he prove it. He had hoped to get access to the house with the help of Sara, but how?

Sara came strolling back from the paddock. She was still wearing her cream coloured breeches and dark green polo neck jumper and black boots.

"Where's Mr Travers?" she asked.

"What was he talking to you about?" asked Liz.

"I don't know really," replied Sara. "He said he used to work for daddy. I think he was going to tell me something about the accident, when you came along. Where is he?"

"Gone," she said. "Good riddance. He's a troublemaker, a thief and a liar. That's why your uncle had to sack him. He was stealing from the company."

"That's awful," said Sara. "But why would he come here?"

"I don't know," said Liz. "That's what worries me. I don't want you talking to him again, do you understand me?" She was gripping Sara's arm tightly, making her wince.

"Okay, okay, mother."

Liz relaxed her grip.

"It's just that he seemed such a nice man," said Sara.

"Well he's not," said Liz, "and until I find out what he wants, I don't want you here. Telephone those people in London you are going to stay with and ask if it's convenient for you to go tomorrow."

That's when she called Emma.

CHAPTER 15

Grant paced up and down the platform at King's Cross. He looked at the station clock – 11.20. He had checked the time of the train and it was on schedule. He had taken the day off work – not just to pick her up, but he had some running around to do for the party. He was dressed in a pair of faded denim jeans, Reebok trainers and a San Francisco 49s football shirt – a present from Tom.

He had parked in a multi-storey at the back of the station. He looked at the clock again. 11.22. This was ridiculous. He felt like a kid on his first date. His stomach was turning somersaults and he had been to the station toilet three times since he arrived.

He sat down on a bench occupied by a sanguine-faced vagrant clutching a can of Carlsberg Special Brew. The man was balding with thin ginger hair. On top of his head was an old scab, remnant of a possible fall, or fight. On his feet he wore navy blue deck shoes that could have seen service under Nelson. The sides were split and a black knobbly toe stuck out from the side of the left shoe.

He was probably about the same age as Grant,

What twist of fate gave him this life, and me mine, thought Grant. He looked at the clock.11.29. A minute to go. Then what? Then she'll step off the train, walk over and shake my hand saying hello Mr Campbell, how nice to see you again. All that business in Menorca will have been forgotten. She is just your daughter's friend coming to stay for the weekend. The platform announcer's voice broke Grant's concentration.

"The train now arriving at platform 12 is the 8.40 from Bradford."

Grant stood up and walked to the ticket barrier. He was behind three British Rail officials collecting the tickets. One was a Sikh whose turban was obstructing Grant's view. He moved to the side of the gate.

The train stopped and the doors swung open like the oars of a Roman galley. He scanned the exodus of passengers, his eyes darting from one form to the next. There was a mix of grey suited businessmen, students with backpacks, mothers with pushchairs, crying children. The station was an astrodome of noise, a cacophony of confusion.

No sign of her. Did she miss the train? Did she fall asleep? His mind raced. He wished the train had done the same. Now there were only a few stragglers disembarking, mainly elderly, the stick brigade. A guard helped a woman off in a wheelchair. Then he saw her. She stepped off the train from the same compartment as the disabled woman. She leaned back inside the carriage and pulled out a large black suitcase. Most of the passengers had gone through the barrier, so Grant moved past the barrier onto the platform.

Sara lifted the heavy case from the floor and looked up along the platform and saw him. She dropped the case and it fell on its side. She too was wearing jeans, a black polo necked sweater and a short burgundy coloured coat, a bag thrown over her left shoulder.

She ran towards Grant and he sprinted towards her. They met half way in the middle of the platform and he caught her in his arms and swung her around. Her shoulder-length blonde hair flew out like a carousel. Their lips locked and the world spun wildly. Her feet were still off the ground and she hugged him like she was clinging to life itself. The disabled woman in the wheelchair gave them a cautionary glance as she propelled herself past their locked embrace. When eventually they surfaced for air and pulled their mouths apart, Grant found himself drowning in the liquid green pools of her eyes. Never before had he seen anyone with such bright white eyes, such iridescence. But the eyes were moist with tears. Grant felt the tears in his own eyes forming.

His throat was hot, his mouth dry. He gently lowered her to her feet.

"Hello," she said, a tear now running down her cheek. "Did you miss me?"

He crushed her to him and in that single moment in time, he knew he was completely lost to her. He clasped her head and pressed their foreheads together. He tried to swallow, tried to speak. He moved back and looked into her tear stained face. He wiped the moisture from her cheeks.

"Yes, I've missed you," he said almost in a whisper, gently kissing her sweet pink lips.

A cleaner armed with a mop and bucket opened the carriage near where Grant and Sara stood.

"Isn't love grand," she said, and gave out a shrill laugh. "It's lovely when the children come home from college."

Grant looked at Sara and she laughed out loud and hugged him.

Yes, she was young enough to be his daughter, but he didn't care. She was the most important person in his life.

He went back to pick up her case where she had dropped it and she threaded her arm though his as they walked back towards the barrier.

Nobody seemed to be taking any notice. Even if they had, Grant wouldn't have cared. He was re-united with his Sara.

"Where do we go from here?" she asked.

"Do you mean us?" Grant asked seriously.

"No, not US, silly," she said. "Where's the car?"

Grant laughed.

"Have you had anything to eat?" he asked.

"I had some coffee and toast in the buffet car," she replied. "But I could murder something now."

They passed into the main concourse and Grant noticed a flower stall. He wanted to buy Sara the entire stall, but realised he couldn't even buy her a single bloom. She read his mind, "It's the thought that counts," she said and hugged his arm tighter.

"The car's in the car park around the back. I didn't book anywhere for lunch as I didn't know what you would want to do."

"I know this is London, but you don't have to book Macdonald's down here, do you?"

She laughed again. Grant realised how much he had missed hearing her laugh.

"If that's what you fancy," said Grant.

"What I fancy you can't get at Macdonalds," she teased. "But a Big Mac will do for now."

Grant pecked her lightly on the lips.

"What sort of car have you got?" asked Sara.

"What sort of car do you think," said Grant playing the game.

"A Morris Minor," she laughed.

"So you see me as an old crock, eh!"

"Only joking," she said. "I see you as a Ford Mustang, or a Ferrari."

"You were closer with the Morris Minor," he laughed. "This is us."

They had arrived at Grant's Mercedes 450SL cabriolet. It was metallic blue.

"Wow," said Sara. "I'm impressed."

Grant flicked the fob and the car unlocked. He loaded the case in the boot and Sara got into the passenger seat.

"Very impressed," she said, doing up her seat belt. Grant got in.

"I'm not trying to impress you," said Grant.

"I know you're not," she said, then reached across and kissed him on the lips.

CHAPTER 16

The red Bentley Mulsanne turbo glided to a halt in the car park overlooking Devil's Dyke. The only other car there was a Jaguar. Inside sat Alan Mattherson. He watched the Bentley come to a halt and opened his driver's door. There was no movement from the other car, and as the windows were tinted, he couldn't see inside. His brown ankle length Chelsea boots crunched on the gravel as he walked towards the limo. When he got to within three yards the driver's door opened and a squat, bull-necked man got out. He was oriental, his head shaved. He looked like a sumo wrestler except he wore a smart chauffeur's livery, not a set of Pampers.

He walked around the side of the car and opened the near-side rear door. He motioned Alan Mattherson to climb inside. He was hit by a draught of cold air from the air conditioning. He sat down heavily on the cream calf leather seat next to a painfully thin man dressed in a silver grey silk suit.

They had met once before, in Hong Kong, where he and his brother had gone to negotiate a joint agreement between Mattherson's Industries and a conglomerate of Chinese businessmen.

The man was Xian Wang, the conglomerate's financial officer. His sallow complexion was not enhanced by the round gold rimmed glasses which made his face look like an owl in a distorted fairground mirror. Xian spoke perfect English with an Oxbridge accent.

"Good morning Mr Mattherson," he said.

"Have you got it?" Alan asked nervously.

"All in good time my dear sir," said the Chinese man.

"First I must convey to you certain anxieties being expressed by some of my associates with regards to…" he paused searching for the right phrase. "…certain loose ends."

"What loose ends?" snapped Alan.

"Your Mr Travers," said Xian. "Our information is that he is no longer with your company."

"That's correct," said Alan, unsurprised by the Oriental's information network.

"He is being dealt with."

"Another unfortunate accident?" smiled Xian.

"Something like that," replied Alan. "Now have you got something for me?"

Xian reached to the floor well and picked up a black Samsonite briefcase. He put it on his lap and snapped open the two locks. He lifted the lid. Alan's eyes lit up at the sight of the contents.

"Take great care, my friend," cautioned Xian closing the lid and snapping the case shut.

As if on cue, the door to the Bentley was opened by bull-neck. Alan took the case and returned to the jag. He gripped the leather covered steering wheel in both hands and looked at his eyes in the rear view mirror.

"You've done it," he told himself. "You've got it all."

Paula Travers stuck the note she had left for George under a cucumber magnet on the fridge door. It read "Have taken Kirsty swimming. Be back around six. Love Paul."

She knew George would find it when he came home because the first thing he would do would be to go to the fridge for a cold beer. He had been drinking a lot lately. He had told her he resigned because of a clash of personalities, but Paula knew there was more to it than that. They had been married for six years – Kirsty was nearly five now – and she knew him almost as well as he knew himself. Something had been troubling him, but he wouldn't say what. George would tell her, but in his own time.

She left the house in her two year old Peugeot having strapped Kirsty in her seat, unaware she was being watched.

Twenty minutes later George arrived back at the house. He had been back to the stables to try and see Sara, but had arrived to discover she had already gone to London. George hoped she would find the envelope he left in her tack box in Scout's stall.

True to form, he went to the fridge for a beer. He popped the ring pull and put the can to his lips taking a good third of the contents in one go. He was about to raise it to his lips again when the front door bell rang.

He went to the door and could make out the uniforms of two policemen through the frosted glass. He undid the latch and opened the door. The officers stood on the raised brick step.

"Mr George Travers?" asked the larger of the two men.

"Yes, I'm George Travers. What is it? What's wrong?"

"I'm afraid it's your wife," said the policeman. "She's been involved in a road traffic accident."

George didn't hear the rest of what the officer said. His mind raced back to the boardroom confrontation.

"It would be such a shame if anything happened to that lovely wife of yours."

"I would be very careful if I were you George. I wouldn't try and see Sara again," wasn't that what Liz Mattherson had said. He had tried to see Sara. Someone at the stables must have seen him and told them. They'd killed Paula.

"Mr Travers?" said the second officer. "Your wife is perfectly all right, a bit shaken, but no serious injuries."

"Oh no, not Kirsty, my baby, how is my baby?" Panic erupted like a volcano in his chest, constricting his breathing.

"She has some minor injuries, but she's asking for you. Come on, we'll take you to the hospital."

His mind wasn't working properly. He had to get to them. He picked up his jacket and felt in the pocket for the keys to the MG.

"I think it would be better if you didn't drive," said the younger officer. "You've had a shock. We'll take you."

The other officer held the door open as George brushed past. The other man closed the door with a gloved black hand. There was a dark grey Sierra parked behind George's MG on the drive. George walked across to the car and the older man opened the rear door. Just as he bent down to get in, George saw, through his peripheral vision, a large black object hurtling towards his skull. It was the last thing he ever saw.

They found George's body, or what was left of it, at the wheel of his MG at the bottom of Devil's Dyke. A near empty bottle of whisky was found in the wreckage. An autopsy found he had large quantities of alcohol in his system. The inquest recorded an open verdict, but it was widely assumed he was a victim of drunk driving. Some thought it was possible suicide, having lost his job and all.

His young widow was inconsolable. All Kirsty kept asking was "When is daddy coming home?"

CHAPTER 17

The drive back from Macdonald's had been unnaturally quiet. Grant and Sara were uneasy. Grant swung into the large driveway of the white-fronted house. Emma had been waiting for them and rushed out to greet her friend.

"Hi you," she said excited and renewing their friendship. "Have a good trip?"

Sara climbed out the car and hugged her.

"Hi dad," she called to her father who had gone to the boot of the car to get Sara's case.

"Come on," said Emma, taking her friend by the hand. "I've got loads to show you and lots to talk about."

Sara looked back at Grant and smiled. He managed a faint smile back and the two girls ran in to the house. Jill was in the kitchen when she heard the excited giggling.

"Hello Mrs Campbell," said Sara on seeing Jill wiping her hands on her apron. Sara thought how much older Jill looked since the holiday. Jill thought the same of Sara.

"No need for Mrs Campbell," she said. "Please, call me Jill."

"Oh come on," said Emma tugging at her friend's jacket. "Come and see my bedroom. We're sharing."

Sara nearly toppled off balance as Emma pulled her towards the stairs. Just then Grant came in carrying Sara's case.

"Hi," he said to Jill greeting her with a peck on the cheek – a different sort of greeting to the one he had given Sara a few hours previously.

"Was the train on time?" asked Jill. "I thought you would have been back before now."

"No, it was on time," replied Grant. "She was starving so went for a Macdonald's."

"Did you pick up the wine for the party?" she added.

"Shit. I forgot," he bit the inside of his lip again. "I'll pick it up later."

"I don't know why you didn't let the caterers bring it," said his wife rolling out pastry.

"They charge an arm and a leg," said Grant. "We're paying enough for the food without paying a mark-up on the drink."

Jill grunted and sprinkled more flour on the board.

"Well, you're the one who insists on lobster, salmon and king prawns, and why you've ordered that suckling pig – it looks hideous." Grant had bought the 22lb piglet from Smithfield Market the previous day. He was going to have it barbecued at the party. Jill had gone ape when she saw it.

"The head looks hideous," she had said. "Can't you cut it off?" So he did, but then when she saw the headless corpse she said it looked even worse and made him sew it on again!

Grant and Jill were still in the kitchen when Emma came running down the stairs. She was wearing a blue bikini with white spots.

"Is it OK if Sara and I go for a swim?" asked the still excited youngster.

Jill shrugged her shoulders. "I suppose so. Where's Sara?"

"Just getting changed," said Emma. "Send her down to the pool."

A few minutes later Sara came down the stairs. She was tightly wrapped in a bath towel which covered her from knee to armpit. She had piled her hair up on top and reminded Grant of the Greek goddess in his bedroom.

"Emma's down at the pool," said Jill. "Just follow the path down the garden.

Grant watched as she walked cat-like down the path.

"She seems to have grown up a lot since the holiday, doesn't she?" commented Jill. She put the pie she had finished making into the oven.

"Do you think so?" said Grant nonchalantly. "I suppose she has. OK, I will go and pick up the wine. Do we need anything else?"

"I don't think so," said Jill. "We've got everything."

On the drive to the wine shop he found himself biting his inner lip. He should never have let her come.

Jill roasted a leg of lamb for dinner. It was obvious Sara loved meat, the way she piled it on her plate.

"How do you stay so slim?" asked Jill, as Sara added more roast potatoes to her plate.

"I get a lot of exercise," said Sara. "I ride a lot which keeps me fit, and I love to swim."

"Sara's got her own horse," interrupted Emma, "imagine having your own horse. I'd love a horse."

"You can't even ride," said Grant spearing a Brussel sprout on the end of his fork.

"Sara says she'll teach me when I go up to Yorkshire," said Emma.

"And when is that?" asked Jill. "It's the first I've heard about it. Grant?"

"Don't look at me," said Grant.

"I can go, can't I?" pleaded their daughter.

"We'll see," said Jill.

"I thought Sara and I could go out tonight," said Emma. "There's a dance on at the youth club and I want to introduce Sara to my friends."

"What time does it finish?" asked Jill.

"Midnight," said Emma, "but it's okay because Nicola's mum said she will pick us up."

"And how are you getting there?" added Grant.

"Well, I was hoping you might take us."

"If it's okay with mum," he said taking the last mouthful of roast potato. He flinched and almost choked when he felt a hand squeeze the inside of his thigh. As the same time Sara said; "Thank you for a lovely dinner, Jill."

The telephone rang and Emma answered it.

"Dad, it's uncle Tom," she called from the hall.

Grant went to the phone.

"Hi Tom, how's things?"

"I was phoning about the party," said the American.

"You're still coming, aren't you?" asked Grant.

"Sure," said Tom. "I just wondered if it would be okay to bring a plus one. I met this gorgeous red-head in Stockholm the other night, red head, no hair!"

"Of course," said Grant. "See you tomorrow."

He went back into the dining room.

"Is Tom still coming?" asked Jill.

"Yes, he's bringing his new girlfriend – Claudia."

"I can't keep up with his love-life," said Jill disapprovingly. "He'll catch something the way he carries on." She didn't like him. She thought he was a chauvinist and a womaniser. She was right of course, but was that any reason to dislike the man.

Grant sat in his favourite armchair in the lounge and wondered why Sara had grabbed his leg under the table. He drifted off to sleep. It was the sound of his daughter's voice that woke him.

"Da dar!" she said announcing herself. "What do you think?" She did a twirl. She was wearing a pair of grey fitted trousers with six brass buttons on the front arranged in two rows of three. She had black patent shoes with black bows on the toes. The outfit was topped off with a white lace top and black sequined waistcoat.

"Oh la la," said her father, "tres chic!"

"Very nice," said Jill. "Where's Sara?"

"She's just coming," said Emma. Grant kept that thought to himself.

Then she walked in and Grant did a double take. So did Jill. Sara wore a plain black mini dress cut four inches above the knee. The neckline was modest, but when she turned around the dress had a large vee-shape cut out of the back which clearly would have showed her bra had she been wearing one.

She had platform heels on which made her look three inches taller. She had washed her hair and wore it down, the undried golden threads cascading like a waterfall around her shoulders.

"Don't you look lovely?" said Jill motherly. "Doesn't she, Grant?"

"They both look nice," said Grant tactfully.

"Come on, let's go," said Emma. "I'll squeeze in the back. You've got longer legs than me."

When they got to the car the roof was still down.

"I'd better put that up," said Grant.

"I'd like to have it off," said Sara mischievously, looking at Grant.

"You'll get blown to bits," warned Grant, but both girls just laughed and got in the car, Sara's dress riding up her thighs even higher.

The drive to the youth club took ten minutes. Sara's hair flew out in front of her and she giggled all the way there.

When they pulled up there was a group of five boys outside the entrance, one astride a Norton Commander 1200 bike.

"Who's the hunk on the bike?" asked Sara.

Hunk, thought Grant, greasy yob more like.

"His name's Jake," said Emma. "He really fancies himself."

As long as Sara doesn't, thought Grant.

The girls got out of the car.

"Have a good time," called Grant.

"We will," said Sara looking back over her shoulder and winked.

Grant sat and watched hopelessly as they crossed the car park to become enveloped in the group of lads outside the doors to the club.

Emma introduced Sara to everyone. Grant noticed how the nerd on the bike held onto her hand just a fraction of a second longer than the others. Christ, I'm jealous. There's no other word for it. He wanted to get out of the car, storm across to the club, pick her up and throw her over his shoulder and carry her back to the car. He didn't get the chance. They disappeared inside. At least the 'hunk' was still on his bike, but as Grant pulled away he saw the object of his jealousy climb off the machine and put it on its stand and follow the girls inside.

Grant looked at the carriage clock on the mantelpiece in the lounge. Its incessant ticking had been annoying him all evening. Everything and everyone had been annoying him all evening. He had put the other children to bed, but declined the offer of reading Sally a Mr Men story. Now he felt guilty about that.

He drained the brandy from his glass and went to pour another. It was his fourth. What the hell, it was officially his birthday now. It was gone twelve. Where were they? His mind was tortured by the thought of Sara with the biker. What if he gives her a lift home? What if they stop on the way? What if…

The front door chimes rang. Grant went and opened the door. Both girls were on the step. Behind them on the drive in a blue Vauxhall a blonde haired woman waved to Grant. The girls went past Grant and flopped on the settee.

"Did you have a good time?" asked Grant.

"The best," said Emma stretching her arms. "Sara was a hit, she's been dancing all night."

"Lucky Sara," said Grant grudgingly,

"One of the guys asked her out," said Emma, now yawning.

"Which one, the biker?" asked Grant.

"Jake? No, not Jake, Andrew, Nicola's brother. He was all over her."

"Em he was not," protested Sara primly.

Emma giggled. "He couldn't keep his eyes off you, or his hands."

"Emma, you're terrible," said Sara. "She was too busy having a good time herself," said Sara getting her own back.

Emma stood up. "I'm going to bed. Night dad," she said and bent down to give him a goodnight kiss.

"Wait for me, Em," said Sara going after her. Then she turned back and looked at Grant. "Night," she whispered, then blew him a kiss.

CHAPTER 18

Grant didn't sleep very well. In his dreams he was tormented by mermaids, tortured by the Spanish police chief, won a Reader's Digest free draw competition despite having sent back the 'no' reply envelope, but then lost the £180,000 cheque when it was eaten by a lobster.

He left Jill sleeping, just put on his dressing gown and made for the en suite. He was busting for a pee. The house was eerily quiet. Grant liked early mornings, it was the best time to think.

His first job was to clean the pool and check the temperature. He opened the backdoor of the kitchen and walked out onto the terrace which ran the length of the rear of the house. He leaned on the ornamental iron railings which separated the terrace from the garden. On the lawn a group of young starlings were fighting over the leg of lamb bone Jill had put out for them. There was a heavy dew on the grass, but Grant enjoyed the feeling of the water between his toes and the softness of the turf as he made his way down to the pool, avoiding the shingle path.

He checked the temperature. It was 30 degrees, a bit too hot for Grant, but he knew the pool would be in use during the party and the guests would like it. He removed the solar cover and set up the vacuum system. He had just sucked up a spider when two young female hands clamped him around the eyes. It was all he could do to stop himself toppling in.

"Happy birthday to you, happy birthday to you, happy birthday dear daddy, happy birthday to you."

It was Emma.

"You're up early," Grant said accepting a kiss from his daughter.

"It's Sara," said Emma, "she snores worse than you."

Grant laughed. "Is she awake too?" he asked.

"You must be kidding," laughed Emma. "She's sound asleep! I thought we could go sightseeing when she eventually gets up."

"I won't have time to take you," said Grant. "I've got too much to do here."

"That's fine," said Emma. "We'll be okay," and off she skipped back to the house.

"Come here, let me do that," said Jill taking hold of the small gold cuff-link Grant was trying to thread through the cuff of his shirt.

"How people with one arm cope, I'll never know," said Grant frustrated. Jill threaded the link through the double cuffs and fastened it. She then did the other one.

"What tie are you going to wear?" asked Jill going to the wardrobe.

"Do I have to?" he said. "It's my party. You know how I feel about wearing ties."

"It's your party," said his wife. "You do what you want."

Just then the doorbell rang.

"I'll go," said Jill. "You finish getting dressed." She hurried out of the bedroom, along the landing and down the wide sweeping staircase into the hall. Through the stained glass front door she could make out two figures. She opened the door.

"Hey Jill, how's it going?" said Tom. Next to him was a tall slim girl with long flame red hair.

"This is Claudia, Claudia this is Jill."

The two women shook hands.

"Where's the birthday boy?" asked Tom.

"He'll be down in a minute. He's just getting ready. Can I get you a drink, Claudia?"

Claudia sat on the arm of the settee.

"Just a fruit juice if you have it."

"Tom?" said Jill.

"White wine if there's one open," said the American.

She was pouring the wine when Grant walked in.

"Happy birthday, buddy," said Tom walking over to him and giving him a hug.

"This is Claudia. Isn't she something?"

"Tom, you're embarrassing the girl," said Jill coming over with the glass of fruit juice. Claudia got off her perch and stood up. Grant came over and gave her a platonic peck on the cheek.

"What sort of work do you do, Claudia?" asked Jill.

Before she had a chance to reply Tom interrupted.

"She's a fashion model. In London for a product shoot, isn't that right, babe?"

"What sort of product?" asked Grant going across to the bar to get himself a drink.

"Kitchen furniture," said Claudia in a strange accent.

"Where are you from?" asked Grant.

She sipped her drink. "I was born in Brazil, but I have lived in Scandinavia since I was 13. I was brought up in Oslo, but now I live in Stockholm. That's where I met Tom."

"How long are you in London?" asked Jill.

"Only three days," replied Claudia. "I have to be in Paris on Tuesday."

"Another photoshoot?" asked Grant.

"No, to see my mother," added the model. "She lives there with my stepfather."

"Well, it all seems a far cry from shopping in Sainsbury," said Jill, and they all laughed.

By six o'clock more than fifty guests had arrived. Only a few had braved the pool. Grant was on the patio talking to Claudia when Emma and Sara came back from their day out.

".....so when the photographer said I had to get up at 3am because of the sunrise I told him...."

"Excuse me Claudia," said Grant. "I'll be back."

He went into the lounge. Sara's eyes locked on him the moment he came through the doors. He threaded his way through his guests oblivious to the slaps on the back. He stopped a foot in front of her.

"Hi," he said.

"Hi, birthday boy," she said taking a gift wrapped parcel from the bag slung across her shoulder.

"Happy birthday," she said almost in a whisper. Grant took the gift and their fingers touched. He winced. It was like receiving an electric shock.

He opened the package at one end while Sara watched. Emma had her back to them chatting to her godfather – Tom. Grant pushed his fingers into the soft package and drew out the contents, a grey and brown silk Balenciaga tie. Holding it between finger and thumb it dropped open. Sara took hold of it and offered it up to his neck.

"You shouldn't have," he said feebly. "It's lovely."

"Let's put it on," said Sara, and reached up behind his neck. She lifted his shirt collar and fastened the button on the neck. Her face was only inches from his and he could smell her perfume, almost taste her breath. She crossed the tie over twice and made a knot before turning the collar back down. All the time she did it her eyes never left his.

"Happy birthday," she said again and kissed him lightly on the cheek.

"Hi dad," said Emma turning around. "Do you like Sara's present? She got it in Harrods. Come on Sara," she said, tugging at her friend's coat.

"We've got to go shower and change." With that the two of them went upstairs.

Clutching a large glass of Jack Daniels, Grant made his way back out to the patio. Claudia was surrounded by three men and looked as though she was enjoying the attention. He made his way down to the pool where he found Tom relaxing on a lounger. Grant sat on the empty chair next to him. "How you doing buddy?" asked Tom.

"I'm not sure," replied Grant. "You remember the girl I told you about from the holiday?"

"Sure," said Tom adjusting his baseball cap against the glare of the evening sun.

"Well she's here."

The American looked at his friend.

"Here, at the party? Are you fucking crazy?"

"It's a long story," said Grant, "she's staying for a few days."

"She's staying here?" said his friend incredulously. "Grant, my friend, you are heading for serious trouble."

"I just want you to meet her," said Grant. "She's different."

"Of course she's different, she's only fifteen for fuck's sake."

Grant turned on his friend. "So how old is Claudia, 18?"

"18 is a fuck sight different to 15, my friend. Ask any lawyer. You got to sort this thing out, man," said Tom and left Grant staring into the water as he went back up to the house.

Grant drained his glass and walked back up the garden. No sign of her. She wasn't in the kitchen, or the lounge, or the dining room. He went into the hall.

"Looking for me?" said a voice from the top of the stairs. Slowly she began to descend running her hand provocatively along the bannister rail. She wore a dark green knitted woollen dress which hugged her body. A wide brown belt accentuated her slim waist. The hem of her dress was shorter than the one she had worn the night before. As she got closer, Grant could see she wore a thin gold chain with a St Christopher nestled in the vee of her neck. Her golden hair fluttered down to her shoulders. The curls bounced softly around her neck as she glided down the stairs.

Grant stood open mouthed.

"You look…wonderful," he stammered.

She smiled. "Why thank you kind sir."

Then Jill walked out from the lounge.

"Sara, oh there you are. Emma has been looking for you. Come on, I'll introduce you to some people. I'm afraid there are no boys your age here, but come and enjoy the party. Don't be shy."

Sara laughed and joked with Emma's aunts and uncles. She and Emma danced the feet off everyone else.

"I can see your problem," said a voice in Grant's ear. It was Tom. "It's hard to believe she is only 15. She's going to be a stunner when she's older. She was talking to Claudia earlier on. She seems to have an old head on a young body."

"She's been through a rough time," said Grant.

"You mean losing her father?" said the American.

"You know about that?" asked Grant.

"Sure," said his friend.

"It was a tough break."

Grant offered Tom another drink, but he declined.

"Claudia and I are going to make a move. I've left a bottle of Dom Perignon on ice down by the pool for you and Jill. Enjoy."

The party starting thinning out and by one o'clock the last of the guests had left. Jill flopped down in an armchair.

"I'm bushed," she said. "Come on, leave the clearing up, we can do it in the morning."

"You go up to bed. I'll make a start on the glasses."

Jill levered herself out of the chair and kissed him on the cheek.

"Don't be too long," she said, "or I will be asleep."

"Are all the kids in bed?" he asked. "They didn't say goodnight."

"They went up ages ago. Probably all sound asleep. Don't be long."

It took him thirty minutes to collect the glasses and stack the first load into the dishwasher. He went onto the patio for one last check and looked down the garden. He saw an eerie blue glow coming from the pool area, yet he was sure he had turned the lights off an hour ago. The leather soles of his white moccasins crunched on the gravel path as he made his way down the garden away from the house. The pool lights were on, casting dancing shadows onto the white stone columns. He went through the rustic arch and stepped onto the pool surround. Then he saw her. Sara, naked in the water.

She pushed off underwater and swam towards him, her body gliding silently, effortlessly, the lights casting her grey shadow on the pool floor.

Her head broke the surface by the side of the pool where Grant was standing. Her hair, darker now, plastered to her head.

She looked up at him.

"Well?" she said.

Grant bent down on his haunches.

"Why are you doing this?" he said quietly, as though someone was listening. She shook her head from side to side clearing the water from her ears. As she did so her hair slapped the water sending a spray over Grant's trousers.

"Oh dear, I've got you all wet. You might as well come in and join me."

"You'd run a mile," he laughed.

"Not like this I wouldn't." she said and pushed off from the side of the pool on her back. The mounds of her breasts broke the surface of the water. She floated on her back, the light triangle of hair of her pubic mound clearly visible. She turned and swam back to him.

"Come on birthday boy, where's your birthday suit?" He looked up at the sky. It was a cloudless night and there was an over-abundance of stars. He thought if he looked hard enough he would find some celestial help, but none came. He took off the tie she had given him and tossed it onto the lounger, then unbuttoned his shirt. In the pool

Sara was enjoying the spectacle and hummed the tune to The Stripper. Grant was grateful he had already taken out his troublesome cuff-links when he was loading the dishwasher. He tossed the shirt aside and kicked off his shoes. He sat down and peeled of his socks, then stood up and unbuckled his belt. Sara hummed louder. Grant's trousers fell in a heap around his ankles. He stepped out of them. Now he stood before her in just a pair of blue slips. He walked down the steps, frightened that the sound of diving in might wake someone in the house.

"Wait a minute, that's not fair," said Sara swimming over towards the steps.

"I have got nothing on, come on, get them off."

For a fraction in time the world froze. Everything stopped, even the stars stopped twinkling. In that moment Grant rationalised everything. He knew the consequences. It was as if God himself had said "Okay Grant, I gave the choice to Adam and Eve and now I'm giving it to you. You know what you should do, but can you do the right thing and walk away?"

Grant took off the briefs and dived headfirst over Sara into the water. He surfaced at the far end of the pool. Sara had remained by the steps. He ran his fingers through his hair to brush it away from his face. Using the breast stroke they swam silently towards each other, the lights reflecting off their faces as though in some macabre ritual. They met in the middle and Sara's arms snaked around Grant's neck. His hands encircled her back and he crushed her to him. Their mouths met in a hungry, wanton embrace as they slipped beneath the water.

Sara brought her legs up and wrapped them around him holding his body in a vice-like grip. Small bubbles of air escaped from her nose, but their mouths remained clamped together, their life forces joined to sustain one another in this watery sanctuary where they were locked away from the world.

When they eventually broke the surface, Grant lay on his back and kicked for the deep end trawling Sara with him. When they reached the wall Sara kissed him again, this time lightly on the lips. Grant wanted the kiss to last longer, but she pulled away. Then she kissed him on the nose, then the cheek, then on his eyelids and his ears. She smothered him in butterfly kisses. She licked the water from his cheeks and her tongue danced across his lips. He caught it and hungrily drew it into his mouth. Despite the cool night air the water in the pool was warm and Grant felt that warmth, her warmth spreading though his loins.

Now it was his turn to pepper her with kisses. She laid back, her head resting on the pool surround. She breathed deeply and her chest swelled as Grant's hungry mouth searched for her rosebud nipples. He drew first one, then the other into his mouth, suckling her gently, snaking first his tongue and then his teeth across them. She gasped and wrapped her legs around him once more.

Grant stopped and looked at her. She opened her eyes, their faces inches apart. Her eyeslashes were like pelmets from which glistened droplets of water. He cradled her face in his strong hands as if he were holding the most fragile egg-shell in the world.

"I mustn't make love to you," he whispered. A droplet of water fell from the corner of her eye. Grant wasn't sure if it was a tear.

"I shall die if you don't," she said. Their lips met softly and Grant felt himself tremble. He ran his hands down her side to her hips and gently lifted her towards him, the motion of the water washing them back and forth like a tide. She pushed forward to meet him and moaned as she felt his hardness push into her. Their union was tight, tighter than anything Grant had experienced before.

"Are you okay?" he asked, concerned that he may be hurting her.

She smiled at him and her eyes sparkled brighter than the stars which stood sentinel above them.

"It feels wonderful," she said and rocked backwards and forward. The muscles of her sex clamped him as his movements became more and more frenzied. Sara threw back her head as her own climax began to build to an undeniable crescendo. Her breath quickened and her moans were getting louder, but Grant was lost in hedonistic delight. He clung to the side of the pool as he thrust deep into her tender young body. She clung to him and sank her teeth into his shoulder as the waves of orgasm washed through her. The pain of the bite and the pressure in his loins sparked a climax of cataclysmic proportions. He erupted inside her, flooding the very essence of her being. Now she wept. The tears flowed freely from her crystal gaze. As the spasm subsided Grant held her closely, kissing her gently on the forehead. His chest was still heaving, his breathing laboured.

"I love you Sara," he said, and then thought how inadequate it sounded.

"I know you do," she whispered, "but do you know how much I love you?"

"This much?" he said indicating a couple of inches with his fingers.

"Look up there," she said tilting her head back and looking at the night sky.

"To the stars and beyond, that's how much."

CHAPTER 19

They stayed locked together for what seemed an eternity. Grant was the first to speak.

"I think we'd better get dried." He looked at his Rolex. It was 3.30. He slipped out of her and kissed her gently on the lips. Levering himself up on his arms he pulled himself from the water, his nakedness no longer an embarrassment. He stretched down a hand which Sara took and with one pull he lifted her out of the water. Dripping water across the patio they crossed to the timber changing chalet. Grant opened the door for Sara and she stepped inside. The light from the pool danced across the log lapped walls. Grant reached up to one of the shelves on the back wall and pulled down a large beach towel. He undid it and wrapped it around his illicit lover. He held it tightly around her and she snuggled into the safety of his arms. He released her and got a towel for himself. She sat down in the Lloyd Loom chair to dry herself.

He looked at her while she dried her hair.

"Did I ever tell you how beautiful you are?" he said softly.

She looked up at him and the lights danced across her face. She smiled and carried on drying her hair. Grant wrapped the towel around himself and secured it at the waist. He went across and knelt at her feet.

"What happens now?" he said softly.

"What do you want to happen now?" she replied.

She stopped drying her hair and took his hands in hers. She lifted them and bent her head and kissed them each in turn.

"All I know is that I never want to be apart from you," and gazed deep into his eyes, the windows of his soul.

"What about your family?" he asked.

She paused before answering.

"I can't go back there…to Yorkshire I mean…" Grant squeezed her hands.

"But your mother, Sara, what about your mother, she needs you, now more than ever since your father died."

Grant saw a coldness creep across her face. Her eyes were no longer looking at him, but through him.

"She has Alan," she said coldly.

"Is that your uncle?" asked Grant.

"Bastard!" she spat the word out. "That bastard, I hate him."

Tears welled in her crystal clear eyes and streamed down her face.

Grant put his hands around her shoulders.

"Sara, Sara, what is it? Don't cry darling. It's all right everything is going to be all right."

Her sobs continued. He lifted her head up and dried her tears with the towel.

"Why don't you want to go back there?"

She sniffed and drew in a deep breath.

"When we made love in the pool did you know I wasn't a virgin?"

Grant was shocked by the question.

"I didn't know, I didn't think about it at all. All I know is that I love you as a woman, like no other woman. It doesn't matter what you have done before."

"But it does matter, Grant," she said. "Until I met you I didn't think anyone would want me because I am dirty, dirty because of what he did to me." She hugged him tighter.

"Who, your uncle?"

She nodded.

"Do you remember that night in Menorca on the beach?" she said looking into his face again, "the night they said I didn't go back to the apartment?"

"How can I forget," said Grant. "It was the night I realised how much I loved you."

She put a finger to his lips.

"I did go back after I left you. I felt wonderful as though I was floating on air. But when I got back he was waiting for me."

Grant was frightened by what he might be about to hear.

"What about your mother," he asked, "wasn't she there?"

Tears rolled down her cheeks again.

"Yes," she was there, collapsed on her bed in a drunken stupor," she said, now trembling.

Grant was ashen faced.

"You mean he…" he struggled with the word.

"Raped me?" she said. "He tried to. He got on top of me and tried to have sex, but I fought him off. I ran out the apartment and hid in the sand dunes in case he came after me. When mum woke up and found I wasn't there she called the police and reported me missing. Alan must have been spooked because he wasn't there when I went back. I tried to tell mum what had happened, but she didn't believe me. She said I was wicked to make up stories about him. She called the police and told them I had been out all night at a disco in Mahon."

Her tears erupted again. She leapt off the chair and flung herself against the window of the chalet. The towel fell to the floor and she stood naked and shivering and in total despair.

Grant went across to her and pressed her to him.

"You poor darling," he said.

It was inadequate, but in his state of shock it was all he could think of saying. He rocked her gently from side to side the way he had comforted his children when they had fallen over or woke from a nightmare.

"Why on earth didn't you tell me when we were on the island?"

"I was too ashamed," she sobbed. "I didn't know if you would believe me, or if you would think I was just making trouble."

"We must go to the police," said Grant.

She stopped crying and looked at him sharply.

"No! No police! I couldn't stand it. Nobody must know. Promise me. I will never forgive you."

"Okay, okay," said Grant trying to calm her. "If that's what you want, but they shouldn't be allowed to get away with it. What happened when he came back?"

"He acted as though it never happened. He steered clear of me on that last day and since we got back home I haven't seen him. That's why I don't want to go back. I want to stay with you," she said, "if you still want me."

"Want you?" he repeated her words. "I want you more than I have wanted anything or anyone in my entire life."

He bent down and kissed her lips.

"I promise I will never let anyone hurt you ever again."

As they dressed it dawned on Grant what they must do.

"We'll run away together." The words dropped out of his mouth as though they had been spoken by someone else.

"What?" said Sara now more confused.

"Tonight, we'll go now."

"But what about Jill, what about Emma and the children?" she asked.

Grant looked at her hard.

"There's no other way. I can't live a lie. They will be okay, I will explain to them later."

"But where will we go?" said Sara, pulling on a pair of Levis.

"I don't know. I'll think of something," said Grant. "Go up to the house and pack a few things. Use Emma's rucksack, it's in her wardrobe. I'll do the same. Be careful not to wake anyone. I'll meet you at the car."

The adrenalin was pumping.

"Do you realise what you are giving up?" asked Sara.

He took her hand, "Come on."

The house was in darkness except for the kitchen light. They crept upstairs. Sara went off to the left to Emma's room, Grant to the right to the master bedroom. He heard the deep even breathing of his wife and knew she was in a deep sleep. He opened the wardrobe and took out his sports holdall. He emptied it of its contents and wondered if he would ever play squash again. He took a leather jacket off the coat rail. That would have to do. He grabbed some socks and underwear from the chest of drawers and stuffed them in the bag. He added a couple of shirts and a pair of trousers. The towel fell to the floor. His heart was thumping. He decided there and then he could never be a burglar.

He put on a pair of jeans and a navy blue Aran sweater. He paused at the door and looked towards the bed. He couldn't see her face and thought it was just as well.

On the landing he stopped outside the boys' bedroom. He eased the brass handle downwards and pressed against the door. The boys always slept with their curtains open so the room was lit by the street lamp outside. Ben was curled up into a tight ball, the duvet drawn up around him. Tim was as straight as a beanpole, his covers unruffled.

He moved to Sally's room. His hand reached for the handle, but something stopped him. He knew if he saw her he would never leave. He rested his forehead against the white gloss paint of her door.

"Grant, Grant, are you alright," whispered Sara coming out of Emma's bedroom holding the rucksack.

His conscious screamed at him "What the fuck are you doing?"

"Yes," he said holding out his hand to her. She took it and they crept downstairs.

Grant picked up his wallet and car keys from the hall table. He opened the front door and they went out into the night air quietly closing the door behind them.

The car was parked in front of the closed garage doors. He opened the boot and put the luggage in.

"I'll roll it to the end of the drive," he said in a whisper, "before I start the engine. Wait at the bottom." Grant opened the driver's door and released the handbrake. Checking it was in neutral he put his shoulder to the doorframe and pushed. The wheels began to turn as Grant moved the Mercedes along the drive. When he got to the entrance he reached in and secured the handbrake. He opened the passenger door and Sara got in.

"Seat belt," he said. She buckled up.

"Are you really sure you want to do this? Are you sure this is what you want?" He leaned across and kissed her. He turned the key and the engine purred into life. He selected drive and the car swung out into the night.

"First stop is the bank," he said. "We're going to need money. Have a look in my wallet and see how much cash is in there," he told Sara reaching into the pocket of his jeans. She opened it and thumbed through the notes.

"About £200," she said.

"That's not going to get us very far," he said, keeping his eyes on the empty road ahead.

"We'll have to get more. I can't use my credit cards or cheque book. They'll be able to trace us,"

She twisted in her seat.

"Do you think they will come after us?" asked Sara.

"I'm sure they will," said Grant. "Kidnapping a minor?"

"What will happen if they catch us?" asked the youngster.

"They won't," he said and held out his left hand. She took it and squeezed it tightly.

"Oh Grant, I feel so safe with you. Everything is going to be all right, isn't it?"

"Sure it is," he replied. "Look, here's an ATM," He pulled over.

"Here, give me the wallet." She handed it to him and he got out of the car and went across to the cash dispenser. He withdrew £250 from his personal account, £500 from his business account and £500 on his Barclaycard.

He returned to the car and handed Sara the wallet.

"Did you get it?" she asked.

"Some," he said, "but we need more. I need to find an Amex machine. "There's one in the Haymarket."

The traffic was light until they got to the West End. Sara stared out of the open window in wonderment.

"Where on earth do all these people come from?" she asked. She looked at the clock on the dashboard. It was nearly 4am.

"It's a different world here," said Grant. "It never stops."

He turned into the Haymarket from Piccadilly Circus and parked outside the American Express office.

Sara looked across the road to the Prince of Wales theatre where Phantom of the Opera was showing.

"Have you seen that?" she asked.

"Three times," replied Grant. "I've got the CD in the car."

He got out of the car and withdrew £500 from the ATM on his platinum card. He folded the cash and put it and the card in his back pocket. Just as he was getting back in the car a police patrol car cruised slowly past. The officer in the car gave the couple in the sports car a glance, but that was all. Grant knew that from now on they would always be looking over their shoulder.

"So where is it?" asked Sara.

"The money?" said Grant.

"No, silly, the Phantom of the Opera CD," giggled Sara.

"I didn't know you liked opera," said Grant enjoying finding out new revelations about his young lover.

"I like all sorts of music," she said. "I wouldn't say Lloyd Webber was really opera, more musicals."

"When you think about it there is so little we know about each other," said Grant.

"We know we want to be together," she said, "At the moment that's all that matters to me."

She put her head back on the headrest and closed her eyes. Grant reached under the dash for the remote control for the CD and selected Disc 3. By the finale the runaways were speeding down the M4 towards Bristol. When the music stopped Grant turned the machine off. Sara was fast asleep.

Dawn was not quite breaking when Grant stopped at the service station just outside Bristol. Ignoring the car's petrol warning light, Grant passed the petrol pumps and pulled into the car park. The lack of motion woke Sara.

"Where are we?" she asked looking around.

"Bristol," he said.

"What are we doing here?" she asked lazily.

He leaned across and kissed her on the lips.

"You'll see."

They left the car and Grant locked it with the remote.

"Do you need the loo?" he asked.

"I'd better," she said. "Where shall I meet you?"

"I'll be in the shop," he said. "Do you want something to eat?"

"Not really," she replied, "just a cold drink."

She disappeared into the loos. Grant made for the shop. He picked up a basket and filled it with ten large cartons of milk and a bottle of diet coke. He threw in two packets of sandwiches, one chicken, one prawn.

When he got to the cash desk the young female assistant looked quizzically at the purchase.

"I know milk's good for you, but that's ridiculous," she joked as she scanned the items. Grant smiled, but said nothing. He paid with a £50 note and pocketed the change. He saw Sara coming out of the toilets. She had brushed her hair and applied some make up.

"You look beautiful," he told her.

"You don't look too bad yourself," she replied. "What's in the bag?"

"Milk," said Grant, "and your coke."

"What do we want with all that milk?" she asked. Grant pushed open the service station door. "All will be revealed," he said.

They went back to the car and Grant started the engine. He pulled over to the corner of the car park where there were no other cars. He got out and took the carrier bag of milk to the rear of the car and opened the petrol cap. Sara leaned out of the window to see what he was doing. He was pouring the milk into the petrol tank.

"Grant, what are you doing?" asked the confused youngster.

"Just wait," he implored her. When he had emptied all the milk into the car, he put the empty carton back in the bag and put the bag in a rubbish bin.

He got back in the car and turned the key in the ignition. The car started, but soon began to splutter and finally stop.

"Oh great," said Sara. "Now we have no car."

"Wait here," said Grant. He left Sara and walked to the rear of the garage where he had previously seen an AA hut. The patrolman on duty was watching an American game show on a portable TV when Grant walked in.

"Morning," said Grant. "The car's packed up and I wonder if you can take a look? I'm hopeless with cars." That was a lie. A few years earlier, Grant had restored a 1963 E-type jag.

"Are you a member, sir?" asked the patrolman getting out of his chair. He was at least four stones overweight. The belt on his trousers cut into the overhang of his stomach and he had spilt something down his shirt. Grant took out the plastic membership card from his wallet and handed it to the man. He checked it and handed it back.

"What make of car is it?" he asked raising a flap on the counter.

He'll never squeeze through that, thought Grant, but turning sideways the patrolman forced his way through the gap.

"It's a Mercedes 450 sports," said Grant. "Problem is we've got to catch an early morning flight from the airport. We were just on our way there."

"Well, we'll have to take a look," he said.

When they got to the car Grant released the catch and the AA man lifted the bonnet.

"Just try and start her up," he said, his head now buried under the bonnet.

Grant reached inside and turned the key. The engine turned, but wouldn't start.

"Again," said the patrolman.

Grant tried again, but to no avail.

"Half a tick," said the patrolman and walked back to the hut.

"Why have you sabotaged the car?" asked Sara.

"We have to dump it," replied Grant. "Trust me."

The patrolman returned carrying a diagnostic kit.

"How long will this take?" asked Grant. "We don't want to miss our flight."

Flight, thought Sara, what flight?

"Stan will fix it," said the patrolman.

"I'm sure you will," said Grant, "but our priority is to get to the airport. If you could drop us off I would be happy to make if worth your while." With that Grant pulled out the wad of notes from his back pocket and peeled off a £50 note.

"What about the car?" asked Stan.

"If you could arrange for it to be towed to the nearest Mercedes garage, they can fix it and I can pick it up when we get back."

The patrolman rubbed his chin.

"Well I am about to go off duty, so I don't suppose I will be missed." He took the £50 note and stuffed it in his pocket.

"If you and your daughter would like to wait in the Range Rover over there, I'll lock the office and be back in a minute."

He turned back to the hut.

"Come on, Sara," said Grant. "This is where we change."

"What's this about a plane? Where are we going?"

Grant just smiled, so far so good. He went to the back of the car and took out his holdall and Sara's rucksack and carried them across to the AA rescue vehicle. They both got in the back. A few minutes later the patrolman came out of the hut and locked the door behind him. As he climbed into the car Grant and Sara felt it sink on its axles. The man's stomach was pressing against the steering wheel.

"Off anywhere nice?" asked the patrolman.

"Just a spot of sunshine for a few days," said Grant.

Twenty minutes later they pulled up outside the terminal building. Grant and Sara got out. Stan stayed in the driving seat.

"Have a good flight," he called before pulling off.

"Thanks said Grant, "we will."

"Now where?" said Sara.

"Follow me," he said and picked up the luggage and headed towards the terminal building with Sara in tow. They walked in the main entrance and across the concourse and out of the side door to the taxi rank. The driver at the head of the rank was reading a Daily Mirror when Grant approached and opened the rear door.

"Coach station please driver," said Grant. He and Sara got in the back.

"Been anywhere nice?" asked the cabbie heading off the rank.

"Just a few days in the sunshine," said Grant looking at Sara.

The cab dropped them at Bristol coach station. Grant paid the fare and gave the driver a small tip.

Grant carried the bags into the coach station and dumped them on an empty seat.

"You stay here while I get the tickets," he told her.

"When are you going to tell me where we are going?" asked Sara.

Grant sat down beside her. "Have you ever been to Islay," he asked,

"I've never even heard of it, let alone been there," said Sara. "Where is it?"

"It's an island off the west coast of Scotland," said Grant. "We can lie low there until we decide what to do."

He went to the ticket desk where he found a fat woman behind the counter. Make a good partner for Stan the patrolman, thought Grant.

"When's the next coach to Scotland?" asked Grant.

Without looking at the timetable she looked up at the clock on the wall.

"The Glasgow coach leaves in three minutes she said. You'll have to be quick. Bay nine."

He paid cash for the tickets and sprinted back to Sara who was applying some lipstick.

He grabbed her arm, and the lipstick smudged a line on her face.

"Sorry," he said. "We've got to be quick. The coach is about to go."

They sprinted down to bay nine just as the doors of the coach were closing and was pulling out. Grant banged on the door and the startled driver applied the airbrakes which made a hissing noise. The coach stopped and the doors opened.

"You're cutting it a wee bit fine, laddie," said the driver in a broad Glaswegian accent.

"I'm sorry," he said in gasps.

"Is the wee lassie with you?" he asked seeing Sara just behind him.

"Yes," panted Grant. "We are together."

"And is that all of the luggage you have?" he asked motioning to the case and holdall.

"That's all," said Grant now regaining his breath.

"Hop on," he said, "there is plenty of space at the back."

Grant held out his hand and helped Sara on board. As she made her way up the aisle with Grant behind her, the doors swished shut and the coach pulled out the Marlborough Street station.

The back seats were occupied by a group of Scouts. They sat a few seats in front. They were on their way to Scotland as dawn broke.

CHAPTER 20

It was gone nine o'clock when Jill woke up. She turned over expecting to find her husband beside her, but immediately saw his side of the bed had not been slept in. He had been doing that a lot lately since the holiday. She swung the duvet back and sat on the edge of the bed, her feet looking for her slippers. She stood up and the hem of her nightdress fell to her ankles. She reached for her dressing gown from where it hung on the back of the bedroom door. She slipped it on and fastened it.

The house was quiet, no television on in the children's bedrooms, only the steady tick of the grandfather clock in the hall. When she reached the bottom of the stairs she crossed to the front door and went to take the safety chain off as she did every morning, but it was already hanging loosely. Perhaps Grant had forgotten to lock up. She opened the front door and took the four pints of milk off the step. She closed the door with her backside and clutching the bottles made her way along the hall. He was probably in the lounge. She poked her head around the door. The settee was empty. She walked through the dining room into the kitchen. She put the milk bottles on the working surface and a moment of terror seized her. He's drowned! He had too much to drink, went for a swim and he's floating face down in the pool.

She hurried down the back steps and half running, half walking, made her way down to the pool. She breathed a sigh of relief when she saw it was empty. She checked the changing hut. Nothing.

Maybe he had to go out, work or something. If he did he must have left a note.

She went back indoors and looked for a note, but couldn't find one. Maybe he left the note in the bedroom. She ran back upstairs to check.

No note. Impulse, intuition she wasn't sure what it was, but she went straight to Emma's room. Her entrance woke her daughter. The put-you-up bed which Sara had been sleeping on was empty.

"Where's Sara?" barked Jill.

Emma sat up and looked across to where her friend should have been.

"I don't know," she said. "Isn't she downstairs?"

"No she's not," she said quietly, "and I can't find your father either."

"Don't worry, mum. Maybe they went for a run. Maybe they're in the pool."

"No I've checked," said her mum. The tears began to well up in her eyes. She looked at Emma through blurred vision and wiped her eyes. Emma pushed back the bed covers and put a comforting arm around her.

"They won't have gone far," she said. "They'll be back soon."

The tears came followed by uncontrollable sobs, infectious sobs because Emma started crying too.

"He wouldn't leave us would he mum, would he?"

Together they cried, united in fear and sorrow, closer than they had been for some time.

CHAPTER 21

Rain splattered the windows of the coach as Sara awoke to look at the North Yorkshire moors. Grant was still asleep, but when she lifted her head from his chest he woke up.

"Morning," she said kissing him lightly on the lips.

"Any idea where we are?" asked Grant.

"I think we're near my home," she replied. "The moors look familiar."

"If you're right we're only a couple of hours from the border."

"I hope we get there soon," said the teenager. "I'm starving."

Grant reached into the holdall and fished out the two packets of sandwiches.

"Chicken or prawn?" he asked.

She chose chicken. He thought how refreshing it was to be with someone who made up their mind, knew what they wanted. If he'd asked Jill the same question she would have said she didn't mind. Perhaps that had been the trouble with their marriage. There was too much I don't mind. Sara was different, so different.

"What will we do when we get to Glasgow?" she asked her mouth half full of sandwich.

"We've got to get to a place called Tarbert to catch a ferry. The problem is I can't hire a car because it will flag up on the system when I show them my driving licence. No, we'll have to get another coach."

"We could hire bikes," said Sara. "Don't need a licence for those."

"It's a great idea," said Grant, "but it's too far. It's 100 miles or more from Glasgow, but we could hire bikes for the island."

"See, not just a pretty face," she said with an impish grin.

They finished their sandwiches and Grant laughed out loud.

"What's tickling you?" Sara asked.

"I was just thinking of all that milk," said Grant. "I could do with some of that right now."

The coach pulled into Glasgow's Buchanan Street coach station just before 2.30pm. The journey had taken seven hours.

"First let's find a Macdonald's," said Sara. "I'm starving again."

There was one just around the corner. Grant settled for a modest cheeseburger and coffee while Sara polished off a Big Mac, large coke and fries.

"How come you look so terrific when you eat so much?" Grant asked as Sara licked a spot of relish from her lips.

"All that riding, I guess," she said, then went very quiet.

"What's the matter?" Grant asked, leaning across the table towards her.

"Oh nothing," she said swirling the ice around the bottom of the cardboard drinks container.

"Come on, no secrets remember, what are you thinking?"

"I was just thinking about my pony," she said. "I don't suppose I will ever see him again. They'll probably have him put down."

He took hold of her hand.

"I'm sorry, Sara. I can't see what we can do."

She looked up from the beaker.

"I love Scout," she said and squeezed his hand, "but I love you more."

They had an hour to wait for a coach to Tarbet and arrived in the small town two hours later.

The last ferry from Kennacraig had already left for the day, so there was no way they could get to the island.

"So what now?" asked Sara.

From a previous trip to Islay he remembered a nice hotel overlooking the sound.

"There's a pub come hotel called The Anchor," said Grant. "Let's hope they have got some accommodation."

The hotel was a short walk, tucked away at the back of the small harbour. Being at the start of the Kintyre Way walking path, the Anchor was a popular spot for hikers. The bar was busy when they arrived. The adjoining Sea Bed restaurant was heaving with early evening diners. They went up to reception. The girl on duty was tall, slim and had bright purple hair.

"How can I help you?" she asked.

"We're looking for accommodation," said Grant.

"Let me get the book and I'll have a look," she said. She reached under the bar and produced a red folder and flicked through it. He couldn't help noticing the sleeve of tattoos on both her arms.

"We only have twin rooms left, if you don't mind sharing with your father," the girl said looking at Sara.

Before Sara could answer Grant stepped in.

"Two twins will be fine," he said producing his wallet. "She's a terrible snorer and I wouldn't get a wink of sleep if we shared."

"He's right," chipped in Sara. "He wouldn't get any sleep!"

"How long will you be staying?" asked the receptionist.

"Just the one night," said Grant. "Is there anywhere in town we can hire a couple of bikes. We want to go touring?"

She reached behind the counter and handed Grant a flyer. Bike Hire.

"Excellent," he said.

The girl pushed the registration book towards Grant and handed him a pen.

"If you could just register," she said. "And if I could take the payment now to save any delay in the morning."

Grant took the pen. "I take it cash will be okay," he said. He registered in the name of Devereaux, Dr Malcolm and Jennifer Devereaux.

"Will you be requiring dinner tonight…doctor?" she asked noticing the prefix in the register.

"I only ask as last orders in the restaurant are at 9.30. Do you need any help with your luggage?"

"No, we can manage," said Grant.

"In that case I will get William to show you to your rooms," and with that she pressed a brass bell on the counter. A few moments later a liveried porter appeared. He was seventy if he was a day, grey whiskered moustache and beard. Captain Birdseye's father, thought Grant.

"If you could show the doctor and his daughter to their rooms, please William," said the receptionist. They followed him up two flights of stairs.

"Here we are Miss," he said fumbling for the keyhole. He turned the key and opened the door. Sara went in, followed by Grant then William. The room was large, very large, with two single beds set apart by a big antique dresser. The ceilings were high with ornate plasterwork. The room had two large windows which extended down to a window seat. The green and blue tartan curtains were mirrored by the bedspreads and on the headboards.

"The bathroom is away to your left, lassie," said William. "And if you will come with me doctor, I will show you your room. It's next door." The room was almost identical to Sara's except the tartan was different. Between the twin beds was a painting of a stag on the side of a mountain. It must have measured six feet by four feet,

"What a magnificent beast," observed Grant.

"Aye it is," said William. "Are you a hunting man, doctor?"

"I'm not," said Grant.

"More's the pity," said William. "There's no finer place to hunt stag than here in the Highlands. Will that be all?"

"It will," said Grant, and reached into his wallet for a five found note, handing it to the porter.

"Thank you William. Goodnight."

The warm suds caressed him as he laid back, the hot water enveloping his neck and chin. Between his legs with her back resting on his chest lay Sara, her eyes closed, totally relaxed. Her long blonde hair, now wet, was scooped over one shoulder and partly covered one breast. Her nipples were soft pale strawberries perched on top of two perfect mountain mounds. The hot water covered most of her firm abdomen, only her breasts and toes exposed to the steam saturated air of the bathroom.

They were happy to lay there, to be with each other, to share the warmth of the water and the warmth of their love.

"What's all this doctor Devereaux business?" asked Sara.

"We have to remain incognito," replied Grant. "It's less suspicious if we are travelling as a father and daughter and being a doctor adds an element of respectability."

"So is there a real Dr Devereaux?" she asked.

"Yes," said Grant. "It's the name of an American I met in London, a friend of Tom's."

"Do you think they are looking for us yet?" she said swirling the bath water with her hand.

"I'm not sure," he replied, "but we will be safer when we get to Islay tomorrow."

She leaned her head back to try and look at him. He kissed her head.

"Come on lady, I'm thinking dinner."

She levered herself up. Grant looked at her firm young bottom and the thick clump of wet hair that adorned the triangle of her sex. He felt the stirrings of an erection. She stepped out of the bath and reached across to the heated towel rail for a bath towel. He stood up in the bath and she looked first at his face, then at his groin. "I thought you said you were thinking about dinner." She laughed and threw the towel around her shoulders. Grant looked down at his semi erect penis.

"Are yer referring to ma wee haggis here?" he said taking off William's accent.

"If that's what's on the menu," she said, "I think I'm in for a midnight feast."

At dinner they both ate the same – pate to start with followed by Dover sole. Grant washed it down with a bottle of Chablis Grand Cru from which he gave Sara one glass. Grant declined the desert trolley, but his companion tucked into a mound of profiteroles. He couldn't believe how much she ate.

After the meal they took coffee in the hotel lounge with a high ceiling. It was decorated in traditional Highland style with a tartan carpet and lots of wall cabinets containing prize species of fish. There were only three other people in the lounge, an elderly couple probably in their seventies and a younger man with ginger hair. The couple were watching the television while the younger man was writing.

"Good evening," said Grant to the couple. The woman replied, but her husband either didn't hear or chose not to.

Sara drained her coffee cup and picked up a magazine from the table.

"I think I'll go up to bed, dad," said Sara and came across to kiss him on the cheek.

"Night, Jennifer," he said.

After she'd left the room the woman turned to Grant.

"What a lovely girl," she said, "pretty little thing."

"Yes, she has her mother's looks."

"Are you on holiday?" asked the woman.

"Just passing through," said Grant, "on a cycling holiday. And you?"

"We're here for a week. It's our golden wedding anniversary present from our children. We go back on Saturday. They booked us a tour, didn't they Reg?"

Reg just grunted and kept his gaze firmly on the television. Grant wanted to do the same. He had a dreadful fear of suddenly seeing his face pop up on the screen in a news bulletin saying that police had launched a manhunt for this child abductor.

He excused himself and went upstairs. He stopped outside Sara's room and knocked gently on the door. There was no reply. He tried the handle and the door opened. The room was in semi darkness but there was enough light to see a bundled shape under the covers of the nearest bed. Then he heard the snoring. He went back to his own room. The moose in the painting looked down on him disapprovingly. He turned the light out, got undressed and went to bed.

It was eight o'clock when he woke up, a shaft of bright sunlight streamed in through a chink in the curtains throwing a wedge of light across the bed. He got up and opened the curtains, wincing as the sunlight hit his eyes. It took him a moment or two to adjust. He looked out across the loch. The surface of the water was like glass. Grant could see three small fishing boats stuck to its mirrored surface. The sky was a cloudless blue and the newly risen sun hung like a golden orb. He showered and dressed in jeans and a jumper. He'd slept well and felt refreshed.

He stopped outside Sara's room and gave a loud knock.

"Hold on, just a minute," she shouted from the room. "Who is it?"

"Room service," said Grant mimicking William's accent.

She came to the door wrapped in a bedsheet. She reached up and kissed him on the mouth as if she were eating a ripe strawberry.

"Where were you last night?" she asked. "I tried to stay awake, but guess I must have dozed off."

She kissed him again on the lips, this time letting her tongue snake into his mouth. Speaking as best as her kisses would allow he asked her what she fancied for breakfast. She pulled the sheet from her so she stood naked in front of him

"I think I'll try some wee haggis," she giggled.

CHAPTER 22

The WPC handed Jill the cup and saucer. "Try and drink this," she said. Her hand trembling, Jill took the china crockery and held it on her lap. It was part of a set they had been given as a wedding present. "So how long has your husband known this girl?" asked the uniformed police sergeant his pen poised over the regulation issue note book.

"About four months," said Jill her voice strained with emotion.

"And you say they met on holiday on Menorca, is that correct?"

"Yes," replied Jill.

"And this girl, how old did you say she is?"

"Fifteen," whispered Jill.

"I'm sorry I didn't catch that," said the sergeant.

"Fifteen," she repeated.

"And have you any idea where they may have gone?" pressed the sergeant.

"If I knew that I wouldn't bloody well be calling you lot," she snapped with rage. The cup and saucer dropped from her lap depositing its milky load onto the lounge carpet. The WPC came across to comfort her.

"There there Mrs Campbell, we don't know the circumstances of their disappearance. They could both turn up with a perfectly rational explanation."

"We have informed the girl's mother in Yorkshire," said the sergeant. "We have a photograph of the girl, but we need a recent picture of your husband."

Jill stifled her sobs. The WPC had picked up the cup and saucer and gone to the kitchen to get a cloth to mop up the spill.

"Am I so unattractive that he would go off with a child," she said looking at the sergeant. "Am I?"

Embarrassed by the question the sergeant put his notebook down.

"Look Mrs Campbell, what makes you think they are in some sort of relationship? I mean, has he done anything like this before?"

Jill clenched her fists. "Do you mean has my husband got a history of child abuse? Are you asking me if he is a paedophile? Of course he isn't!"

"Take it easy, Mrs Campbell, I'm sorry I have to ask these questions. We will find them, now about that photograph?"

CHAPTER 23

Grant called the first number on the bike hire flyer, from the phone booth in the hotel, but it was engaged, so he tried the second. No answer. "Third time lucky," he said turning to Sara.

A voice answered: "Good morning Gales cycle hire."

"Hi there," said Grant in the Californian accent he often used to mimic Tom. "My name is Dr Martin Devereaux and I'm here on vacation with my daughter and we would like to hire a couple of mountain bikes. You have. Gee I appreciate that. Can we pick them up right away? Excellent, we're staying at the Anchor Hotel, how far away are you? That's great, we'll see you soon."

He put the phone down. "It's just the other side of the harbour," he told Sara. "Let's get our things and make tracks."

"Sure thing, doc," she laughed.

They found the cycle shop in Harbour Road. Grant pushed open the front door and a bell rang. The noise alerted a man in the back of the shop. He was tall, but thin faced with round wire framed glasses. He stooped slightly which made the loose fitting grey cardigan he wore hang like a tent from his bony frame.

"Hi there," said Grant dropping back into his American accent. "Dr Devereaux. I called earlier about leasing a couple of mountain bikes."

He reached inside his coat for his wallet and took out a business card which the real Dr Devereaux had given Grant when they had met at the conference. He handed it to the shopkeeper.

"Ah, yes doctor," said the man examining the card. "You spoke to my wife."

"A most helpful lady," said Grant.

"How long will you need the bikes?" asked the thin man.

"A couple of weeks," replied Grant.

The shopkeeper reached under the counter and brought out a laminated card.

"They are £8 a day and there is a £50 deposit on each bike." He picked up a calculator and started punching in the numbers. As he did so a stout woman wearing a bright turquoise two-piece suit emerged from the back room.

"Are you managing, dear?" she asked her husband. Momentarily her sudden appearance had caused him to lose concentration and he started again.

"I'm just dealing with Dr Devereaux," he said.

She came forward and extended her hand, a hand weighted down with a gaudy collection of rings and bracelets.

"Ah, doctor," she said, "so nice to meet you. Is my husband attending to you?"

Grant took a closer look at her. She looked like an over-inflated sex doll. He imagined sticking a hat pin in her and watching her fly around the shop getting smaller and smaller.

"He was just explaining about the deposit," said Grant.

"Henry, let me deal with the doctor," brushing her husband aside. She picked up the business card.

"I see you're from Philadelphia," she beamed. "I have a penfriend in Florida. Do you know any people in Florida, doctor?"

"No mam," said Grant politely, "we are New England stock."

"How nice," she beamed.

"Now how long do you need the cycles?" she asked, "a couple of weeks did I hear you say?"

"Yes mam," said Grant. "My daughter and I are touring. I have a second cousin on my mother's side who lives in Kinross."

"We have a lot of Americans among our clientele," said the woman. "Will you be paying cash or card?"

"Cash if that's acceptable, mam?"

"Very acceptable, doctor, and I don't think we need to bother with the deposit, do you Henry? After all if you can't trust a doctor, then who can you trust?"

Grant paid in cash and Henry wheeled out two Muddy Fox mountain bikes, one lime green, the other orange.

"I can't tell you how pleasant it is to have met you Dr Deveraux," she said holding out her hand. Grant politely shook it.

"See you again in a couple of weeks." He was just wheeling the bikes out of the shop when she called him back.

Dr Devereaux, you've forgotten something," and went to hand him the business card.

"That's fine thank you mam. You keep it."

Sara was twenty yards up the road looking in a baker's shop window when he came up behind her.

"Looking at food again?" he joked.

"Wow, those look the bizz," she said seeing the bikes. "Can I have the green one?" Grant pushed it towards her and she climbed on. "Perfect size," she said, "so where to now?"

"Now we go and sort out the ferry," said Grant.

Grant and Sara stood on the deck of the Caledonian ferry and watched the mainland slip away as they headed for the Inner Hebrides. The journey took two hours and twenty minutes before docking in Port Ellen. They wheeled their bikes down the gangplank.

"Where to now?" asked Sara.

"Have you ever stayed in a castle before?" asked Grant.

"Oh all the time," said Sara.

"So are you afraid of ghosts?" he added.

She turned and smiled. "Not if you are with me."

They mounted their bikes and Grant took the lead.

"I hope I can remember where this place is," he said. "I came here years ago when we were putting together an ad campaign for one of the distilleries on the island. The photographer I used had a place here in the grounds of an old castle. He only uses it once in a blue moon. It's very basic and very isolated so it should be ideal for us."

The rode past the Laphroaig, Lagavulin and Ardberg distilleries on the A846, thereafter the road deteriorated the closer they got to Kildalton. Grant pulled onto the verge.

"Look for a footpath off to the right," he said. "Probably best if we pushed the bikes from here."

After about five minutes Sara shouted; "I think I've found something, but it just leads into the bushes."

"That could be it," said Grant. "I remember it being buried in a rhododendron forest."

They took the path and followed it for half a mile, the bushes getting thicker.

"Are you sure this is right?" asked Sara doubtfully. "There's no sign saying Castle This Way."

Grant laughed. It was becoming almost impossible to push the bikes through the undergrowth, but not once did Sara complain.

"How much further Dr Livingstone?" she quipped, "or should I say Dr Devereaux?"

Twenty yards on they came to a clearing and there, on a large swathe of grass, were dozens of rabbits. Behind them was the façade of the castle. Although the roof had fallen in, the walls were sound. It was built as a country house in 1870 on a 2,000 acre estate for a whisky distiller, but it fell into disrepair in the 1920s.

They wheeled their bikes around the back of the castle down a narrow path to a stone building that had once served as the laundry for the big house. It was a rectangular building about 12feet wide and 30 feet long. It had a wooden front door and three windows on each side. The back wall was solid. The roof was slightly pitched and topped with slate tiles which had become covered in moss. The bottom half of the windows were curtained, but the glass was so filthy you couldn't see inside.

"I hope you've got your front door key," joked Sara.

"Key? What key?" said Grant and turning the brown handle pushed the door open.

Sara stepped inside. The centrepiece of furniture was a large brass double bed pushed up against the back wall. It was unmade, but there was a pile of bedlinen on top. A worn leather armchair stood one side of the open fire. The floor was flagstone, the only covering, an Indian rug stretched under the bed and reappearing on either side. On the wall opposite the fireplace was a large pine dresser with an assortment of clutter.

"What's through there?" asked Sara pointing to a doorway in the corner.

"Come on, I'll show you," he said taking her hand.

The room contained a large refractory table surrounded by a mismatch of chairs down one side and a church pew on the other. There was also a wood-burning stove and a sink without a tap. The walls were whitewashed and there were cobwebs everywhere.

"Not exactly five stars," said Grant. "It doesn't look as though anyone has been here for quite some time."

Sara hugged him again.

"Don't worry," she said. "I'll soon get it into shape. I'll do a bit of spring cleaning tomorrow."

He put his hands on her shoulders.

"Do you know, I think you are marvellous," he said and kissed her gently on the lips.

"I think you're pretty terrific too. What about a cup of tea?"

"Well," said Grant.

"Well what?" replied Sara.

"Well," repeated Grant. "The water's in the well."

"You're kidding me," said the youngster. "No running water?"

"Nope."

"So what about the toilet?" said Sara cringing at the thought of no proper loo.

"There's a chemical toilet around the back," he said. "Is it too awful?"

"It's not ideal," she replied. "Look, you go and get some water and I'll make up the bed."

"You'll be okay on your own?" he asked. She smiled and headed back to the other room.

"Of course I will I'm not a child."

Grant looked at her. It was true, she wasn't.

He found a large water carrier in the kitchen with a length of rope attached. It was partly full, but Grant didn't know how long the water had been in it.

"If I'm not back in three days, send out a search party," he joked. He made his way through the bushes at the side of the cottage. He remembered the well was no more than twenty yards away, but in which direction he wasn't sure. He wished he had bought the machete he had seen hanging on the wall by the stove and wondered if he should go back for it. He thought better of it and pushed on through the undergrowth. After ten minutes of searching he found the wooden cover of the well. He prised it up with the tips of his fingers. It lifted up and he slid it off. He peered inside. The water was no more than two feet down. He reached down and cupped a handful of the ice cold liquid. He tasted it. It was sweet and pure. Removing the cap on the water carrier he lowered it into the well using the rope. He immersed it and waited for it to fill.

Back at the cottage Sara was busy making the bed. There were no sheets, only blankets which smelled musty, but they would have to do. She was bending over the bed smoothing the blankets when the creak of the front door made her jump. She spun round and screamed when she saw the figure standing in the doorway.

Grant sprang to his feet the instant he heard the blood curdling cry. He let go of the carrier and tore through the bushes back towards the cottage, the thick branches scratching his face. As soon as he broke through the clearing he saw the tall figure in the doorway. He flew at it with a rugby tackle even Will Carling would have been proud of. They crashed onto the slate floor.

"Please don't hurt me," cried the man suffocating under Grant's weight. Grant kept the intruder pinned to the floor. Sara was sat on the bed looking terrified.

"Who are you? What are you doing here?" snapped Grant. "Sara, are you okay? Did he hurt you?"

"Please, let me explain," said the stranger struggling to get up.

"If you've so much as touched a hair on her head," Grant said menacingly, his face a twisted mask of insanity.

"No, he didn't touch me," said Sara. "Grant, please let him up."

Grant released his grip and the man scrambled to his feet.

"I'm the laird," he said trying to compose himself.

"I'm the laird of Kindalton. I own the castle. I own this cottage."

Grant looked shocked.

"I'm so sorry. I don't know what to say. I thought this place belonged to a friend of mine, Mike Walters."

"The photographer?" said the laird. "He leases the cottage from me. He only uses it occasionally and he always lets me know when he's coming. I have to check it from time to time in case I get squatters or poachers. I've had trouble with both. Mr Walters didn't tell me you would be staying."

"No, it was a bit of a last minute decision," said Grant. "I hope its okay."

"It's not a problem," replied the laird, "now I know who you are. The accommodation is very basic. I hope you will be all right here."

"I've stayed here before," said Grant. "We'll be fine."

"Well, if you are sure, I'll bid you a good day," and with that he left.

Grant closed the door behind him and leaned back. Sara got off the bed and hugged him.

"My hero," she said snuggling up to him.

"Some hero, I feel a right idiot, and I dropped the container down the well. I'd better go back for it. Will you be okay?"

"Sure," she replied, "but don't be too long."

Grant went back to the well, retrieved the container and filled it with water. He replaced the lid of the well before returning to the cottage. Sara was kneeling by the fireplace watching the kindling she had lit crackle into life.

"I didn't know you were in the Boy Scouts," said Grant. She smiled.

"I thought it's going to get chilly. I found a stack of firewood under the stove and there's a calor gas camping stove in the other room. At least we can make a cuppa."

"We can go into Port Ellen tomorrow and pick up some supplies," he said. "I don't know how long we will be here."

Sara put more wood on the fire and the reflection of the flames flickered on the walls. The light was fading. Grant found a saucepan hanging from a nail on the wall and filled it half full with well water. He lit the camping stove and put the saucepan on top. In the store cupboard he found a jar of instant coffee, albeit a bit on the lumpy side. There were also a couple of tins of minestrone soup, a tin of sardines, tin of baked beans and a dribble of Worcestershire sauce.

Grant felt Sara's arms envelop him.

"Not much in the store cupboard," she said.

Grant turned around. "You'll be surprised what I can do with a tin of baked beans," he joked. "I will make the coffee, you look after the fire."

The water seemed to take an age to boil. While he waited he carefully examined the wood burner. He opened the front to see the unburnt remains of some hefty logs. If they were to stay there he would need to find a lot more wood. The water began to boil and he poured the contents onto two powdered mugs.

"You'll have to have it black," he called from the back room. He turned the gas off and carried the two mugs into the front room. Sara was under the blankets with only her shoulders bare. Grant knew she was naked. Despite all that had happened between them they had never slept in the same bed before. He felt a mixture of nervousness and excitement.

The fire was now roaring, great yellow flames flicking up the narrow chimney, orange sparks spitting onto the stone hearth.

The light from the fire augmented the candles Sara had found, lit and dotted around the room. The light gave Sarah's hair a golden glow. Her skin looked honeyed and smooth. Her green eyes shone like jewels and her white teeth gleamed. Grant put the mugs down on the floor beside the bed. He pulled off his jumper and threw it on the foot of the bed. Sara looked admiringly at his firm torso and the carpet of dark hair on his chest. He undid the buckle on his belt and loosened the top button. He undid the zip and slid the tight denims down his athletic legs. His erection was already straining at the front of his boxer shorts. He lowered them allowing it to spring free. Sara pulled back the blanket on the spare side of the bed exposing a slim naked leg. Grant sat on the bed and caressed her ankle. He kissed it lightly moving his mouth down to her toes. He kissed each of them in turn before turning his attentions to the sole of her foot. He kissed that too tracing a line from her heel to the big toe with his tongue. He continued the line back to her ankle up the front of her shin. She shifted in the bed. Grant looked up and could see she had removed the blanket exposing her breasts. Her left hand rested on her left breast and Grant could see the erect nipple jutting out from between her fingers. His tongue went back to her shin and dragged along the fine hairs which covered her long golden limbs. He stopped at her knee and peppered it with kisses, then slowly snaked his tongue along the inside of her thigh. She flung the blanket off completely and spread her legs wide, pinching her nipples and arching her back in anticipation of what was to come. Grant kissed the inside of her thighs then moved higher, but he made her wait. He could smell the muskiness of her sex, but concentrated all his ministrations around her thighs and belly.

She arched her back again lifting her bottom off the bed.

"Oh please, please, Grant, don't tease me," she whimpered.

It was then his insatiable mouth found the point of her pleasure. She moaned and writhed as Grant's tongue explored her femininity. The smell of her sex and the ambrosia taste of her juice drove Grant into a frenzy of love, lust and passion. She cried out as a tidal wave of pleasure and emotion wracked her young body then she collapsed back on the bed.

Grant kissed the light golden hair of her pubic mound, moving up her body until his mouth found her hardened nipples. He licked gently at the jutting buds taking each into his mouth in turn, sucking, nuzzling. Then his mouth moved to hers and they kissed ferociously. Grant now lay on top of her and the tip of his rock hard organ nudged at the entrance to her dripping sex. She gasped and brought her legs up around his back as he slid deeper and deeper into her, pinning her to the mattress, a butterfly mounted on the velvet cushion of desire. His movements were slow and circular as if he were trying to write his name with an invisible quill clutched between the cheeks of his buttocks. They both glistened with sweat, Sara's eyes only partially open as she groaned under the body of her mature lover.

The pace of movement increased as Grant felt the explosion building inside him. She felt it too and was ready for him. Her own pleasure intensified until, locked together in wanton abandonment they both cried out as Grant pumped the hot seed of his love inside her. He collapsed on top of her. She traced fairy light patterns across his back with her long nails as he lay there exhausted. Finally he rolled off and lay face down on the bed, his head tilted towards the fire. She covered him with the blanket and stroked his hair.

"I was afraid I wouldn't be any good," she whispered.

Grant looked at the flames racing each other up the chimney and wondered if they, like him, were on their way to Hell.

"Good?" he said his mouth muffled by the mattress. He turned over to look at her.

"You are fantastic, so beautiful."

She rested her head on his chest and he stroked her hair.

"I never thought it could ever be like that," she said quietly. "It hurt so much when Alan tried to do it."

Grant carried on caressing her.

"That was in the past, he will never hurt you again."

She nuzzled his chest and ran her fingers through its hair.

"I know," she said," but I want to tell you everything. I have wanted to tell somebody. That night I told you about on holiday wasn't the first time he abused me. I remember when I was little, probably five or six I think, when he used to come and visit and give me piggy-backs up to bed.

"I'll put Sara to bed," he used to say. But when he was putting me to bed his hands would always stray. At first I didn't think anything of it, but as I got older it got worse. He used to play with me, down there. Then he used to make me touch him. He said it was a game that it was his snake and if I rubbed it, it would spit at me. I knew it was wrong, but he said if I ever told anyone they wouldn't believe me and I would be taken away to a children's home. I was too frightened to tell."

Grant brushed her hair. "But you say you think your mother knew?"

"That was later," said Sara. "After daddy died she changed. She became dependent on Alan, controlled by him, I guess. She started to drink heavily. I thought there was something going on between them, but I was never sure until that night of the holiday."

The conversation lapsed then Sara asked: "Was it like this with Jill?"

Grant stared up at the ceiling.

"Never like that," he said.

"Not even at the beginning?" asked Sara.

He paused and thought honestly before answering.

"I suppose at the beginning it was better, but sex was never really important to her."

"So did you stray?" asked Sara. "We're you ever unfaithful to her, before me?"

"A few times," he said.

"So why did you never leave her?"

Grant felt her smooth skin against him. "I guess I was afraid to," he said.

"And now?" she asked.

"Now I'm more afraid than ever."

The two mugs of coffee were stone cold when they woke in the morning and the fire was a pile of ashes.

Sara was awake first. By the time Grant had opened his eyes she had washed, paid her first visit to the chemical loo, made two fresh cups of coffee and heated up the baked beans. She knelt on the bed and handed him the coffee.

"You're up early," he said wincing slightly by the heat of the mug.

She walked across to the front door and flung it open.

"It's a beautiful day and I am hopelessly in love with a beautiful man," she said doing a twirl in the sunlight.

"You're mad," he said taking another sip.

"Madly in love," she said. "Come on lazy bones, you've got work to do."

She tried to pull the blankets off the bed, but Grant held them, which made Sara giggle even louder and pull harder.

"Trying to protect your modesty?" she laughed.

"Bit late for that, I would have thought," said Grant. "I love you Sara Mattherson."

"Good," she said. "So would you do anything for me?"

"Anything," he replied.

"Good," she said again, "because that chemical toilet needs emptying."

Then she grabbed a cushion from behind him and playfully hit him on the head with it.

Most of the morning, they spent working. Sara set about cleaning the cottage while Grant saw to the loo, chopped a pile of logs and refilled the water container. Sara set a new fire, dusted, cleaned the windows and hung the blankets on a line she rigged with string from a drawer in the refractory table.

Grant came in for a drink of water after chopping the wood and watched her dust and sweep.

"What are you thinking?" she asked seeing him look at her.

"I was thinking it's like watching Snow White getting the place ready for the Seven Dwarfs," said Grant. "One day you're going to make someone a lovely au pair."

Sara raised the broom as if to attack him. He shielded his face and backed away to the door.

"Okay, okay, I surrender. Finish up and we'll ride into town for a spot of lunch and some supplies."

The rabbits were still on the lawn as Grant and Sara wheeled their bikes back to the road. They cycled in to Port Ellen without seeing a single car on the four mile ride. They stopped outside the Port Ellen Hotel, opposite the quay where they had landed the day before. They propped their bikes up against the wall of the whitewashed building and went inside. It was lunchtime, but there were only four people in the bar – all men. Sara took a seat at the table in the corner while Grant went to the bar.

"Hi," said Grant when the burly landlord came over.

"Good day, what can I get you?" he said looking past Grant and across to Sara.

"A pint of bitter and an orange juice," he said," and can I have a look at the menu, if you have one?"

The landlord turned away and reached for a black plastic folder which he handed to Grant. The other customers looked at Grant and then across to Sara, talking in hushed tones. The landlord poured the drinks and handed them to Grant.

"Can you put them on our bill?" asked Grant.

"Aye," he replied.

Grant took the drinks over to Sara.

"Friendly lot, not," said Sara sarcastically.

Grant handed her the menu. "What do you fancy?" he asked.

Sara looked impishly back at him.

"To eat?" he added.

"Steak and salad," said Sara, "medium and some fries."

Grant took a mouthful of beer and went back to the bar.

"What will it be?" said the landlord in anticipation.

"A couple of medium steaks and salad with a portion of chips," said Grant.

"Be about fifteen minutes," said the landlord. "I'll bring them over."

Grant went back to sit with Sara.

"Why do you think this place is so quiet?" asked Sara. "The place is like a morgue."

"Out of season, I guess," said Grant, "but the fewer people we see the better."

Twenty minutes and two pints later the meals arrived. Each steak filled the plate. The salad and chips came separately.

"You'll never get through all that," said Grant, but she did.

They cycled into town which had a dozen or so small shops including a Spa grocery.

Sara took charge of the shopping.

"We have tea, coffee, milk, sugar and bacon. Do you like bacon?" she asked.

"Love it," replied Grant.

"Cheese, we'll get some cheese," said Sara hovering over the refrigerator cabinet. "And pate, let's have some venison pate."

"Remember, there's no fridge at the cottage," Grant reminded her.

"The whole place is like a fridge," said Sara. "I even had goose pimples on my goose pimples this morning."

Grant slipped a packet of chocolate hobnobs into the basket. Sara added another packet.

"See we have the same taste in biscuits," she said.

By the time they got to the checkout the basket was overflowing. They had to queue behind two local women who were deep in conversation with the cashier.

"You stay in the queue, I just want to get some wine," said Grant putting the basket on the floor. He picked up three bottles of wine and a bottle of Lagavulin malt whisky. Sara was unloading the basket onto the counter. The two women in front had not left the shop and were still chattering away by the door. Grant put the bottles on the counter while Sara continued to unload the shopping. Grant moved around her to a pile of newspapers on the checkout counter. They were all copies of the Scotsman. He picked one up and looked at the front page headline: Government defeat on European vote. He turned over the page and his eyes dropped to the small photographs at the bottom of page three. It was him and Sara.

"Police hunt widens," read the headline.

"That will be £44.80," said the girl. Grant closed the paper.

"Erh, sorry," he stuttered, "how much did you say again?"

"£44.80," she repeated.

Grant fished in his pocket and handed her a £50 note. She held it up to the light to check its authenticity. Grant's mouth had suddenly gone very dry.

"You can't be too careful," said the check-out girl opening the till. "There has been a spate of forgeries turn up on the island. My husband

– he's the police sergeant – he reckons they're being brought over from the mainland by a gang posing as tourists. Whatever next? Will there be anything else?"

Grant pocketed the change and they left.

"Grant whatever is it?" said Sara seeing how agitated he had become.

"Later!" he said, "come on, we have to get back to the cottage."

He balanced his two bags of shopping on either side of the bike and waited for Sara to do the same. When they had cleared the village Grant turned off the road and Sara followed. He got off the bike and laid it down. He took the newspaper out of the bag and opened it to page three and handed it to Sara. Her eyes widened when she saw their photographs.

"Read it out," he said, "I didn't have time to read it properly in the shop."

Sara folded the paper in half and read aloud: "Police Hunt Widens. The hunt for a fifteen-year-old girl and a middle aged London advertising executive missing since Sunday has switched to the West Country. This follows the discovery of the man's blue Mercedes sports car in a Bristol garage. Police are concerned for the safety of the girl who disappeared from the north London home of 40-year-old Grant Campbell where she was staying as a guest of the family. Neither of them have been seen since Saturday night.

The sports car was discovered in a Bristol garage following a nationwide television appeal by the girl's mother. It had been towed there by an AA service patrolman after it broke down at a service station on the M4.

Detective Chief Inspector Douglas Templeton of the Metropolitan Police who is co-ordinating the hunt, told a press conference 'We are extremely concerned for the safety of this child and are asking for anyone with any information as to their whereabouts to come forward.'

"That's all it says," said Sara.

"That's all!" said Grant in dismay. "Fear for her safety. Christ, they think I've done you in!"

Sara went over to him and put her arm around him.

"We'll ring them," she said.

Grant looked at her in disbelief.

"We'll what?"

She looked up at him.

"We'll call this Templeton and tell him I am okay and that I came willingly."

"They'll trace the call to the island," he said biting the inside of his lip.

"Not if I don't give them time to trace it," added Sara.

Grant thought for a moment running his fingers through his hair.

"I think it's better if we lay low here for a few days."

"Until the heat cools off," said Sara in a Chicago accent.

Grant was not amused.

"It's not a game Sara," he said solemnly. "You realise if we are caught what will happen to me?"

The smile dropped from her face and she suddenly seemed to age. She flung her arms around his neck and hugged him tightly.

"They won't get us," she said, "you'll see."

They returned to the cottage and spent the rest of the afternoon indoors. They ate bacon and eggs which Sara cooked on the calor gas stove and Grant drank one of the bottles of wine. Their mood was more melancholy than the previous night and Grant fell asleep after they made love.

Sara left him sleeping on the bed and went out to the back room. She fetched a chair and wedged it under the front door handle. She blew the candles out one by one until the only light in the cottage was that supplied by the fire. She moved the curtain on one of the windows to the side and looked out. There was nothing but blackness, but she had an uneasy feeling they were being watched. A shiver ran down her naked spine as she tiptoed back to bed and snuggled up to Grant. For the first time they had been together Sara felt afraid. She closed her eyes, but it was a long time before she slept.

CHAPTER 24

It was a scratching noise that woke her. The cottage was in inky blackness and at first she couldn't tell where it was coming from. She raised her head from the cushion and strained her ears against the dark silence. Then she heard it again, a soft tapping coming from the front door.

"Grant," she whispered, then more loudly, gently shaking him awake. "Grant, wake up."

He stirred unsteadily into consciousness, unaware momentarily where he was.

"Listen," she whispered. "There's someone outside."

Grant looked at the luminous dial of his Rolex. Quarter to five. He propped himself up on his elbows and listened. The scratching, tapping was distinct and it was coming from the front door.

"Where are the bicycle lamps?" he whispered.

"There's one under the bed on my side," she whispered back. "Hang on I'll see if I can find it." She reached under the bed and her hand found one of Grant's trainers. Then she found it and handed it to Grant. The tapping continued.

Grant swung the blankets away and sat on the edge of the bed trying to get his eyes accustomed to the dark.

"Turn the lamp on," whispered Sara.

"I don't want to scare them away," Grant whispered back.

"Scare them!" Sara exclaimed.

Grant crept towards the front door. He was off the rug now and the stone floor felt like ice. Only another pace or two and he would be there. He reached out to search for the door handle when the big toe on his right foot came into contact with the leg of the chair Sara had wedged against the door. He wanted to howl, but stopped himself. The impact shot along his foot, up his leg to his groin. Then his toe went numb.

"What the f…" would all he would allow himself to coarsely whisper. The scratching stopped. He found the arm of the chair and pulled it away from the door. His throat was now completely dry and he had trouble swallowing the tennis ball he felt in his throat. He reached for the handle. The lamp was poised in his other hand. He turned the handle and jerked the door open flicking the lamp on at the same time. Startled by the light, the fawn turned and scuttled away into the undergrowth.

"Who is it?" called Sara from the bed.

"It's not who, it's a what," replied Grant. "It was a deer, a baby deer."

He closed the door and didn't bother to replace the chair. He hobbled back to the bed and the warmth of her arms.

"I'm sorry," she said snuggling up to him. "I guess I'm just a bit jittery."

Grant put his arm around her protectively. "I know the feeling. We won't stay here any longer than we have to. How do you feel about going abroad?"

She curled his chest hair with her fingers.

"Where to?" she asked.

"Europe, Scandinavia, maybe Australia. We could lose ourselves there."

She rubbed the palm of her hand across his flat stomach.

"What about passports and stuff. They'll be looking for us, won't they?"

Grant stroked her hair.

"We'll find a way."

For the next couple of days they stayed close to the cottage not venturing into town. By day they explored the coastline of the Kildalton estate. They had a picnic by the Kindalton Cross, a Celtic monument dating back to AD800. Grant had studied the history of the island and fascinated Sara with tales of the clan feuds between the Macdonalds and the Campbells.

"Strange, isn't it?" said Sara. "Before I met you I loved a Macdonald's, but now I love a Campbell."

By night they lay in bed in front of a blazing fire learning new things about each other. The more they learned the closer they became. They talked openly about their past lives, their fears, their hopes, their feelings. It was a complete purging of their souls. When they had finished they had bared themselves before each other without a single secret in their hearts. What became clear was that Grant felt he could not leave the country without first seeing Jill and his children and at least trying to explain what had happened. For Sara's part she wanted to speak to her mother.

"We'll catch the ferry back to Tarbert, then make our way back to Glasgow," said Grant. "From there we can go to Bradford and see your mother."

"And Scout," added Sara.

"And Scout," echoed Grant. "In the meantime, put your party frock on. Tonight we're going out for dinner."

Sara looked divine when she emerged from the back room. She had washed her hair and pinned it up in a bun leaving just a few strands either side of her face. Grant was taken aback by how much older it made her look.

"Do you approve?" she said, doing a twirl.

The look on Grant's face answered her question. Grant opened the door.

"Madame, your wheels await," he said pointing to the bikes.

They took a leisurely ride into Port Ellen and stopped at the same hotel where they had lunched the first day. The restaurant was busy, but a pleasant waitress who couldn't have been much older than Sara found them a table in the corner. Grant introduced Sara to lobster and she ate it like a New Englander, savouring every morsel.

On their way out, Grant picked up a copy of the daily newspaper from the table in reception and thumbed through it looking for any reference to them. He folded it and put it back on the table. It was then that Sara saw a familiar face on the front page, the face of George Travers.

"Wait a minute, I know that man," said Sara picking up the paper. The headline read 'Driver killed in mountain accident.' Sara read the copy. 'The body of a 29 year-old man was recovered from the wreckage of his car which plunged 400 feet from the car park at a beauty spot in the Peak District. The badly burned corpse was later identified as that of local businessman George Travers. An inquest was opened at Bradford coroner's court, but adjourned.' Sara's face was ashen.

"That's the man who came to see me just before I came down to London," said Sara.

"So what did he want?" asked Grant.

"Well, that's just it," she explained. "He said he needed to speak to me about my father's death, but my mother stopped me talking to him."

"So we'll never know," said Grant.

When they returned to the cottage they fell upon each other. Their lovemaking was frenzied and abandoned and left them both exhausted. They fell into a deep sleep, neither of them aware of the eyes at the torn curtains at the side window that had been witness to their illicit passion.

The laird's hand grasped the bulbous purple head of his engorged shaft and jerked the foreskin back one more time sending a jet of thick white semen spurting onto the stone wall of the cottage. He looked at the naked form of the girl on the bed. He vowed that tomorrow he would have her himself, after all, if they were who he thought they were, she could hardly object.

CHAPTER 25

Grant and Sara stood on the deck of the ferry and watched the islands slip by.

"That was the best honeymoon a girl could have," said Sara wrapping her arms around Grant's waist. "I never knew life could be so wonderful. I must be the luckiest girl in the world."

Grant looked across to Tarbert and wondered how much longer their luck could last. That question was answered when tired and weary they cycled to Inveraray that evening. The poster outside the newsagents read MISSING GIRL; HUNT SWITCHES TO SOTLAND.

Grant's heart leapt in his mouth, Sara saw it too.

"Stay here while I get a paper," said Grant. The woman behind the counter looked up when Grant entered the shop and Grant could see his own reflection in her pebble-thick glasses. He walked over to the magazine rack and flicked through a selection of yachting and boating magazines. He picked up a copy of Yachting World and took it to the counter. There staring up at him on the front page of the newspaper was a photograph of himself and next to it a smaller colour photograph of Sara. Grant's first thought was that he couldn't remember the picture being taken. Jill must have given it to police. The photo of Sara looked as though it had been taken on the holiday. He even remembered the dress she was wearing. He picked up the paper and folded it in half and handed it to the shopkeeper along with the magazine.

She scrutinised the price on the magazine cover and tapped it into the till. Then she unfolded the paper and checked the cover price. No glimmer of recognition. He handed over the correct money and left without speaking. He crossed the road to where Sara was sitting on a bench.

"What does it say?" she asked impatiently.

Grant read it out 'The hunt for a missing teenager and a 40 year-old London businessman took a bizarre turn today. Following new evidence police have now discounted earlier theories that the man, Grant Campbell, may have taken her abroad. They were last seen in the West Country following their disappearance from Mr Campbell's £600,000 luxury home.'

"That's a joke," said Grant, "It's not worth that."

He continued reading; 'Following the discovery of Mr Campbell's Mercedes sports car in a Bristol garage it was thought they may have left the country via Bristol Airport. However, a local taxi driver has confirmed picking up a man and young girl fitting their description from the airport and taking them to Bristol coach station. Following a nationwide appeal police have been inundated with possible sightings of the couple. The man in charge of the hunt, Detective Chief Inspector Douglas Templeton issued this statement. "There is reason to believe the girl is alive and well and may be in Scotland. We are appealing for information. The girl's uncle Mr Alan Mattherson has offered a £10,000 reward for information leading to the safe return of his niece."

"What do we do now?" asked Sara.

Grant put his arm around her.

"We'll just have to move things forward. The sooner we leave Scotland the better. Come on, we're going shopping."

He spotted the shop he was looking for in the High Street – Beaumans –specialist in Highland dress. They propped their bikes up outside.

Entering the shop was like stepping back in time 30 years or more, parquet floors, acres of polished wood panels and highly polished glass counters. The only difference was they wouldn't have had the American and Japanese tourists rummaging through the piles of Pringle sweaters.

An elderly sales assistant without a spot of tartan on came over. He looked emaciated and wore half rimmed glasses perched on top of a thin nose that twitched at the end when he spoke.

"Can I be of assistance?" he asked in an effeminate voice.

"G'day," said Grant in his best Crocodile Dundee accent. "I'm looking for a pair of strides for the girl here, something in tweed."

Sara looked at him. The assistant looked at her.

"Perhaps the young lady would like to walk this way," he said.

She already does, thought Grant.

"What size?" asked the assistant looking at Sara's trim waist.

"She's a 10," said Grant, "a 22 inch waist."

The assistant turned and plucked three pairs of tweed trousers from the rail.

Sara took them into the changing room and re-emerged wearing a grey herringbone pair.

"Ripper!" cried Grant. "We'll have them. Keep 'em on Shirl, now what about a nice sweater, and one of these tweed caps?"

Bloody Australians, thought the assistant. So uncouth, but they do spend.

"And any footwear?" the assistant asked, eyeing up a nice commission.

"These Doc Martens are beaut," said Sara picking up the Aussie accent. "And they're my size."

When Sara emerged with her new clothes the transformation was complete. Her hair tucked up inside the cap, boots, trousers and baggy sweater, she had lost her girlish charm.

"Where to now, cobber?" she asked.

"Now we put it to the test," said Grant. "From now on you are Sam, all right my son?"

It was 8pm when they knocked on the door of the bed and breakfast. The sign that hung in the window clearly stated there were vacancies. The door was answered by a round-faced woman who reminded Grant of his auntie in Dagenham. She was softly spoken with bouncy curls of grey hair and piercing blue eyes.

"Good evening," she greeted them. Sara stood with her hands in her pockets facing slightly away from her.

"Good ev-er-ning," said Grant now in his best Maurice Chevalier accent. "I am sorry to trouble you this late, but I was wondering if you ave ze room for us, no?"

The woman's smile broadened. "You are French," she said delighted with herself for being so astute.

"Oui monsieur," she said, "entre."

"You speak French?" Grant asked.

"Well only a few words," she said, "a room for just you and your son?"

Grant smiled and took her arm turning her away from Sara and into the hall.

"Yes, we are only two. His mother and I are, how you say, not simpatico anymore."

She looked at Grant and blushed.

"Will you be staying long, monsieur…?"

"Dupont," said Grant stopping to kiss her on both reddened cheeks.

"Max Dupont et mon fils Phillipe."

Sara kept her head down and her cap in place.

"Perhaps if we could see ze room," asked Grant, his eyes never leaving hers. She was lost in his gaze and hadn't taken in what he had said.

"Madame, ze room?" She blinked. "Of course, I've only recently had it decorated."

She led them into a large double room with twin beds.

"There's a bathroom through here," she said crossing to a door at the side. "There's plenty of hot water."

"The room is very beautiful," said Grant escorting her back to the door. "We will be very 'appy 'ere."

"Will you be requiring dinner?" she asked now captivated by her new lodger.

Grant thought quickly.

"Sadly, Phillipe is not feeling too well and will be better in bed. For me also I have to sleep as we are returning to Paris tomorrow."

At the mention of Paris her eyes took on a new iridescence.

"Paris, so you are from Paris?" she said wrapping her arms around herself.

"How wonderful, I would love to go to Paris, so romantic."

She blushed again.

"You have been there, non?" asked Grant.

"Non," said the landlady.

"But you speak such good Francais," he flattered.

The redness of her cheeks turned crimson.

"Only a little," she said coquettishly. "Perhaps I could fix you a little supper, some smoked salmon from Lock Fynne and I think I have a bottle of Chablis?"

Grant had to extricate them from what was becoming an embarrassing situation.

"This is most kind madame. I will have it in our room. Phillipe is a nervous boy and I do not like to leave him toute serle."

The smile dropped from her mouth.

"Of course," she said. "It was foolish of me to think you might like to ..."

Before she could embarrass herself any further Grant took her hand and lifted it to his lips.

"You are very kind," he said, and ushered her out.

After she had gone Grant turned to Sara. "Looks like she's fallen for it," he said.

"Looks like she's fallen for you," said Sara. "She can't keep her eyes off you – or her hands given half the chance."

"I do believe you are jealous, Phillipe!" Grant laughed.

Sara grabbed a cushion off the bed and threw it at him.

"Jealous, what of her?" said Sara.

Grant went across to her and took off her cap. He lifted her chin and kissed her tenderly on the mouth leaving her aching for the embrace to never end.

"Go and have a bath," he whispered.

Ten minutes later the landlady returned with a tray of brown and white smoked salmon sandwiches, a bottle of chilled Petit Chablis Grand Cru and a glass of freshly squeezed orange juice. Grant took the tray and thanked her. He put the tray on the dressing table and undressed. His erection was the first thing Sara saw when he entered the bathroom carrying the tray. Sara lay naked in the bath, her breasts breaking the surface of the water, her nipples already hard and erect. The water swirled over the blond thatch of hair that pointed like an arrowhead to the cleft between her legs.

"Some room service," she joked watching his penis bouncing as he crossed the bathroom.

"Can I interest you in any of this?" asked Grant. She shifted upright in the bath as Grant now stood beside her, his hardness directly in front of her face.

"No, but I'll have some of this," she said and cupping his scrotum in one wet soapy hand fed the head of his swollen manhood into her mouth.

Grant gasped. It was the first time she had done this. He had wanted her to, but only when she was ready. Boy was she ready, and boy was she good. Grant had always believed some women were natural when it came to giving oral sex and some weren't. Jill had never been a natural, but Sara was altogether different. Within minutes Grant felt the old heave-ho as several million sperm decided it was time to leave the family home. His gasps told her what was coming – him! He made the gentlemanly gesture of withdrawing, but she was having none of it. She clasped both hands to his buttocks and held on tight. The tension in his testicles was unbelievable and he was sure they were going to burst. It was when she slipped a wet finger into his anus that he erupted like a gusher feeling the hot fluid pumping the length of his shaft. She made a strange muffled noise as she withdrew her mouth for a moment, then clamped back on his penis, sucking and licking. His legs turned to jelly and he cried out.

Within seconds there was a knock on the bedroom door.

"Monsieur Dupont, is everything all right?" called the landlady.

Grant grabbed a towel from the rail and wrapped it around his waist. He went to the bedroom door and opened it a fraction.

"My foot," he said. "I stubbed my big toe on ze bath," and showed her the blackened toe he had injured at the cottage.

"I heard a cry," she added. "I was worried."

"I'm fine," said Grant. "Thank you for your concern." He closed the door.

They ate their sandwiches and shared the wine. They slept together in one of the beds, but Grant ruffled the duvet on the other one before they left the next morning.

Inverary has no railway line, so Grant and Sara abandoned the bikes and caught a bus into Glasgow. Grant didn't want to risk taking the bikes back to the shop. He knew that Dr Devereaux in Philadelphia would receive a call from the shop, but as Grant had only met the man once at a conference in London where he had given Grant his business card, Grant knew he would deny all knowledge of the rental.

On the journey to Glasgow Sara seemed calmer, more relaxed. She wore no make-up and kept the cap pulled down over her eyes. They finished the packed lunch the landlady had prepared for them just before the coach reached Glasgow. Grant noticed two policemen at the station, but hoped they were looking for a man and young girl, not a father and son. At the Queen Street ticket office Grant bought two singles to Bradford. They had a 30 minute wait for the train, time they spent shopping. Grant bought a pair of scissors and a football. When they returned to the station Sara said she needed the loo. It was only as she was about to go into the ladies that Grant stopped her.

"Come on Phillipe," he said motioning towards the gents.

It was the first time Sara had been in a gents' toilet and her jaw dropped when she caught sight of a man tucking his pecker away as they walked in. Fortunately he was the only other person in there. Grant made for the furthest cubicle from the door and pulled Sara in with him.

She was taken by surprise.

"Surely, not in here?"

Grant laughed remembering a line from the film Airplane.

"Take your cap off and stop calling me Shirley."

She removed the cap and sat on the seat. Grant got out the scissors and picked up a length of Sara's hair.

"I hate to do this," he said, "but you can't hide under the hat the whole time."

Sara knew he was right. They had talked about it the previous night, besides she knew it would grow back. Fifteen minutes later they emerged from the stall with Sara's hair cropped.

"How does it look?" she asked.

"Like a cross between Sinead O'Connor and a boiled egg," he said. "But I still love you."

"What about the ball?" she asked.

"Just hold it under your arm and bounce it every now and then."

CHAPTER 26

They arrived in Bradford at three o'clock.

"We can catch the bus from here," said Sara. "I'm so looking forward to seeing Scout again. I know you'll love him."

"Then we must go and see your mother," replied Grant.

They caught the bus and Sara pointed out all the familiar landmarks. When the bus slowed on a bend Sara rang the bell and jumped up.

"Come on, this is our stop."

The bus came to a halt at a shelter which Grant thought seemed miles from anywhere. Sara took his hand.

"Come on it's not far."

They walked a little way along the road to a small turning on the left. It led to a narrow unmade lane. A dilapidated sign hanging by only one hinge read Fordingham Stables. They walked up the lane for half a mile until a large house came into view, the entrance guarded by a wooden gate.

"Where will he be?" asked Grant.

Sara's pace quickened.

"I'm not sure," she said, "sometimes they leave him in the paddock or turn him out to the big field at the back." They climbed the fence and skirted around the back of the stable block. There was nobody about and most of the stables were empty.

"He's usually in the end one," said Sara. They picked their way along the stalls, Grant looking furtively around for any sign of life. Before they reached the end stable a huge black head protruded from the open door and the animal gave a huge snort and whinny, shaking its head, its massive brown eyes widening when it saw Sara.

"Scout," she cried running to the horse and hugging its head.

"Scout, oh Scout," she repeated, "have you missed me?"

Grant felt slightly embarrassed at being an interloper at such a personal reunion. Then Sara turned to him.

"Grant this is Scout, Scout meet Grant."

The horse whinnied again and nodded its head as much to say "Hi Grant, nice to meet you."

She opened the stable door to go inside. It was then she saw the deep welt marks along the horse's side. Tears flooded her eyes. The lacerations extended from the horse's back along to its hindquarters. It had been beaten.

"My God," gasped Grant as he saw the injury. "Who would do such a cruel thing to such a beautiful animal?" Sara was sobbing now, her arms still around the animal's head.

"Only one bastard that I know," said Sara between sobs.

"You mean your uncle?" said Grant.

"Who else?" She spat out the words. The venom in her voice startled Grant. Her character had completely changed.

"Is there something we can do for him," asked Grant "a vet or something?"

Sara sniffed and wiped her cheeks with her hands.

"There's some ointment I keep in my tack box. The vet gave it to me in case he hurt himself on the barbed wire fence. I think there's some left." She went to the rear of the stall to a large cupboard. She opened it and lifted out a brown wooden box about the size of a medium suit case.

"I keep all the grooming brushes in here," she said flicking aside the locks. The horse looked around and nodded its head again. She opened the box and saw a brown envelope with her name handwritten in ink.

"What…?" she picked it up and undid the butterfly clip which sealed it. Inside were a number of pieces of foolscap papers. Her eyes went to the top of the first page.

"Well, what is it?" said Grant. Sara began to read out loud.

'Dear Sara, I tried to talk to you here at the stables, but your mother stopped me. I was trying to tell you that I don't think your father's death was an accident. I think he was murdered.'

Sara's voice faltered and Grant could see her welling up with emotion.

"Your father and I were not close friends, but he did confide in me in matters of business. He expressed fears that his brother was trying to make a private deal with a powerful Chinese business consortium to smuggle heroin into the UK using the canning factories of Mattherson Industries.

'After your father's death I went to see your mother, but when I arrived at your house I found her in a compromising position with your uncle. When I confronted them they laughed and said I had no proof and nobody would believe me. They threatened that if I went to the police they would hurt my wife and daughter. That's why I am arranging to go away, and take them somewhere safe. I felt I had to let you know what was going on. If I do not get in touch with you personally it means that something has happened to me and you must do what you think fit. Enclosed are copies of the documents your father refused to sign with the Chinese, invoices, shipment details. I trust I am not too late. George Travers.'

Sara's hand dropped to her side.

"I'm afraid he was too late," rasped a voice from behind them. Grant and Sara whipped around. Standing in the doorway of the stable pointing a 9mm Beretta automatic at them was Alan Mattherson.

Sara went to charge at him, but Grant grabbed her around the waist and restrained her.

"Oh how touching," mocked her uncle, "saved by her knight in shining armour. You don't look like a kidnapper to me. More of a child molester, I'd say."

"And you would know all about that," said Grant.

Alan Mattherson smirked.

"So our little Sara has been telling tales out of school," has she. He switched the gun from his right hand to his left and moved inside the stable door.

"I take it you've had a piece of the action. Nice tight cunt she's got, hasn't she?"

Now it was Grant's turn to lunge at their tormentor and Sara's turn to hold him back.

"You bastard," spat Grant. "You murdering bastard."

"Ah yes," said Mattherson, "my brother? Didn't he do well? He got a double first at Manchester. I got a lower second. He got married and had a kid and I stayed single. He ran the company and shat all over me. That dear fucking father of yours was always one step ahead of me. Nobody recognised the work I did. I never got one word of praise or thanks. Oh good old Alan, he'll do that. Alan won't mind, but Alan did fucking mind.

"Everyone always thought your dad was so smart. Smart? Crap! He didn't know I was frigging his little girl when I put you to bed of a night. He didn't know I was fucking the arse off his wife when he was away on business. He was so smart he couldn't see the deal with the Chinese would give us more money than we could ever dream of. All right so it's dirty money, drug money, who gives a fuck? If there are stupid cunts like your mother who want to take that shit, who am I to stop them."

A broad evil grin spread across his face.

"But that's all in the past. You're just a couple of loose ends that need tidying up, like your father, like George Travers."

"You'll never get away with it," said Grant.

"Oh I don't know," said the gunman. "I knew you'd come back here sooner or later. You came here to demand money. You were holding a gun, we struggled, the gun went off and, well, you know the rest.

"It's a shame I would have liked to have fucked her properly, just for old time's sake." He pointed the gun at Grant's head which was now beaded with sweat. Grant was praying his bladder and bowels wouldn't let him down.

"Who wants it first," he said moving the gun to Sara, "you, your lover boy or old Scout here?"

At the mention of his name Scout threw his head round and caught Mattherson on the back of his head knocking him forward. Grant seized his chance and grabbed the arm holding the gun. The man struggled furiously and discharged a shot. The sound of the blast reverberated around the stall throwing the horse into panic. It reared up thrashing wildly with its legs. Grant wrestled the gunman to the floor trying to knock the weapon from his grasp. They rolled on the floor under the hooves of the terrified animal.

"Get him out of here," cried Grant as he desperately fought for their lives.

Sara was in two minds what to do. She wanted to help Grant, but they were rolling around so wildly she couldn't aim an accurate attack on her uncle. Instead she grabbed Scout's head and dragged him out of the stable. It was then she heard another shot. She froze. My God, Grant's dead she thought. Then a figure rushed out from the stable. It was Grant, the front of his shirt stained in blood.

"You're shot," she screamed and rushed over to him.

"I'm okay," he panted. "We've got to get out of here."

He put his arm around her for support.

"What about Alan?" she asked.

"I've killed him."

In the driveway of the house was a dark blue Jaguar.

"It's Alan's car," said Sara. They broke into a run. The car was unlocked and the keys in the ignition.

"Quick, get in," said Grant.

"Shouldn't we go to the police?" said Sara "We can tell them everything?"

Grant didn't know, couldn't think. He had to get away, away from this waking nightmare. He headed back towards Bradford. No, they'll be looking for the car. Have to dump it. Then how could they get away? He'd just killed someone, how do you get away from that?

On the outskirts of town he picked up a sign for the motorway and headed south towards London. They spent the journey in virtual silence too wrapped up in their own thoughts to talk; each needed time to digest the magnitude of what had happened.

They reached London by nightfall and dumped the car in an underground car park in Park Lane. The blood on Grant's sweater had dried leaving an ugly stain, but in the darkness it could pass for being part of the design.

They hailed a cab and asked for West Halkin Street, where Tom lived.

CHAPTER 27

The cab pulled up outside the cream painted Georgian terrace. As Sara waited for Grant to pay the driver, she noticed a group of fur clad women standing outside a large white building sixty or so yards down the street. The building had a red illuminated letter M above the main door arch. Grant saw her looking.

"It's Anton Mossiman's," he said, "one of the best restaurants in London."

The name was lost on her.

"I thought it was a posh Macdonald's," she joked.

Grant took her by the hand and led her across to a plate glass doorway. On the side were a row of buttons linked to an intercom. He pressed 4B and waited for a reply. There was none. He reached in to his pocket and took out a set of keys. He selected a long Chub key and opened the door. She stepped inside and sunk into the deep pile carpet. It was gone ten and Grant knew the commissionaire would be off-duty. Had he been there it wouldn't have posed a problem. He knew Grant from when he had stayed there when Tom was away on business and he was always very discreet.

"Wow!" said Sara as she looked around the reception area. It was a combination of pink marble, gilt and glass. The huge glass chandelier which hung over the commissionaire's post had once hung in the Grosvenor House ballroom.

"Come on," said Grant taking her hand again, "this way." He led her along the plush oak-lined corridor down two flights of stairs to the basement. At the end was a heavy white door with large brass numbers – 4B. He took out the keys again and inserted another Chubb key into the lower lock and a Yale key in the latch. The door opened.

"Quick, inside," said Grant. "I have forty seconds before the alarm is triggered."

Sara entered the apartment and Grant swiftly followed. He closed the door and went to the security system on the wall which was flashing red meaning the alarm was activated. He punched in 1409 and the light turned green.

"How did you know the number?" asked Sara. "The code could have been changed."

Grant allowed himself a smile. "It's Tom's birthday, September 14 – 1409. He never changes it."

Grant flicked the lights on.

"Come on, I'll show you around." He led her into the dining room. A large tropical flower arrangement stood in the centre of the glass table. A card nestled among the flowers. It read 'Thanks a bunch for the other night. Love, Claudia.'

He took her into the lounge and had flashbacks of him and Barbara. He put her from his mind and showed Sara the kitchen. The units were brilliant white gloss and the accessories were bright yellow. Sara opened what she thought was a cupboard, but it was the fridge. Inside there was a carton of fresh orange juice and two bottles of Bollinger Special Cuvee and a bottle of Perrier water. Nothing changes, thought Grant, except now he was here with Sara.

Grant next showed her the two patios.

"Looks like he does a lot of entertaining," she said.

"Wait until you see the bedrooms," he smiled.

He opened the first door off to the left of the passageway. It led to a large shower-room, more marble, mirrors and gilt. He opened a door to a bedroom without a bed, just lots of glass fronted wardrobes.

"Where's the bed?" asked Sara.

Grant winked and flicked what looked like a light switch. A quiet whirring noise startled Sara and she jumped as three mirror doors tilted forward towards the floor.

"I can see you've been here before," said Sara giving him a disapproving smile.

"You ain't seen nothing yet," he said and took her to the room at the end of the passageway. It was already ajar so Grant pushed it open.

The room was huge, almost as big as the lounge. A king-sized bed stood centre stage on a raised floor canopied in great swirls of pale yellow silk which matched the bedcovers and curtains. The room was immaculate, nothing out of place. Grant opened the closet doors to reveal rail on rail of suits, jackets and trousers, shelves of freshly laundered hand-made shirts, racks of ties, rows of highly polished Gucci shoes.

"Look in here," said Grant opening the door to the en suite. It had a sunken double Jacuzzi complete with gold fittings. On the marble shelf, were a mass of aftershaves and colognes. On gold coat pegs fastened to the marble walls hung bathrobes from some of the world's top hotels. Tom always made a point of "borrowing" one from each hotel he stayed at.

Sara turned the tap on the bidet and jumped back when a fountain of water erupted from the basin.

"Some pad," she said, "but where's Tom?"

"Hong Kong, Honolulu, who knows. He could be anywhere."

They went back into the lounge and sat on the settee.

"So what do we do now?" asked Sara. "Are you still going to see your family?"

Grant thought long and hard.

"I've got to," he said. "I must try and explain. I can't leave without letting them know I'm not a murderer."

Sara pressed herself close to him.

"It was all my fault – going back there."

Grant squeezed her shoulder.

"Don't be silly," he comforted her. "It was your uncle who pulled the gun, not that the police are likely to believe that."

"They will if I tell them what happened," said Sara. Grant raised her face.

"Do you want to go back?" he asked softly. His eyes searched deep inside her soul for any sign of doubt, but found none.

"Not if it means us being separated," said Sara and she kissed him tenderly on the lips.

"Would it be all right if I had a bath," she asked getting off the settee.

"Sure," he said. "You go and run one. I'm just going to pop out and telephone the family and arrange a meeting tomorrow."

"But what if the line's tapped?" she asked.

"Don't worry," replied Grant. "I've thought of that."

Sara went to the en suite and switched on the Jacuzzi and got undressed. Grant left the flat and walked to the phone box on the corner of the street. He dialled home. A voice answered, it was Emma.

"Dad? Where are you?" said his daughter with a mix of relief and excitement. "Are you okay? Where's Sara? What's happening?"

"Hold on, hold on," said Grant trying to calm her. "Em, is your mother there?"

There was a pause. "I'm sorry dad, she's out." There was another pause although Grant could hear muffled voices in the background. Then Emma came back on the phone.

"Dad? She's terribly upset, we all are. We have been so worried. Where are you? When are you coming home?" Grant heard a click as though a tape recorder had been switched on. His mind raced.

"Em, how are the boys?"

"Worried about you," she replied. "None of us have been to school. It's all in the papers."

"I know darling," said Grant, "but I can explain. How's Sally?"

"She cries a lot," said Emma.

Grant bit the inside of his lip.

"Listen carefully Em. Is she still reading her favourite Mr Men book?" Grant asked pointedly.

"Ye-e-e-s," said Emma. "When will we see you?"

"It's a shame I can't see you tomorrow for lunch, but I will not be in London, you can bank on that, with all the police around. It just wasn't meant. I'll call again when mum hasn't got the needle with me. Give everyone my love." He put the receiver down and hoped his coded message had got through to his bright young daughter.

It was a game Grant and Emma had played when she was younger. Her favourite Mr Man was the same as Sally's, Mr Topsy-Turvy who always said everything the wrong way round. If he said he was going out it meant he was staying in, if he said one thing it meant the opposite. Grant and Emma had shared countless reverse conversations, but the cypher was now up to Emma to decode.

Ben, Tim and Sally crowded around their sister wanting to know the news. Emma was puzzled by the conversation and began turning it over in her mind.

"He said he loved us all very much and would see us soon," she told the others. She told them only what they wanted to hear. Jill appeared from the lounge. She'd aged ten years in as many days. She was under sedation from her GP and looked as though she hadn't slept for a week, which wasn't far from the truth.

"What did he say?" she said in a zombie like monotone, her eyes vacant.

"He said he was all right, but couldn't talk," said Emma.

"Is that all?" asked her mother.

"He asked how we all are," said Emma. Jill turned and went back into the lounge.

"Come on you lot, off to bed," said Emma. "It's late."

When she had got her siblings settled down she sat at her bureau in her room and took out a pencil and paper.

"I won't be able to see you tomorrow lunch time," she said to herself. That means he will be able to see me tomorrow, but where?

She racked her memory for what else he had said. "I won't be in London," which means he will be in London. She wrote down all the words she remembered him saying. There must be a clue as to where he wants to meet, but why can't I find it.

She looked again, "Wasn't meant," "You can bank on it". Bank? Does he mean the Bank of England? "Bank? Meant? The Embankment, that's it, the Embankment."

Her brain was now moving into overdrive. Where on the Embankment? What else did he say? "I'll call again when mum hasn't got the needle. Needle? Cleopatra's Needle. That's it!

CHAPTER 28

Sara was enjoying the sensations of the hot jets of water bubbling between her legs as she lay back and luxuriated in the Jacuzzi. With the noise of the jets she didn't hear the front door open.

Tom saw the lights on and knew he must have company. He wasn't expecting any and thought his cleaning lady may have left them on by mistake. He put his Louis Vuitton brief case on the dining table and took off his jacket and hung it over the back of one of the dining chairs. He picked up the note on the flowers and smiled. He headed towards the bedroom. The door was half open and he could hear the Jacuzzi running. Maybe it was Claudia. He'd left her in bed when he'd flown to Brussels that morning. Maybe she was still there.

"Darling, is that you?" he said opening the bathroom door and walking in.

Sara was so relaxed she was half asleep, but she sat bolt upright when she heard the American's voice then realising how exposed she was slid down the bath to cover herself.

"Christ!" said Tom, turning away. "Sara, is that you? I'm so sorry, I had no idea."

He backed out and pulled the door to.

"Just a minute," called the teenager. She climbed out from the tub and dripping water across the marble floor, reached for a bathrobe. He caught a glimpse of her naked form through the narrow opening in the door. He pulled it shut. Seconds later it opened and Sara stood in the doorway looking hot and flustered.

"Jeez, what happened to all your hair?" he said, then realised how rude that must have sounded adding;" I mean, you look great, it's just, I didn't expect to see you here. Where's Grant?"

Sara sunk her hands into the deep pockets of the Bali Laguna Beach Hotel robe and scrunched her toes into the deep pile of the carpet.

"He'll only be a minute," she said. "He's gone out to use the phone. He's in a state, Tom. He shot and killed my uncle this afternoon."

Tom's jaw dropped. "He did what?"

She took her hands out of the pockets and clenched her fists in desperation.

"He killed my uncle," she repeated.

"Holy shit!" said the American. "This is getting fucking unbelievable." He sat down.

"Do you want us to leave?" said Sara quietly, her head bowed.

Tom turned his head from side to side. "No, no, you can stay here. There's half the fucking country looking for you out there."

They both heard the key in the front door. Tom remained seated while Sara went to meet Grant.

"Tom's here," she said. The American emerged from the bedroom.

"How are you doing buddy?" asked Grant.

"A lot better than you are by the sound of it. What's this about Sara's uncle? You wasted the guy?"

Grant recounted the afternoon's events over one of the bottles of Bollinger from the fridge.

"Seems to me you're in deep shit," said the Californian – ever the pragmatist.

"So what do you suggest?" asked Grant "turn ourselves in?"

Sara moved closer to Grant on the settee pulling the robe together at the front where it had parted to reveal rather too much of her thighs.

"Well Sara's in the clear," said Tom. "A good lawyer, claim self -defence, a suspended sentence at best."

"And at worst?" said Grant.

Tom remained silent and shrugged his shoulders.

"I won't let him," said Sara. "They're not going to separate us."

The conversation dried up.

"Have you two eaten?" asked Tom. Grant shook his head.

"Want some take away – Chinese, Sara?"

"I'm starving," she replied.

"She's always starving," added Grant.

Tom ordered food, Sara ate most of it.

They polished off the second bottle of champagne and Grant noticed how Sara was drinking more than she used to. She was quite merry when she got up from the settee and declared she was ready for bed.

"Are you coming?" she asked Grant bending forward to kiss his forehead. As she did so Tom had to avert his eyes as her breasts swung down inside the robe.

"You go on ahead," said Grant. "I won't be long."

Sara turned to Tom and smiled.

"Night Tom," she said and sauntered off to bed.

As soon as she had left the room Tom looked at his friend.

"Fifteen? Fucking unbelievable."

CHAPTER 29

Chief Inspector Doug Templeton stood at the picture window looking impassively out over the Bradford skyline, his hands dug deep in the pockets of his beige trench coat.

"You can go in now chief inspector," said the nurse in a soft Irish lilt, "if you would like to follow me."

"How is he?" he asked, following her out of the waiting room. She turned and looked at him over her shoulder.

"Dr Munro will fill you in on his condition," she said.

She opened the door to a private room. In it, wired up to a drip and an assortment of monitors was Alan Mattherson. The man standing at the foot of the bed looking at the medical charts which hung there turned when they walked in. He offered his hand to the policeman.

"Doctor Munro, senior registrar," he said introducing himself.

"How's our patient?" asked the policeman.

"He's lucky to be alive," said the doctor. "A single bullet entered through the fourth and fifth rib puncturing the left lung. It missed the fourth thoracic vertebrae by less than a centimetre and exited the lower lumber region."

"What's his condition now?" pressed the officer.

"Well, he had lost a lot of blood when one of the stable hands found him, but he's now in a stable condition. Forgive the pun."

"Is he off the danger list?"

"Yes, I would say so," said the medic.

"How long before he regains consciousness?" asked the detective, "it's vital we talk to him to establish the identity of his attacker?"

The doctor picked up the patient's wrist and felt his pulse.

"Do you think it was the same man who kidnapped his niece?" he asked.

"You're well informed," said Templeton.

"Not really," said the doctor. "I read the newspapers and watch the television the same as everyone else."

"Let's just say the sooner we find Mr Campbell the better. I will leave a man outside the door."

CHAPTER 30

Sara clutched Grant's arm and turned away in disgust. The body on the floor in front of them was that of a young woman no more than 25. She had been split open from her throat to her navel her intestines had been dragged out and lay in a twisted putrescent tangle across her groin. Deep cuts to each of her turkey white breasts had congealed leaving gouts of congealed black blood across her chest. The body was twisted as though frozen in time during some frenzied dance.

"Not a pretty sight," joked Grant. "Come on, there's more gruesome goings on in here."

He led Sara to the next tableaux. He had been the one who had suggested the London Dungeons, but now wasn't sure it had been such a good idea.

"At least it's dark and we won't be recognised. Are you sure you'll be okay here on your own? I shouldn't be long. I'll just meet Emma and explain everything, then meet you back here."

"Course I'll be all right," she said trying to convince herself. "You just go and sort things out."

Grant left Sara in the tourist attraction and walked to Swan pier where he had to wait five minutes for a river bus. From the river he knew he would get the best view of the Embankment and would be able to see if his daughter was waiting at Cleopatra's Needle.

He purchased his ticket from the machine and watched the river traffic, mostly barges, going up to Tilbury or Dartford, or pleasure craft taking tourists on scenic tours.

The river bus arrived on time. The only other passengers on deck were an elderly couple with their grandchild.

As they passed the Egyptian obelisk Grant could see Emma standing by the wall. She was wearing the bright red hooded coat he had bought her for her 13th birthday. She was alone. Grant got off at Charing Cross Pier and walked back on the opposite side of the road. He stopped when he had her in view and bent down to pretend to tie his shoelace. She had one hand in her pocket and kept glancing at her watch on the other. Grant walked through the Embankment Gardens and positioned himself on a bench from where he could still see his daughter.

He watched her for ten minutes, pretending to read a newspaper. The only other people in the vicinity were two workmen digging a hole in the pavement. Grant put the newspaper on the bench and exited the gardens by the same gate. Emma now had her back to him and was looking out onto the river. Now he was almost directly opposite her. He waited for the traffic to clear and crossed half way. Now only twenty yards away, he waited for the green Harrods delivery van to pass then crossed.

"Em," he called.

She whirled around at the sound of his voice. He moved forwards, his arms outstretched to embrace her. He looked at her face, but instead of the broad smile he was so used to, he saw more of an icy glare. It was then he felt his arms being ripped behind his back and felt himself being propelled forward with animal ferocity. The two workmen had abandoned the nearby hole and pinned him against the wall. He thought his arms would snap as the pain burnt through his shoulders. Then he felt the coldness of the cuffs on his wrists and heard them click shut. One of the men spun him around. He looked at his daughter and saw tears dripping from the corner of each eye. Still winded by the ferocity of the attack he gasped to regain his breath.

"Don't worry darling, it wasn't your fault, they must have followed you."

She wiped the tears from her face with her gloved hand and an iciness Grant had never seen in her before contorted her features.

"Follow me? They didn't follow me. I told them where you would be. I hate you! I hate you for what you have done to us."

Screaming and fists flying her eyes full of tears she launched herself at her father.

One of the workmen – part of Templeton's undercover team, pulled the teenager off.

Everything happed so quickly. A police patrol car siren sounded as the vehicle screeched to a halt. The doors were flung open and uniformed officers sprung out. Seconds later another car, this time unmarked screamed to a halt in front of the patrol car. Lunch time joggers along the Embankment looked on in amazement as the arrest unfolded, though none stopped jogging.

Another policeman climbed out of the back of the unmarked car and climbed into the back seat of the car where Grant had been thrown.

"Grant Campbell," he cautioned, "I am arresting you on suspicion of kidnapping and attempted murder. You do not have to say anything, but anything you do say may be taken down and used in evidence against you. Do you understand?"

Grant was bewildered by his daughter's betrayal. He sat and watched as she was escorted to the unmarked police car. Even when he heard the cell door close at Charing Cross police station he was unable to fully comprehend what was happening.

Sara waited at the Dungeons until they closed at 5.30pm. Grant had not returned and she knew something was wrong. She caught a taxi back to Tom's apartment and let herself in with the key he had given her. There was nobody at home.

Grant was pacing up and down his cell, six feet by eight feet, no windows, no toilet and no wash basin.

God, I can't go to prison, he thought to himself. I'd rather be dead. He heard the lock turn and the heavy metal door swung open.

A middle aged policeman, 50ish with grey hair and about three stone overweight stood in the doorway.

"Come on laddie," he said in a thick Glaswegian accent. "You're coming for a ride."

He stood aside and let Grant through the door.

"Where are you taking me?" said Grant nervously, all manner of aberrations tearing through his mind.

"The Chief Inspector wants a word with you," he said.

He led Grant by the arm along a corridor with cells off to each side. He could hear screams of abuse interspersed with loud banging on cell doors.

"Don't worry about them, laddie, it's yourself you should be worried about."

Grant was taken out the back of the police station to the yard where there was a newly registered PTV – prisoner transport vehicle. Before leaving the cell Grant was released from his cuffs. He was bundled into the back of the van. Inside were several small cubicles no more than three feet wide with a bench seat in each. Grant was pushed inside one and the door closed and locked.

It's a good job I'm not claustrophobic he thought. He looked up at the top of the cubicle. It was covered with a thick opaque Perspex cover. He stood on the bench, but could not reach it with his fingertips. Pressing his back to the wall he shuffled upwards using his shoulder blades. Then he heard the engine start and the forward motion of the vehicle caused him to lose grip and he fell back on the seat. He tried again using the same technique, inching his way up the wall to the top of the cubicle. When he was close enough to the emergency escape hatch he bent his right hand backwards and gave an almighty shove with the palm of his hand. The pain sent shockwaves up his arm. He gritted his teeth and struck it again. It moved. The pain in his back was getting unbearable as he wedged himself between the walls. He struck the vent again and this time he could see a small gap. Grant could taste the cold night air seeping through. He hit it again and this time heard a snap. From the pain in his arm he thought he may have broken something. He had – the latch on the hatch. He hauled himself higher and pushed the perplex cover off. He pulled himself through the hole until his chest and torso lay on the roof with only his legs now incarcerated. Almost exhausted by his efforts he sucked in large gasps of air to clear his head. Behind him on the road were lines of traffic. He didn't recognise where he was, but he guessed he wouldn't have long. Keeping as flat as he could, he slithered like a snake onto the roof, keeping hold of the hatch way for grip. The van swung left and Grant was thrown to the right. He only just managed to hold on. All he wanted was a break in the traffic and for the van to slow down. He didn't have to wait long. He looked up ahead and saw traffic lights on green. Please change, please God make them change, he prayed.

Whether it was God or just the traffic computer, the lights turned amber and the van slowed. Red and it stopped. Grant looked behind. No cars. He crawled commando-style to the back of the van swivelled around and dropped silently to the road. He stayed crouched on his haunches as the van pulled away. He rolled to the side avoiding the headlights of traffic coming the other way. His heart was pounding. He stood up and dusted himself down and walked back in the direction of where they had come. He turned up the first side street and looked up at the sign – Bensham Grove. He looked around for a telephone, but couldn't see one. He had to phone Sara to tell her he was okay. He found a phone box around the corner, but he had no money. All his personal belongings had been confiscated at the police station. He dialled 100 and waited for the operator. When she answered he placed a reverse charged call to Tom's apartment. Sara accepted the charge and Grant was connected.

"Grant, are you okay? Where are you? What's happened?"

Grant breathed a huge sigh of relief at hearing her voice. It would have been awful being locked up, but being apart from Sara was even worse.

"I'm okay, don't worry. I'll tell you what happened when I see you. Is Tom home?"

Sara sat down on the chair in the hall.

"Not yet," she said, and as soon as the words left her mouth she heard the key in the front door.

"Hang on a minute, I think that's him."

Sure enough Tom came through the door.

"It's Grant, he wants to talk to you," she said handing Tom the telephone.

Without taking his coat off Tom took the receiver.

"Hi bud, how did the meeting go with Emma?"

"Don't ask," he said. "She betrayed me. The police were waiting and they arrested me."

"So where are they holding you?" asked the American.

"Well that's just it," said Grant. "They threw me in a prison van, but I escaped."

"Holy shit! So where are you now?"

Grant looked for a street sign. "Salmon Lane," he said, "in a phone box opposite a big street hoarding advertising the Independent newspaper."

Tom looked at his watch.

"Stay there, buddy, I'll find you. I'm on my way."

CHAPTER 31

Gary Spalding looked at his watch; it was 8.30pm another three hours and he would be off duty. It was his day off tomorrow and he had arranged to play golf with two other men from the shift. He hoped his new putter would give him an edge. He was playing the eighteenth in his mind when a doctor in a white coat and with a stethoscope around his neck approached him from the end of the corridor. He sat upright in his chair trying to look alert.

As the doctor got closer he could see he was Chinese, of slim build, dark black hair and round rimmed glasses. He stopped in front of the policeman.

"Is this Mr Mattherson's room?" he inquired in a heavy Chinese accent.

"Yes sir," said the constable. "You chaps have been in and out all day, but he's still unconscious."

The man smiled.

"I am a specialist," he said, opening the door and disappearing inside.

Alan Mattherson was still unconscious. The main light in the room was off, but a lamp over the bed cast a light upon the sallow features of his face. The Chinaman moved across to the bed and lifted each of the man's eyelids in turn. He reached into his pocket and produced a hypodermic syringe and an ampule of clear liquid. He removed the safety cover from the needle and inserted it into the bottle and drew off most of the liquid. He lifted the hospital shirt covering the patient's right arm. He deftly inserted the needle and emptied the contents into the arm. He replaced the safety cover and put it back in his pocket. He stooped and lifted the eyelids again.

Alan Mattherson blinked and a murmur escaped his parched throat. The first face he had hoped to see when he woke up was maybe Liz, or at least a pretty young nurse – not Xian! He tried to focus, but the room was swimming. It was like trying to look through a fish eye lens. All he could make out was the distorted face of the Chinaman.

"Welcome back to the land of the living Mr Mattherson, can you hear me?"

He tried to move his body, but felt as though he had been nailed to the bed. His head began to clear as the effects of whatever had been pumped into his body started to work.

"Xian, is that you? Thank God."

"My employers were concerned about your health."

"Campbell tried to kill me. He and that bitch niece know everything. Travers got to her before we killed him. She has all the files, all the invoices, everything, she has enough to bury all of us."

"Not so," said Xian. "Mrs Mattherson found the documents in the stable and had the good sense to hand them over to us, so you see the only people who know about our arrangement are Campbell and the girl, and you."

"So what are you going to do?" he asked, again trying to move. He couldn't.

"We're going to take care of them," said Xian reaching into his pocket for the syringe and another ampule of liquid, "just like we are going to take care of you."

Through blurred vision Alan Mattherson saw the fine spray of liquid erupt from the end of the needle. He felt the sharp prick as it entered his skin. Thank God I'm not paralysed, I can feel that, he thought. But it was the last thought he ever had.

"How's the patient then, doc?" asked constable Spalding as the Chinaman emerged from the room.

He smiled inscrutably at the officer.

"I think he will be unconscious for some time."

CHAPTER 32

The telephone rang in Doug Templeton's office. He picked it up.

"You've what!" he screamed. "You had better be fucking joking." The veins in his head erupted to the surface like swollen rivers of blood. "How the hell did he get away? He's an advertising executive, not fucking Houdini. I'm going to have someone's bollocks for this." He slammed the phone down and stared at the desk. If his eyes had been lasers they would have sliced it in two. He was still fuming when there was a knock on the door. A pretty auburn haired WPC walked in carrying a message.

"What?" he snapped.

"It's from the hospital, sir. They say Alan Mattherson died twenty minutes ago without regaining consciousness."

CHAPTER 33

Grant was waiting opposite the telephone kiosk when he saw the familiar black Porsche pull up. Tom was at the wheel and Sara was in the back. He raced across and climbed in the passenger seat. Tom floored the accelerator and the car sped away. Sara leaned over and kissed Grant hungrily on the mouth, a deep searching embrace of lovers separated for an eternity.

"Hey knock it off you two! So tell us pal, what happened?"

Grant recounted the story from the time he met Emma on the Embankment to the escape from the van.

"You two are turning into Bonnie and Clyde," said Tom trying to relieve the tension. "So, where to now, buddy boy?"

"I've been thinking about that," said Grant. "It's not going to be safe at your place. Now they know we're in London they'll be watching all the places I'm likely to go. Besides, you've risked enough for us already."

"So where do we go?" asked Sara.

"First, we will need a car," said Grant.

"No problem there," said Tom. "You can have one of the pool cars from work. I sometimes borrow one when the Porsche is in for service."

"Can we pick it up tonight?" asked Grant.

Tom looked at the clock on the car's dashboard.

"We can give it a try, but even if you get the car, where are you going to go?"

"I think it best you don't know," said Grant.

Twenty minutes later Tom parked the car at the side of the bank.

"Wait here," he said and disappeared into the building.

"Where are we going?" asked Sara.

"Scandinavia, because I think I may have thought of a way of getting there without our passports."

Fifteen minutes later the huge chain metal security gate to the car park opened and a car's headlights shone like twin beacons up from the basement slope. Tom appeared behind the wheel of an Audi. He swung out of the garage and the grill closed. He parked behind the Porsche and got out.

Grant and Sara alighted the sports car.

"There you go," said Tom. "She's all yours."

"And the other thing I asked you for?" said Grant.

The American reached inside his jacket pocket and produced a large brown envelope.

"Five big ones," he said handing it to Grant.

"Thanks pal," said Grant giving his friend a bear hug. Tom broke the embrace and gave Sara a brotherly kiss on the cheek.

"Those clothes look better on you than they do on Claudia," he joked

"You take care of each other, do you hear?"

Grant put the envelope in his inside jacket pocket and opened the passenger door of the Audi for Sara. He got in the driver's door, put the key in the lock and turned on the ignition. The car had a full tank, more than enough for where they were heading.

CHAPTER 34

Grant pulled into the entrance to the mobile home park ignoring the 5mph sign. He took the left fork which took them down towards the river, the quietest part of the site. It was the jolt of driving over the first sleeping policeman which woke Sara. She looked around as the car's headlights picked out mobile homes on either side of the narrow lane.

"Where are we?" she asked.

Grant looked at her and smiled. "We're on our holidays. Haven't you ever stayed in a caravan before?"

"Once I think," she replied, "when I was little. Mum and dad took me to Whitby and we stayed in a caravan. I can still remember the sound of the rain on the roof when I was tucked up in bed. I felt so secure."

Grant pulled up outside a large green 26ft van and parked on the embankment overlooking the river. He turned off the engine.

"Stay here while I check it out," he said.

"Be careful," replied Sara.

The tide was out and the riverbed was littered with small boats imprisoned in the silt waiting for the water to release them. The wind blew in from the sea making a cacophony of sound as the wire riggings beat a nautical tattoo against the masts. There were no lights on in any of the vans. This was a holiday site and Grant knew it should not be occupied overnight out of season. He knew the homes would be locked, but hey, if he could break out of a prison van he could sure as hell break into a caravan. He climbed the three stairs leading to the rear door and examined the lock. The door was fitted with both

Yale and Chubb locks. He went to the back of the van and checked the windows. They were all closed and too high off the ground to make it easy to climb through.

He abandoned the green van and moved on to the next one, a white thirty-two feet luxury eight berth. Security on that was just as tight. He examined six other homes along the river front, but they were all the same. Then, parked behind the last one was what he had been looking for, an old van with a flimsy looking padlock on the door. He went back to the car.

"Any luck?" asked Sara.

"Maybe," replied Grant. He went to the boot of the car and took out the wheel brace and a flashlight. He inserted the tip of the brace into the lock and wedged the end onto the door frame, then with a sharp jerk snapped the lock. He was in. The inside smelt a bit musty – a bit like the Islay cottage. There were blinds at the windows cutting out the little light from outside. He used the torch to look around the inside. It was very basic, but at least there was a bed.

He went back to the car for Sara. Getting into the driver's seat he started the engine.

"No good?" said Sara.

Grant smiled.

"No, perfect," he said. "I just want to hide the car." He reversed it between the first two lines of vans so it would not be noticed from the road. Switching off the ignition and lights he climbed out.

"Come on," he beckoned.

Inside the van Sara asked: "Are there any lights?"

"Probably," said Grant, "but we don't want to bring attention to ourselves. We can make do with the torch. Not scared of the dark are you?" he nuzzled the back of her neck.

"So what about heating?" she asked. "It's colder than the cottage. At least there we had a fire."

"We have our love to keep us warm," he smiled, and took her in his arms and kissed her passionately.

Grant lay exhausted by their lovemaking. Sara kissed him lightly on the tip of his nose.

"Does this mean I've joined the Caravan Club?" she giggled.

The screaming call of circling seagulls stirred Grant from a deep slumber. He'd slept like a log. Daylight seeped through the curtains illuminating the small bedroom of the van. The walls were papered with small floral patterns, a picture of a windmill the only adornment to the walls. Grant turned on his side and looked down into the face of the young girl next to him, the young girl who had changed his entire life. Her hair was cropped short, but losing her long locks hadn't taken away her beauty. Grant noticed her long eye lashes, like those of the fawn that had visited the cottage on Islay. Her face was as soft and fresh as a new born baby. Her nose small and slightly turned up at the end, her lips so pale and pink and full. He noticed the tiny blonde hairs which covered her upper lip. Her breathing was deep and regular. He thought what she must be going through, learning that her father had been murdered by his own brother, of her mother's infidelity and drug addiction, of her own years of abuse and now being hunted like a wild animal.

As he gazed into her face, her eyelids flickered and opened. Grant drowned once more in the clear liquid green pools of her eyes, so white, so bright, so clear.

"Good morning," he said softly.

She smiled. "Good morning," she murmured. She brought her arm out from under the blankets and put a soft hand against his whiskered-cheek. He leaned his head to one side trapping her hand between his cheek and his shoulder.

"Promise me you will always be here when I wake," she whispered.

Grant felt tears welling up and his throat tightening.

"I love you so much," he said, his voice now strained with emotion. A tear trickled from his cheek and fell softly onto her arm. She cradled his neck and pulled him closely to her, roles now reversed. It was she who was providing the comfort and reassurance. It was Grant who felt cocooned from the troubles of the outside world. He lay with his head on her chest staring at the windmill on the wall and its sails, sails that was it, that was their way of escape.

CHAPTER 35

"He can't have disappeared off the face of the earth," stormed Templeton. "Somebody must know where he is. Someone must be helping him."

The squad of detectives in his office said nothing.

"Well?" he snapped.

Jack Williams, a sergeant with rapidly receding hairline shifted uncomfortably in his chair. "We have contacted all his friends and associates, guv. Nobody has seen him since the party."

"What about the girl?" barked Templeton. "Have we had anything from the mother?"

WDC Kay Carpenter, the petite short haired brunette who had only been on the squad for two months spoke up.

"We have interviewed her since the death of her brother-in-law, but she's still in a state of shock. She's heavily sedated at the moment, sir. We have photographs of Campbell and the girl at all airports, rail and bus stations, ports and ferry terminals. They can't get out of the country."

"Like we didn't think he would escape from the fucking prison van," raged Templeton. "We're a laughing stock. Somewhere, somehow we have missed something. Where's that list of known associates?"

Sergeant Williams flicked through a thick folder containing dozens of statements. He handed it to the inspector.

"The crosses are against the ones we haven't been able to contact. There are only two left, one is an American friend of Campbell who is away on business in Japan. The other is the American's girlfriend. She's a model and lives in Denmark. I shouldn't think she knows anything."

"What about the wife and daughter. Have they got any idea where he may have taken her, past places they have been on holiday, anywhere remote where they might hole up?" asked Templeton.

"We're checking those now," said Carpenter. She handed her boss a list.

"Do any of those tie in with any of the sightings," he asked.

Carpenter pointed to one place.

"This one," she said, "Islay. It's an island off the coast of Scotland."

Templeton glared at her.

"I know where it is," he barked. "What have we got?"

Carpenter handed him another file.

"These are statements from the licensee of the White Hart Hotel. He has positively identified Campbell and the girl.

"And how do we know Campbell has been on Islay before?" asked Templeton.

"His partner," said the sergeant. "He said Campbell spent two weeks on the island filming a commercial."

Templeton paced the office and stopped at a photo of Grant pinned to a board.

"If he was in Scotland, why would he go to Bradford to murder the girl's uncle and why come back to London?"

"To see his family?" pondered Carpenter. "Maybe one last time before he flees the country?"

Templeton looked at his team. "We check every private airfield, every coastal town. This man's very resourceful, we know that, but he can't move on his own, especially if he has the girl with him. He needs money and he needs help. If we don't find him quickly we will never find him. I want this bastard back behind bars, capisce!"

Carpenter raised her eyebrows at the sergeant. She hadn't seen the chief this worked up before, not even when he was having sex with her on his office desk the previous night. Their affair had endured for six months now and was the worst kept secret in the department. It was Templeton who had arranged her transfer from uniformed branch and they had often been seen leaving the office within minutes of each other.

Kay Carpenter was 29 years old and divorced. She married another copper when she was 20, but the marriage only lasted four years. Since then she had lived alone and despite vowing never again to get involved with another member of the Firm, she had fallen hook, line and sinker for Templeton. He was 43, married without children. His wife didn't want a family. He made chief inspector at 38 and was hotly tipped for promotion to superintendent – before his indiscretion with the pretty police woman. He had fallen for the temptation and knew he was going to have to pay the price. Kay was like a drug and he needed a regular fix. She was like no other woman he had ever been with and in the course of his career he'd had his fair share of 'office bikes'. Kay was the ride of a lifetime, unashamed and abandoned in the bedroom. She catered for his every fetish – and he had plenty.

She handcuffed him to the bed and rode him like a rodeo bull. She would allow him to act out all his bizarre fantasies. She wondered what the rest of the office would make of him if they had seen him dressed in nappies and a pink chiffon tutu pleading to be punished for being a naughty little girl. It was difficult to believe he was the same man.

When the meeting broke up Sergeant Williams picked up the telephone in an empty office and dialled. Xian answered the call. "Looks like you need to be talking to the American friend – Tom Cody – he's flying back into Heathrow tonight. I will expect a bonus for this."

CHAPTER 36

Grant and Sara walked hand in hand along the river bank with only the gulls circling overhead for company. The tide was now in and the small boats which littered the water bobbed easily to and fro. The wind from the east was cold on their faces and Sara's cheeks glowed bright red.

"So how did you know about this place?" asked Sara, the wind taking her words away.

"About 18 months ago one of our clients chartered a boat for a party. It started at St Katherine's Dock in London and we cruised down to Southend. Then we sailed the River Crouch and that's when I noticed this place."

"How long before you think they'll find us?" asked Sara.

Grant put his hand around her shoulder and stopped.

"We'll be long gone by then," he said trying to sound confident.

They walked for an hour following the line of the river towards the mouth of the estuary until they came to a deep water terminal. There, tied up to the jetty was the 25,000 tonnes cargo vessel Virage.

Huge cranes and a small army of dock workers were busy unloading its cargo of Russian timber. Grant and Sara sat on a capstan watching the activity. A fleet of trucks scuttled backwards and forwards across the acres of concrete which made up the handling yard of Baltic Wharf. They neatly stacked the mountains of timber being unloaded from the belly of the giant orange ship.

Sara shivered.

"Come on," said Grant and pulled her to her feet. He pulled the hat she wore down over her ears. Dressed in jeans and a baggy jumper she had borrowed from Tom, Grant hoped she was sufficiently disguised to avoid attention. They crossed the terminal entrance and Grant knocked on the door of the security hut. A middle aged man dressed in a dark navy blue uniform complete with peaked cap opened the door.

"Sorry to trouble you," said Grant. "I've been sent down here by the Jobcentre for an interview with the captain of the Virage, erh…" he pretended to rack his memory for the name … "oh they did tell me, funny name, foreign."

The security guard picked up a clipboard from his table and ran his eyes over it.

"Captain Swensson?" he asked.

"Swensson, that's it," said Grant. "Where will I find him?"

"On board, I suppose," said the guard. "If you go up the gangplank and ask for the first mate," he looked at the clipboard again, "Eric Neilmyer," he added. "He should be able to help you."

"Thanks," said Grant going to turn away.

"Hang on a minute," called the guard. "It's not as easy as that."

Grant froze. He turned to the guard.

"You'll need a security pass," smiled the official, reaching into the top pocket of his tunic for a pen.

"Now what name is it?"

"Oliver," said Grant instinctively, "Thomas Oliver."

The guard reached for a plastic lapel badge and inscribed it with the fictitious name.

"What about the lad?" he said looking past Grant at Sara who had been waiting by the door.

"Sam?" said Grant. "Will he need one as well?"

"Everyone needs one," he said filling out the name. "It's procedure."

He looked at his watch and noted the time on a sheet of paper attached to the clipboard. He handed Grant the passes.

"Make sure you hand them back when you leave," he said. "If you don't we'll assume you are a couple of stowaways." He broke into laughter and Grant forced himself to join in.

"We will," he said taking the passes, "shouldn't be long."

The guard raised his hand with his fingers crossed.

"Good luck with the interview," he said, and then went back to his mug of tea and the copy of Caravan World.

Sara followed Grant up the gangplank.

"What are we doing?" she asked.

"Playing it by ear," answered Grant. "Let me do the talking."

At the top of the gangplank they found an itinerant sailor leaning on the railing smoking a Disque Blue.

"Morning," said Grant. "Can you tell me where we can find Eric Neilmyer?"

The man looked at him and then at Sara and shrugged his shoulders.

"Do you speak English?" Grant said slowly and phonetically. The man shrugged again and walked away.

"There was nobody else on deck. Grant saw a bulkhead door and looked inside. A flight of stairs led down.

"Come on," he said to Sara. "Let's go find someone."

At the bottom of the stairwell was a corridor which seemed to run the length of the ship. Grant and Sara took the right turn heading up towards the bow. They were intercepted half way along by a man dressed in bright yellow overalls coming up from another stairwell which led deeper into the bowels of the ship.

"Ah," said Grant, smiling. "Excuse me, do you speak English?"

"A little," he replied.

"We are looking for Eric Nielmyer or Captain Swensson," said Grant.

The man nodded.

"The captain left the ship this morning."

"And when will he be back?" asked Grant.

"He had to return suddenly to Copenhagen. Did you have an appointment with him?"

Grant looked him straight in the eye.

"Eleven thirty," he said looking at his Rolex.

"Perhaps Mr Neilmyer can help," said the sailor. "Come, I will take you to him. What name shall I say?"

"Oliver," replied Grant, "Tom Oliver."

Grant and Sara followed him along the corridor up two flights of stairs and into a bright reception area. Through a glass petition he could see a young man sitting behind a large desk talking on the radio phone.

The man in overalls knocked on the door, opened it and put his head around. The man on the phone took the receiver away and looked up. The sailor said something in Danish. The man behind the desk nodded. The sailor closed the door and turned to Grant and Sara.

"He will not keep you waiting very long. Please be seated." Then he left.

They sat on two of the four chairs.

"Grant!" said Sara, but the office door opened and Eric Neilmyer stretched out a hand to greet them.

"Good morning," he said in perfectly clipped English. "Mr Oliver. How may I be of service? I understand you had an appointment with Captain Swensson. I am sorry, but I see no note in his diary."

Grant looked at Sara, then at Neilmyer.

"Perhaps I can have a private word," said Grant, "in your office."

Intrigued the young officer motioned to the office door and followed Grant inside leaving Sara wondering what the hell was going on.

"Please sit down Mr Neilmyer," said Grant in an authoritarian voice.

"I am afraid I have a confession to make," he said walking over to the desk. "I am not Tom Oliver."

The officer looked confused.

"Captain Swensson left the ship this morning, correct?" stated Grant.

"Yes, that is correct," said Neilmyer.

"And do you know the reason for Captain Swensson's sudden recall to Copenhagen?" asked Grant.

The second officer shifted uncomfortably on his seat.

"He said his wife had been taken into hospital, a problem with the pregnancy."

Grant stopped pacing and leaned on the desk.

"How long have you known Captain Swensson?" he asked.

The Dane ran a finger around the front of his collar to loosen the pressure on his neck.

"Almost two years," he said, "why all these questions, who are you?"

Grant raised an eyebrow.

"Who I am is of no importance. What is important is that for the past two years you have been under investigation. We believe that Swensson is part of an organisation that has been responsible for the trafficking of narcotics and underage sex workers between Scandinavia, Germany, Holland and the UK."

The officer's mouth dropped open in disbelief.

"The boy outside is in fact a 15-year-old girl in disguise. She is the only eye witness we have to tie Swensson in with the traffickers. She is the only one who can identify the South American contact. We had to get Swensson out of the way because we have set up a bogus meeting with the traffickers when the ship returns to Denmark."

Grant hoped he wasn't sweating as much as the second officer.

"The girl is under special protection. Two attempts have already been made on her life. You may hear something on news broadcasts. The British government is fully co-operating with our own people and as far as the British press are concerned the girl is missing, assumed kidnapped."

Neilmyer was struggling to take it all in.

"But I know nothing of any of this," protested the officer. "I didn't know anything about drug smuggling or sex workers. It's nothing to do with me. I'm innocent, you must believe me."

Grant looked at him.

"As I say, you have been under investigation for two years and we know you have not been complicit in these offences. That's why I hope I can trust you. Can I trust you Officer Neilmyer?"

"Of course, of course," he replied. "What do you want me to do?"

"This is a sensitive and covert operation," said Grant. "We do not know who else on board may be involved, so nobody must know of our presence. Certain crew members are under suspicion and radio transmissions are being monitored remotely. It is imperative you follow your original orders. Nothing must seem out of the ordinary."

"You mean we still sail tonight?" asked Neilmyer.

Grant smiled.

"Of course, naturally the girl and I will need accommodation away from the crew."

"Not a problem," said the officer. "You can have Captain Swensson's cabin."

Grant went to the door and opened it.

"Come in my dear," he said to Sara. "I have appraised officer Neilmyer of the situation."

He held out his hand.

"Can I have your security pass, please," he said. "Mr Neilmyer will need to return them to the office."

Sara had no idea what was going on, but she had learnt to trust Grant. She unpinned her badge and handed it to the officer and Grant did the same.

"Please see these are returned to security," said Grant handing them to the officer, "and that we are checked out. Now, perhaps you can escort us to the captain's quarters."

Nielmyer was in no mood to argue. He didn't know which government department his visitor was from, but he didn't want to get on the wrong side of him. With Swensson out of the way his chances of promotion were that much better if he co-operated with the inquiry. He had held his Master's ticket for three years and was tired of playing second fiddle to Swensson, but drug trafficking, sex workers, who would have believed it.

Grant told Sara the whole story when they were alone in the captain's cabin. It wasn't as large or luxurious as Grant had imagined, but he would have settled for a broom cupboard providing it had been safe.

"As long as Nielmyer doesn't check, we'll be in the clear," said Grant. "By nightfall we will be out of the country."

Sara was fast asleep. Grant was going through the cabin to see if there was anything that might be of use to them, when there was a light tap on the door. For an instant he thought he would open it to see the boys in blue. Instead it was Nielmyer standing there with a tray of food.

"I thought you might be hungry," he said.

Grant stood aside and let him into the cabin. He placed the tray on the table and looked across to Sara asleep on the bed. She was lying with her back towards him, her legs curled up into her chest.

Grant lifted the lid on one of the two covered plates on the tray. It was a selection of cold meats and salad.

"Are we on schedule?" asked Grant.

The young officer averted his gaze from the shapely contours of Sara's backside.

"We sail on schedule and dock at 20 hundred hours tomorrow."

"Excellent," said Grant. "Nobody knows of our presence here?"

The officer shook his head.

"You are a good man, Nielmyer," said Grant. "Your co-operation in this matter will not be forgotten." He walked to the cabin door and opened it.

"Oh, and Nielmyer needless to say I do not wish to be disturbed until tomorrow."

The officer nodded. "Very well, sir."

Grant closed the door and sucked in a deep breath. Only a few more hours and the nightmare would be over and they would be free. It wasn't until they were underway that Sara woke up. She and Grant picked at the food, too nervous to eat.

At some stage during the night they did fall asleep, Sara on the bed, Grant in the captain's chair. A knock on the cabin door awoke him. It was 10am. Nielmyer had brought another tray of food, bacon, eggs, sausages, toast and a pot of hot coffee. Sara stirred from her sleep when the officer put the tray on the table.

"What do you want me to do when we dock?" asked the officer. Grant poured out two cups of coffee.

"Nothing," he said, "until after the customs inspection." He assumed there would be one.

"We must stay concealed until we slip away to our rendezvous with the traffickers. By that time my men will be in place."

"And what of Captain Swensson?" he asked.

"Act normally. It might be weeks or even months before we can move on Swensson."

"Of course, will there be anything else?" asked the officer.

"Not for now," replied Grant.

When he had left, Sara got off the bed and stretched. She threw her arms around Grant's neck and kissed him gently on the mouth.

"I'm starving," she said sitting down at the table.

"I see you're back to your old self," said Grant. "That didn't take long."

Before they arrived in Copenhagen both Grant and Sara showered in the en suite bathroom. Sara had suggested they shower together "to save water" she joked, but the cubicle was barely big enough for one, let alone two.

"I need a change of clothes," she said padding naked across the cabin.

"We'll get you a new wardrobe," said Grant. "Not that you need it, I think you look nice just as you are."

She laughed and tilted her head on one side to dislodge the water in her ear. Her breasts jiggled from side to side as she shook. He felt a familiar stirring under his bath towel. She noticed it too and with an impish grin crossed to where he was sitting. Facing him she mounted him like she would her horse. Her mouth closed in on his like a patriot missile. Her tongue darted inside the warm wet cavern. His hands travelled slowly over the slippery wetness of her body, upwards until his palms centres on the hardness of her nipples. He kneaded them gently and felt her thrust her groin against his hardness. Now it was her turn to use her hands, resting them on Grant's knees and drawing her legs up she moved her hips forward engaging the head of his purple shaft into the wetness of her sex. Grant gasped as she rocked backwards and forwards enjoying the rhythmic coupling. Grant was a master of control and had learnt in their brief time together how to hold on until her time was right. He could feel the tension build in her body. Her legs began to quiver as the first shock waves of pleasure erupted throughout her tender young body. She leant further back impaling herself deeper on his organ to feel the strength of his manhood pressing deep against her cervix. As Grant sensed her orgasm he relaxed and let nature take its course. His own release came with hers and he groaned at the power of her vaginal muscles as they sucked every last drop of hot seed from him.

She went to climb off, but he stopped her placing his hands either side of her hips to keep her impaled.

"Not yet," he whispered, and kissed her tenderly on the lips.

The ship docked on time and an hour later Nielmyer reported that Customs had been and gone. Grant shook his hand at the end of the gangplank.

"The Virage is a fine ship in need of a new master," said Grant, "a man who can be trusted."

"I understand, sir," he said and watched Grant and Sara disappear into the arms of the Nyhavn night.

CHAPTER 37

It wasn't until they had cleared the docks that Grant finally felt as though a ten ton weight had been lifted from him. He grabbed Sara by the waist, picked her up and swung her round and around, making her squeal.

"We did it," he yelled, putting her down.

"You did it," she corrected him and leaned up and kissed him.

Hand in hand they walked along the Esplanade and turned left in to Bredgade.

"First thing is to find a hotel," he said, "shouldn't be too difficult."

"What about that one," said Sara as they came into the square at Kongens Nytorv, pointing to Hotel Angletterre, an imposing 19th century building.

"Something smaller," I think," said Grant. "Do a left here."

They turned into Nyhavn.

"This used to be the red light district," Grant told her. "It's gone upmarket since I was here 20 years ago. The canals where these boats are now were dug out by soldiers back in 1673. Hans Christian Andersen lived in three different houses along here."

Sara loved listening to Grant talk. He seemed to know something about everything.

"So how come you know about the red light district?" she teased.

"Ah that would be telling," he laughed. They stopped outside Nyhavn 71 hotel, a converted warehouse building overlooking the quay. A little further along was a queue of people outside a cinema.

"Probably showing a porno movie," said Sara, "Can we go and have a look?"

"Certainly not," he said in mock disgust, "might give you some ideas!"

The reception of the hotel was very rustic, lots of old wooden beams. Grant rang the bell on the reception desk and seconds later an attractive young blonde receptionist appeared from an ante office.

"Hi" said Grant, "my girlfriend and I would like a room."

Sara was clinging on to his arm looking at him with big calf eyes. Then she realised what he had said, girlfriend, not daughter, or son. I'm his girlfriend.

The receptionist smiled at them both.

"How long will you require the room?" she said, "the minimum let is two hours."

They both erupted in fits of laughter.

"We were thinking of a few days," said Grant.

"A double room?" she asked.

"The best you've got," said Grant. "The honeymoon suite if it's free!"

The receptionist joined in the laughter.

"We do have a special room which I think you will like," she said "if you could sign the register."

She looked down.

"No luggage?" she observed.

"Nope," he said, "no luggage!"

"And how will you be paying?"

"Better make it cash," said Grant. "Will sterling be okay?"

"That will do nicely, but if you want to change some currency, I can do that for you."

Grant signed the register.

"Welcome Mr and Mrs Smith," she said, and they all laughed.

Grant swiped the room key to suite 27 and heard a click. He pushed it open and inserted the key into the holder. The lights came on automatically. The room was huge, despite a massive king-sized four poster bed. Sara ran over and launched herself on it. It undulated beneath her.

"Hey, it's a waterbed," she said rolling over and over.

Grant crossed to the windows and looked for a cord to open the curtains, but couldn't find one. Instead he saw a remote controller in a bracket on the wall. He picked it up and pointed it at the windows and pressed the button. The curtains opened to reveal a stunning view of Copenhagen's waterfront. Sara was off to explore the apartment.

"Grant, come and look at this," she called. "We've got our own log cabin."

Grant walked through the bathroom, which lead down a small passageway.

"It's a sauna, idiot," said Grant jokingly. "And that next door is a steam room, like a Turkish bath."

"This is great," said Sara, "come on let's strip off and use everything."

Next to the steam room was a sunbed.

"You can even get a tan," he said.

CHAPTER 38

Flight BA 537 from Tokyo touched down at London's Heathrow airport at 8.20pm. Tom Cody cleared the customs hall at Terminal Three forty minutes later. He was going to get a cab into London so was surprised to see a liveried chauffeur in the arrivals lounge holding up a card with his name on it.

"Hi," said Tom. "I'm Tom Cody, are you from the bank?"

The oriental man, no taller than 5ft 2inches bowed his head.

"That is correct sir."

Tom handed him his suitcase.

"I didn't know Dee had laid on chauffeur drive." Dee was his secretary and sometimes bed mate. "What's the big deal?" asked the American.

"I have instructions to take you to an urgent meeting," said the chauffeur.

"What, at this time of night?" he said. "It must be urgent."

Then he remembered the car he had given Grant and wondered if the meeting was about aiding a fugitive.

"I'd better call the office first," he said looking for a phone. But by this time they were in the short stay car park.

"There is a telephone in the vehicle," said the chauffeur, "you can call from there."

Tom lit up a Marlborough.

"It's okay," he said. "It can probably wait."

They arrived at the car, a black stretched Mercedes with black tinted windows. The chauffeur opened the car remotely and opened the rear door for Tom to climb in. He then put Tom's case in the boot. Between the front and rear seats was a glass privacy screen.

I'll call Ginger, thought Tom, see if she fancies coming over tonight. Ginger was a long-time girlfriend, great company and fantastic in bed. She was just what he needed after the long flight. He tried to dial Ginger's number, but the phone seemed dead. He leant forward and tapped on the glass.

"Hey buddy, the phone's dead," he shouted. The chauffeur reached across and flicked a switch locking all the doors. Tom knocked on the glass again.

"Did you hear me, the phone's not working."

The oriental glanced in his rear view mirror. All Tom could see was his dark impassionate eyes.

"Stop the car, godammit," he shouted and banged his first on the glass shield. He reached for the door handle and tried to yank it open despite the fact the car was travelling at speed.

"Let me out of here," he yelled, now gripped with panic. Then he heard the escape of gas as the rear of the car began to fill with fentanyl. Tom was soon slumped on the plush black leather seat, oblivious to what was in store.

CHAPTER 39

Grant and Sara were too hyped up to sleep. Instead Grant suggested they go out and celebrate their new found freedom with a night on the town. The hotel receptionist saw them going out and called them back.

"If you feel like a party, some friends of mine are giving a get together." She reached for a piece of paper from reception. She wrote down an address and handed it to Grant.

"It's not far from here and I expect it will go on until late, so come whenever you want."

Grant put the note in his pocket and thanked her. When they were outside the hotel, Sara turned to Grant.

"I think she fancies you."

"Probably," he replied.

"Shall we go?" asked Sara.

"Do you want to?" he asked.

"Let's see how we feel later," she said putting her arm through his as they strolled off to find some Copenhagen night life.

CHAPTER 40

The Mercedes came to a halt inside a cavernous warehouse in London's docklands. As soon as the car was inside, the corrugated roller doors closed shut. In the headlights of the car, Tom, now awake, could make out three men standing on a raised loading platform on the riverside of the warehouse. The chauffeur opened the door and yanked Tom from the car. Tom was surprised by his strength, it was disproportionate to his size. He pushed the frightened American towards the men waiting on the platform.

"Look, I don't know what this is about, but if it's some sort of kidnap there's nobody out there who's going to pay any money to get me back so you're wasting your time. Do you hear?"

The chauffeur pushed him again and he fell onto the base of the six wooden steps leading to the platform. One of the men waiting above moved to the top of the stairs.

"Mr Cody, we are so pleased you could join us. Please excuse Li Kim; he has no fondness for Americans." Tom climbed the steps. At least this guy seems civil.

On the platform stood a table and two chairs, a lamp and a Nike sports bag.

"Please have a seat," said the tall man.

"What the hell's going on here?" said Tom, aggression substituting for fear. "I am an American citizen, I have rights. I'm not going to…"

He never finished the protest. The tall man struck Tom's face.

"You will speak only to answer my questions," he snarled.

"Where is your friend Grant Campbell and the girl?"

If the penny hadn't already dropped it had now.

"I don't know. I've been in Japan," pleaded Tom.

The man struck again.

"Jeeesus," screamed the banker.

"The British police seem to think you know where they are. They are watching your apartment."

Tom could taste his own blood in his mouth from the split inflicted in his lower lip. "Please, Mr Cody, this is no time for heroics. Tell us where Campbell and the girl are hiding."

Tom managed to raise his head to look at his inquisitor half expecting another blow.

"I told you, I haven't seen them," he said wearily.

The man smiled. "Very well." He turned to the two other men on the platform who could have passed for sumo wrestlers. Before Tom could move one of the two men pinned his arms in a vice like grip. The other moved in front and reached for the waistband of Tom's trousers. Tom lashed out with his feet, but a giant fist pounded into his stomach with sledgehammer force. Vomit spewed from his mouth. The man ignored the remains of Tom's airline dinner spread across his arms and roughly undid the belt and pulled down his trousers and shorts in one movement.

Tom wriggled in the chair trying to free himself.

"Fucking perverts," he hissed.

The tall man went across to the table and reached inside the holdall.

Tom went berserk when he saw the contents, a club hammer and a nine inch railway spike. He struggled and pulled, twisted and turned, but the tall man slowly came towards him hammer and spike in hand.

"I will ask you only one more time, where are they?"

Tears streamed down Tom's face.

"Look, all I did was give them one of the pool cars from my bank. I don't know where they went in it."

Tom felt cold fingers encircle his shrivelled penis. The man pulled the flaccid organ stretching it out like a piece of pizza dough. His icy hand grabbed Tom's scrotum.

"Please, not that," Tom begged helplessly. He felt the cold tip of the metal spike nuzzle behind the head of the coruna. He opened his eyes as the hammer swung down and he heard it make contact with the head of the spike before the vacuous warehouse filled with his own bloodcurdling screams.

CHAPTER 41

The taxi driver dropped Grant and Sara off outside a stylish town house in Gothersgade, opposite the Botanical Gardens. From the lights in the three storey house and the loud music which blasted from the windows they knew they had the right venue. Grant paid the driver with some of the Danish money he had changed up in the hotel. He rang the brass doorbell and waited. A bearded youth, no more than 19 answered. He wore black trousers and a white shirt unbuttoned to the waist. His chest was matted with thick dark curls and around his neck he wore an iron cross on a silver chain.

"We were invited by the receptionist at our hotel," Grant began to explain, but there was no need. They were ushered inside. The hall of the house was littered with bodies, people talking, drinking, smoking, some snogging.

"Welcome," said the youth and disappeared off into one of the rooms.

"What do you want to drink?" shouted Grant trying to make himself heard.

"White wine," said Sara.

Grant forced his way through the partygoers in the corridor towards a room at the end, which looked the most likely place to be the kitchen. On the stairs he noticed an attractive raven haired woman sitting with a black male. It wasn't the fact she was extremely pretty that he noted it was the fact she wore a very short dress and no underwear.

He made his way to the kitchen where the work surfaces were littered with an assortment of booze. He grabbed an open bottle of Sauvignon but couldn't see any glasses, but there were a stack of plastic cups so he took a couple of those.

"Some party," said a blonde woman now next to him. "Are you here on your own?"

Pre Sara, Grant wouldn't have hesitated, but since he had met Sara he wasn't interested in any other girl.

"No I'm here with my girlfriend," said Grant.

"Shame," she smiled. "Perhaps I'll see you later anyway."

Grant made his way back to the hall carrying the wine and cups. Sara was not there.

"So how long have you and your boyfriend been together?" said the hotel receptionist looking in the bathroom mirror at Sara as she bent forward to apply some lipstick.

The receptionist had seen Sara standing in the hall waiting to use the loo, so she had taken her upstairs to a bedroom with an en suite.

"Not long," said Sara. "We met in Spain."

The older girl replenished her mascara.

"Isn't he a bit old for you?" said the girl looking round to face Sara.

"We love each other," she replied.

"Well that's okay then." The receptionist put the mascara back in her bag and took out a small piece of silver paper. Sara thought it was gum until the girl unwrapped it and tipped the contents onto the glass surface of the dressing table. It was a fine white powder.

"Is that cocaine?" asked Sara and then realised how naïve she must have sounded.

"Only the best," said the girl reaching into her bag again and this time bringing out a thin silver tube the thickness of a straw.

"I don't suppose you've ever tried it, have you?" said the receptionist.

Sara shook her head. The girl stretched the powder out into two lines. She bent down putting the silver tube to her nostril and snorted the first line. She stood up and sniffed in deeply.

"You've been told its bad for you and you get hooked, right?"

Sara nodded. "Are you hooked?" she asked.

"Of course not," replied the girl. "I just do a little now and then, go ahead, try it."

Those two little words have been responsible for so much misery, just five letters. Sara felt herself moving towards the dressing table. The girl held out the silver tube. Copying what the girl had done she moved along the line of powder and sniffed it up. She immediately felt light headed and thought for a moment she was going to faint. She rocked slightly on her feet. The receptionist held her and Sara felt her head swimming.

"Come on, you had better sit down for a minute," said the girl. She led Sara across to the bed and sat her down, then sat beside her. "You'll be okay," she reassured the teenager.

"It's strange the first time."

Sara heard her voice, but it sounded distorted, as though she was speaking from another room.

"Everything is strange the first time," she heard the girl say.

"Just lay back and close your eyes." She eased Sara back onto the bed. Sara closed her eyes and she felt more relaxed and more comfortable than any other time in her life.

"You're such a pretty little thing," she heard the girl say. Then she felt the waistband of her jeans being undone and the rough material being pulled down her thighs.

"Such a pretty thing," the words bounced around her head.

She felt sharp nails tracing a pattern from her stomach down through the curls of her pubic hair and kept wondering why it was the voice of the girl she was hearing and not Grant. And then she did hear Grant's voice, booming and angry. He was shouting and she was being pulled off the bed. Her jeans were being yanked up, not down, and she was being pulled from the room and down the stairs. The cold night air hit her and instead of feeling relaxed she felt so alive, more alive than any other time in her life.

"I want to dance and sing and make love all night," she shouted twirling around." Grant caught her before she fell.

"God what have I done?" he whispered. "Sara, what have I done to you?"

CHAPTER 42

Chief Inspector Templeton was looking out of his office window across to Big Ben wondering which nursery outfit to wear later that evening, the yellow or the pink.

Kay Carpenter had promised him "a special" and it had been on his mind all morning. His concentration was broken with a knock on his office door. DC Ralph Ballon walked in.

"It looks like we have got a result, guv. We've found the American – Tom Cody."

"So he's back from Japan?" asked Templeton.

"He is, but I bet he wished he'd stayed there. A couple of dock workers found him this morning in a warehouse in docklands nailed to the floor by his dick!"

The senior man winced.

"Is he dead?"

"He's in a bad way, but no. The docs over at the Homerton Hospital reckon he will survive. Probably won't father any kids though."

"Is he conscious?" asked Templeton.

"He was a few minutes ago, sir."

Templeton moved across to the coat stand and picked up his raincoat.

"Come on then," he said. "Let's get over there before this one snuffs it."

When they arrived at the hospital reception the American was awake, but drowsy due to the heavy painkillers that had been administered. He was also on a drip due to a considerable loss of blood. He felt numb in his groin and had not plucked up the courage to ask the medical staff the extent of the mutilation. He had to take it one stage at a time. He had survived and he must stay conscious long enough to tell the police everything Grant and Sara had told him. He knew the police had to find them before these oriental butchers.

Dr Munira Singh escorted Templeton and the DC to the intensive care unit where the American lay.

"He's very weak," she warned. "He lost a tremendous amount of blood. Who would do such a terrible thing to a man?"

The chief inspector looked straight ahead.

"That's what we need to find out."

They arrived at ICU. The uniformed constable on guard stood up and opened the door to the private room. Templeton walked in. The American was unconscious.

Sara woke with a thumping headache. It was three in the afternoon. The curtains in the room were still closed and the room was in comparative darkness. She threw off the duvet and was surprised to find she was still fully dressed. There was no sign of Grant. She shouted his name.

Grant was in the sauna when he heard her call out. He stubbed his injured toe on the metal water bucket as he leapt off the bench and made for the bedroom.

"Sara," he called. "I'm here, I'm coming."

She was standing by the curtains. He threw his arms around her.

"It's okay, I'm here."

She hugged him and stifled a sob.

"I thought you'd left me."

"He held her tightly, "I will never leave you," he said, "but you must promise me you'll never do that again."

Sara stifled another sob.

"I don't remember much after we arrived at the party. What happened?"

He broke the embrace and moved across to the remote control and opened the drapes. Sunlight streamed into the room and Sara winced at the brightness of the light.

"You remember our hotel receptionist?" asked Grant, "the one who you thought fancied me?"

"Erh, yes" said Sara.

"Well she didn't fancy me, she fancied you!"

Sarah screwed her face up.

"That's gross!"

Grant grinned. "Why did you put me to bed with all my clothes on?" asked Sara looking at Grant's nakedness.

"There didn't seem much point in taking them off, the state you were in," he replied. "You were on another planet."

Now it was her turn to grin.

"Well, I'm back on earth now!"

It was eight hours before Tom Cody regained consciousness. As soon as he stirred, the detective constable by his bedside radioed the Yard to inform Templeton. The Duty Information Officer rang the CI's home, a smart detached house in a leafy Loughton lane. The man leading the hunt for Grant Campbell and the missing teenager was in the first throes of orgasm when the telephone beside the bed rang. Kay Carpenter sat legs astride impaled on him. She leaned forward, being careful not to let him slip out of her and picked up the receiver.

"Yes this is Chief Inspector Templeton's residence," she said, her right nipple brushing against her guvnor's nose. He tilted his head back and licked the underside of the teat.

"No I'm sorry, he's tied up at the moment, can I give him a message?" She gasped slightly as he drew the tip into his mouth and teased it with his teeth. It was true, he was tied up. Two silk ties bound his wrists firmly to the bed head.

"Very well, I'll tell him to come as quickly as possible." She put the receiver back on the cradle just as he jerked his hips forward and did just that.

CHAPTER 43

The interview with the American lasted twenty minutes. In that time he told the Chief Inspector everything he knew – all that Grant and Sara had told him about the events in Yorkshire leading up to the shooting and Alan Mattherson's deal with the Chinese, the murder of Sarah's father and George Travers. When Templeton returned to his office he called a meeting to assemble the team.

"Kay, I want you to get over to the bank and get the number and description of the car Cody gave Campbell and the girl. Then put out an all-points bulletin on it.

"Steve," he said turning to detective sergeant Steve Tanner, "I want you to bring in the mother. If what Campbell and the girl told Cody is true then she's in this up to her eyeballs. The rest of you I want to concentrate around all exit points in the south east. Look for a man and a young boy travelling together. We know they are resourceful so don't rely on them using conventional transport. Check freight and cargo terminals for anything unusual, rail, air and sea." As an afterthought he turned back to Steve Tanner. "While you are in Yorkshire I want a full autopsy report on Alan Mattherson. I also want everything there is on Mattherson Industries, who they are, what they do, who's pulling the strings. If what Cody says is true, if we don't find Campbell and the girl they are dead meat."

Grant and Sara spent the day shopping. Sara bought half a dozen chic outfits from the boutiques in Nyhavn. Grant treated himself to new trousers, shirts, sweaters and jackets. They lunched at the Copenhagen Corner restaurant on the corner of Hans Christian Anderson Boulevard and Vesterbrogade and returned to the hotel early in the evening. There was a new receptionist on duty, a young Dane in his early twenties, blonde, blue eyes and extremely handsome.

"Now I wouldn't mind if he fancied me," sniggered Sara as they collected their key card.

"Down girl," laughed Grant as they headed hand in hand towards the lift.

CHAPTER 44

The car park security guard tucked the Playboy magazine under the blotter on his desk as he saw Kay Carpenter and two uniformed officers approach his booth. He got up from the old cracked leather swivel chair hoping that his erection would be hidden by the long jacket of his uniform. He opened the door.

"Good evening," he said.

Kay scrutinised him. She was sure she could detect a slight bulge in his trousers, but it wouldn't have been the first time that she's had such an effect on a man.

She flashed her warrant card.

"DC Carpenter," she said. "We believe one of the bank's executive's Mr Tom Cody borrowed a car from the company pool," she said.

The guard put his hand on his hips.

"What is it with you lot?" he said. "I already told you people about that."

Kay threw a glance at her colleagues.

"Told what people?" she asked.

"You know the two other guys that were here yesterday asking about that. I gave them all the details".

"Did they show you any ID?" asked Kay.

The guard rubbed his chin. "Well no come to think of it. They said they were Special Branch."

"What did they look like?" said Kay taking out a notebook.

"Well, I thought it was strange," said the guard. "They were both foreign looking."

"Oriental," asked Kay, "maybe Chinese?"

"Could be," replied the guard, "they all look the same, don't they?" He laughed. Kay didn't.

"Give me the make, colour and registration number of the car," she said.

The guard rubbed his head and a shower of dandruff cascaded to the floor. He returned to his desk and rummaged through a pile of papers. He handed her a sheet of pink paper.

"There you go, see, that's Mr Cody's signature, all legal and above board."

Kay took the paper. "We will need a full description of the two men you spoke to yesterday. You may need to come down to the Yard to look through some mug shots to see if you can identify them. May I use your phone?"

The man stepped aside. Kay picked up the receiver and dialled.

"Chief Inspector Templeton," he said.

"Guv, its DC Carpenter. It looks like we've been beaten to it." She explained what had happened.

"Get back here," he ordered and slammed the receiver down. He looked at the clock on the wall and knew that time was running out.

CHAPTER 45

Thor Solberg sat at the smoke filled bar of the Anchor Inn and emptied the content of the pint glass in front of him. He would be glad to get back to Denmark where he could have a decent drink. Lager in Britain never tasted the same as his beloved Elephant beer back home. Nonetheless he had drunk eight pints already that night and was waiting for a refill when two photographs were placed on the bar in front of him. He turned to see who had put them there, behind him stood two large Oriental men in Burberry suits.

"Have you seen these two people?" asked the larger of the two men. Solberg was over six feet and powerfully built, but even he felt intimidated. He recognised the picture of man, not the pretty blonde haired girl.

"Perhaps," he said, placing them back on the bar.

The other man reached into his jacket pocket and produced a wad of £20 notes. He placed them on the bar in front of Solberg. The Dane picked them up and flicked though them estimating the pile must contain £500.

"The man was aboard my ship a few days ago – the Virage. He had a young boy with him. He was looking for the captain. I took him to see the first mate."

He went to pick up the money when a stiletto crashed down between his fingers and stuck in the wad of notes. Solberg flinched.

"Nobody on the ship was supposed to know, but we took them across to Copenhagen. I saw them sneak off the ship after Customs had left."

The stiletto was withdrawn and Solberg pocketed the cash. He turned and saw the two huge dark shapes disappear out of the stained glass door.

CHAPTER 46

Kay Carpenter had a broad smile on her face when she knocked on Templeton's office door. Her boss was sitting behind his desk going through a pile of papers.

"It looks like we have found the car," said Kay. "It was on a mobile home site at a place called Hullbridge in Essex. One of the caravan owners reported a break-in to the local Plod and they found the car nearby, but it looks like our lovebirds have flown the nest."

Templeton got up from his desk and walked across to the map on his wall.

"Where is Hullbridge?" he asked. Kay pinpointed it. He studied the map in detail.

"What's this place, Baltic Wharf?"

"It's a deep water cargo terminal on the river," said Kay. "We're checking it now."

CHAPTER 47

It was midnight before Grant and Sara got back to the hotel. They had dined on board a restaurant ship, one of the top seafood restaurants in Copenhagen. They both had oysters, smoked salmon and caviar followed by lobster thermidor washed down with Montrachet and Bollinger.

They laughed and joked, chatted easily with each other. In the new tight fitting mini dress Sara looked every inch the beautiful young girl she was. They were still laughing when, back at the hotel, they went to collect the key card from the young Dane still on duty in reception.

"Ah, Mr Smith," he said as he saw them approach. "There were some people looking for you earlier on."

Grant's jaw dropped.

"Looking for us?" he said in disbelief.

"Don't worry," said the young receptionist. "I did not tell them you and the young lady are staying here. We are very discreet."

"What did they look like?" said Grant.

"I do not think they were police," said the Dane. "They were Chinese."

Grant felt his world collapsing around him. Sara grabbed his arm to steady him.

"Are you all right, sir?" asked the concerned receptionist. "Perhaps there is something I can get you?"

Grant shook his head. How had they been found? It must have been Nielmyer, he thought. He must have talked.

When they got to their suite Sara poured Grant a large glass of Jack Daniels. He took a gulp and felt the oaky spirit burn a path down his gullet. He sat on the bed and Sara sat next to him.

"Maybe we should give ourselves up," he said looking at her.

She shook her head and put her arm around him resting her head on his shoulder.

"Never," she said. "You promised."

Grant stood up. "Sara, these are probably the same goons who killed George Travers, the ones your uncle was in league with. They are killers and they are after us. I can't let anything happen to you." He crossed the room to the telephone.

"What are you doing?" said Sara.

"I'm calling the police. I'm going to give myself up."

Sara pressed the receiver down.

"No," she said sternly. "We're safe here for the time being, they won't be back. We can get away, go somewhere else. We did it before and we can do it again. We'll go far away, live in the bush, on an island, anywhere as long as we are together. I love you so much."

He held her close so she couldn't see the tears escaping from the corner of his eyes.

"Looks like we're in luck, guv," said Kay Carpenter to her boss.

"There was a ship left the deep water terminal on Wednesday, sailing for Copenhagen."

CHAPTER 48

Neither Grant or Sara slept much. They held each other, just being together was enough.

"What will we do?" asked Sara staring up at the canopy above the bed. Grant bit the inside of his lip.

"Tomorrow I'll catch the hydro across to Malmo and see if I can figure a way of getting out of here. If we've got enough money we may be able to buy false passports."

Sara said nothing, but lay there hoping that sleep would eventually claim her.

Grant left the hotel early without waking Sara. He walked down to the ferry and waited twenty minutes before boarding the hydrofoil for the 40 minute crossing to Sweden. When he arrived at the Swedish seaport he made straight for the myriad of bars. A mixed race barmaid with a low-cut blouse and a 50 inch bust was drying glasses when Grant walked into the Shamrock Bar. Despite it being early morning there were at least two dozen drinkers in the smoke filled room. Grant ordered a lager, trying not to fall into her cleavage.

"Sure a man could drown in there so he could," said a soft Irish voice. Grant turned and saw it belonged to a small fat man with receding hair and bright red cheeks sitting at a table behind him. The barmaid served Grant his lager.

"Would you be English by any chance?" asked the Irishman. Grant sipped his beer.

"Could be," said Grant cautiously.

"I can see you're taken with our Inga," he smiled. "You don't get many of those to the pound back home. Would you care to join me? Sure it can be fearful lonely on your own." He pushed a chair away from the table gesturing for Grant to sit down.

"Are you long in Sweden?" he asked.

"You ask a lot of questions," said Grant returning to his beer.

"No offence," apologised the small man. "There was me thinking how troubled you were looking."

"Girlfriend trouble," said Grant. The Irishman's eyes lit up.

"Now didn't I know that the minute you walked in? Noel, I said to myself, for that's my name, Noel Geary, Noel there's a man with woman trouble if ever I saw one. A row is it?"

This guy hasn't just kissed the Blarney Stone thought Grant, he's swallowed it. "Kind of," he said taking another sip. "I needed to get away. It's her parents, they don't approve. She's quite a bit younger than me and now she tells me she's pregnant. When her old man finds out…" He let the words trail off, but tilted his head back and drew an imaginary line across his throat.

The Irishman gulped.

"So you'll be here to drown your sorrows?"

Grant took another sip.

"No I'm here to try and find somebody to smuggle us both out of the country. Her father has people looking for us."

The Irishman looked at him, paused and then burst out laughing.

"Sure, you're a caution and no mistake. You had me half believing you."

Grant smiled and sipped.

"So what's an Irishman doing here in a bar in Sweden at this time of the morning, apart from the obvious?" said Grant.

"Sure, I own the place," he replied, "me and Inga."

Grant looked back at the barmaid.

"Inga, is she your wife?"

The Irishman burst out laughing again.

"Glory be to God in Heaven. No, she's not my wife. My wife is back in Ennis, County Clare so she is, or scouring the pubs in Dublin where she thinks I am."

The thought of the small balding Irishman and an Amazonian Inga conjured a bizarre picture.

"Can I get you a drink?" offered Grant. The Irishman drained his glass. "Sure have you ever heard of a Geary refuse a drink. I'll have a small Paddy." Grant smiled, he thought he is a small Paddy.

He went to the bar and asked Inga for two refills. Inga said she would bring them across to the table.

Returning to his new acquaintance he sat back down.

"So tell me, Noel, how long have you been in Sweden?"

"Sure now who's asking all the questions, two years, two years this Christmas."

Inga brought the drinks over and Grant could appreciate the full majesty of her figure. She had an incredibly small waist with slim hips and legs that went up to her armpits. Her huge bosom was disproportionate to the rest of her. She walked as if she were clutching a five pound note between the cheeks of her arse. Grant watched her all the way back to the bar.

"Sure she's a grand girl," observed Noel.

"I'm sorry," said Grant slightly embarrassed. "I didn't mean to stare."

The Irishman laughed. "Don't apologise," he laughed. "Inga is used to getting attention. It's the size of her tits!"

Grant nearly choked on his beer.

"See, now you look like a different fellow to the man who walked in here."

Grant was beginning to like this funny little leprechaun of a man, but could he trust him?

"Noel," he said. "What if I wasn't joking about being smuggled out of the country?"

Geary cupped the glass tumbler in his podgy hands.

"Well then I would say you were in more trouble than just having a pregnant girlfriend with an over-protective father."

"But could a man buy passage out of here, undetected?"

Noel's eyes twinkled.

"Sure, Jack the Ripper could buy his way out of here if he had enough money….and knew the right people."

"And how much would be enough for two people?" asked Grant.

Geary raised a bushy eyebrow.

"You would still need new passports, identification etc."

Grant could see his brain ticking over.

"£10,000 would cover it."

"And how soon could it be arranged," asked Grant, "hypothetically speaking?"

The Irishman drained his glass.

"Hypothetically speaking there may be a Russian ship leaving for Malaya on Sunday."

Grant looked at the calendar on his Rolex.

"That gives me 48 hours to get the money."

The Irishman fingered the tumbler.

"Okay, arrange it," said Grant. "I'll get you the money."

The Irishman's demeanour had changed from jovial buffoon to serious businessman.

"I will need a gesture of goodwill," he said, "a deposit of some sort, say half now."

Grant knew he didn't have £5,000. With the money they had spent he'd be lucky to have half of that.

"That's a fine looking watch you have there," said Geary eyeing up Grant's Rolex. "It's not one of those Hong Kong fakes, now is it?"

It was his most treasured personal possession, the symbol of everything he had worked for. He took it off and handed it to Geary.

"It is 22 carat gold, certified in Switzerland. It's worth £10,000 on its own."

The Irishman examined it.

"The watch and £5,000 in cash," he said.

Grant bit the inside of his lip.

"How can I trust you?" he asked.

"You can't," he replied, "but it seems to me you are running out of options."

"Can I use your phone?" Grant asked getting up from the table.

"Of course," said Geary. "Inga will show you where it is."

Grant checked the code for Copenhagen in the telephone book and dialled the number of the hotel which he had written on a book of matches from the room. The operator made the connection to the hotel, but the reception said Sara was not in the room.

CHAPTER 49

She strolled along Isted Grade enjoying the admiring glances from a group of youths sitting on a bench. You didn't need to be a linguist to understand what they were saying. She wore a tight pink dress with black vee neck which showed off her figure to perfection.

She passed a cinema showing hard core porn movies and thought about popping in just out of curiosity. She didn't want to stay in the hotel on her own. Next door to the cinema was the Taboo Club, boasting continuous live shows. At the door stood a blonde haired stud of a man in his early 20s, He reminded Sara of her James Dean poster.

"Free show, free drinks for you," he said. Sara hesitated. She was tempted. After all she would probably never get another chance. She knew Grant wouldn't approve, but, what the hell. She went inside.

Three steps down led into a large room with subtle red lighting. In the middle of the floor area was a large bed on which a young couple were writhing. Around the bed laid out in rows three deep were comfortable velvet padded chairs. There were about twenty people watching the show, mostly men, but some couples. To one side of the room was a bar and behind it a barman stripped to the waist and wearing a red bow tie around his neck. The doorman had followed Sara in and asked her if she would like a drink from the bar. She asked for an orange juice and sat down on a front row chair near the bar.

There was soft music playing and the lighting changed from red to amber to green and then blue. The couple on the bed were humping and heaving. The girl, a pretty Eurasian who Sara thought looked about the same age as her was on her hands and knees. The man was completely hairless, but with a muscular body. He knelt on a cushion and was thrusting his penis into her doggy-style. Nothing new there thought Sara, been there, done that.

The barman brought over her orange juice on a silver tray. She took it and smiled demurely. The couple on the bed changed position. As the man withdrew his penis, Sara's eyes widened when she saw the size and thickness of it.

"He is magnificent, is he not?" said a voice into her ear. She turned and smelled the fetid breath of a dark skinned man who had come to sit behind her. He was an Arab with yellowing teeth all bar one, which sparkled when the light caught the diamond embedded in it.

"Let me introduce myself," he said in a whisper. "I am Tariq Aziz, the owner of this club."

He offered his hand which Sara took nervously.

"Permit me to offer you something on the house, some champagne perhaps?"

Sara turned back to watch the show. Like the bald performer it too was reaching a climax.

"I only drink orange juice," she lied.

The man on the bed was reaching fever pitch. Sara watched as his buttocks clenched forming deep dimples at the side of his hips. Then in a final fury he withdrew his penis and ejaculated thick streams of sperm the length of the girl's back, some matting her jet black hair. The audience applauded, but Sara didn't join in. The Arab came and sat next to her.

"Forgive me for asking, perhaps you are looking for work?" he leered his tooth sparkling as the house lights were raised.

"Not that kind of work," she said as Aziz ran his eyes over her body.

"A great pity," he continued. "A beautiful young girl like you could earn a lot of money here." He reached into his top pocket and pulled out a business card.

"Please take this. Feel free to call me anytime if you change your mind." Sara put the card in the small clutch bag she had bought to match her dress. She left the remains of the orange juice stood up and straightened her dress. She felt the Arab's eyes burning into her as she walked up the three steps. She looked over her shoulder at him and smiled. He ran his tongue across his lips at the thought of tasting her.

Sara was back in the hotel when Grant returned. The first thing he did when he saw her was to kiss her passionately on the lips. The next thing he did was pour himself a large Jack Daniels.

"How did you get on?" she asked.

Grant told her of the meeting with the Irishman and how he had left his watch as a deposit for their passage out of Scandinavia.

"But where the hell we are going to get the other money I have no idea," said Grant "unless I rob a bank."

"Or a banker?" said Sara.

Grant looked at her quizzically. "What are you scheming young lady?" he said, tickling her so she fell back on the bed. "And where were you when I tried to call?"

Sara told him where she had been and her encounter with Tariq Aziz.

"You can forget that right away," said Grant. "You are not working in a sex club!"

"I've no intention to," said Sara, "but I do have a plan."

CHAPTER 50

The following morning Tariq Aziz was in his office auditioning a new girl for the show when the telephone rang. The head of the pretty Vietnamese girl was still bobbing up and down in his lap as he picked up the receiver.

"Aziz," he said and then winced as the girl's teeth raked the head of his shaft.

"No teeth!" he admonished her then turned back to the phone call. "How may I help you?"

Sara sat nervously on the bed back at the hotel, Grant by her side.

"Mr Aziz, we met at your club yesterday. You asked if I was looking for work. I was wearing a pink dress."

Aziz sat upright in his chair dislodging himself from the girl's mouth. She looked up forlornly, but he pushed her away with a ring encrusted hand.

"Yes I remember," he said. "Have you changed your mind?"

Sara took a deep breath to calm her nerves.

"Well I may have a proposition for you. Can we meet?"

Aziz's face lit up at the prospect.

"Of course," he said. "Come to the club at one o'clock."

Grant nodded.

"Fine," said Sara. "I look forward to it." She put the phone down. "I don't believe I did that," she exhaled.

"So far, so good," said Grant, "now for stage two."

Before one o'clock Grant and Sara returned to Nyhavn to do more shopping, this time they were looking for something rather special for Sara. They found it in an Italian designer fashion store. As soon as Sara came out of the fitting room Grant knew it was exactly the right dress – high neck, long sleeves, pleated skirt cut below the knee.

"I thought I was supposed to be getting something sexy," she said giving Grant a twirl. "You know, split up to the waist and showing more front than Woolworths."

"You look just fine," said Grant and turned to the sales assistant, "we will take it. Don't bother to wrap it, she'll wear it now."

Just before one o'clock they arrived at a small café twenty to thirty yards from the entrance to the club. Grant gave Sara an affectionate peck on the cheek.

"Remember," he said," if things start getting out of hand, just scream and I'll come running." She smiled nervously.

"I'll be okay," she said and kissed him tenderly on the lips. She turned and went to keep her appointment.

The same doorman was on duty at the club. He recognised her from the previous day.

"Mr Aziz is expecting you in his office," he said. "Up the stairs and it's the first door on the left."

Sara climbed the narrow threadbare carpeted stairs, her stomach in knots. The door was half wood, half opaque glass with the word manager printed in gold lettering across the glass. She knocked.

"Come," said Aziz licking the palm of his hand and running it across his greasy black hair. She opened the door and walked in. The office was as seedy as she had imagined. Aziz was perched on the edge of a large mahogany desk inlaid with green leather. On it were a computer, telephone, wooden tray and silver framed photograph holder, the contents of which Sara could not see. To one side of the room there was a large leather armchair and a matching four seater leather settee. The casting couch, thought Sara.

Aziz slid off the desk like a lizard and extended a limp hand to greet her. As she went to shake it he took her hand and raised it to his lips and kissed the back of it.

"Now what sort of a job are you looking for?" he asked, keeping hold of her hand.

Sara pulled it away. "One that pays a lot of money," she said.

Aziz ushered towards the settee. Sara sat in the armchair instead.

"In the club you could make £400 a day," said Aziz.

"And what about outside the club?" Sara asked.

He came over and sat on the arm of the chair.

"That depends on experience."

Sara stood up.

"I have no experience," she said looking him straight in the eye. "The fact is I am still a 15 year-old virgin."

The man's eyes widened.

"When I lose it," she continued, "it's going to be for at least £5,000."

Tariq burst out laughing and Sara thought she had blown it.

"£5,000," he said incredulously. "You must be mad."

She stepped half a pace towards him, so close their bodies were almost touching. Her perfume filled his flared nostrils. He was dazzled by the whiteness of her eyes, the depth of colour in her green irises. Then Sara reached up and kissed him on the lips running her tongue across his teeth and felt the diamond implant. Then she broke away.

"Still don't think I'll be worth it? Like I said, the price is £5,000." She turned and walked to the office door pleading with God to let her get out of the place in one piece.

"Where can I get in touch with you?" said Aziz.

"The Richmond," said Sara opening the door.

"What name?" asked the Arab, "I don't even know your name."

"Brady," said Sara, "Flick Brady."

Grant was waiting at the café. "How did it go?" he asked as she rushed into his arms.

"I'll tell you as soon as my knees stop shaking," she said. "I think he took the bait."

The next stop was the Hotel Richmond where earlier that morning Grant had registered Sara in a double room.

"Just stay in the hotel until you hear from me," said Grant, "catch you later."

He caught a cab to Ostergade and instructed the driver to stop outside the theatrical costumiers. He went inside. An elderly man shuffled out of a back room into the cluttered showroom.

"God morgen," he greeted Grant in Danish.

"Do you speak English?" asked Grant. The old man smiled, "English, Danish, Yiddish, you name it I speak it," he said. "What can I do for you?"

"I have to attend a fancy dress function tonight and I have a bet with my boss that he won't be able to recognise me. I thought I would go as a Middle Eastern potentate. I need the make-up, costume, the works,"

The old man frowned.

"Oi ve! me a Jew should keep an Arab costume, come on, round the back." He beckoned Grant to the rear of the shop and began sorting through a rail of costumes. He looked at Grant to size him up, and then continued searching.

"This," he said pulling out a white and gold trimmed robe. "This is you." He held it up against Grant.

"I have the turban to match. This was the Thief of Baghdad. Do you remember the film?"

Grant shrugged.

"No matter," said the old man. "Try it on. If it fitted Burt Lancaster it will fit you."

Grant took the costume and held it up to his chin. "So this was worn by Burt Lancaster?" he asked.

"Burt Lancaster, Victor Mature, who can remember, so many films, so many actors."

Grant tried on the costume in a small changing room and came out to show the shop owner.

The old man lifted the material at the waist. "An inch here, a centimetre there, it will be perfect. I do the alterations while you wait."

"I'd be very grateful," said Grant, "but what about the make up?"

"Make up shmake up. My May could turn Mother Teresa into Madonna." He went out to the back stairs and called up.

"May, May, come down here old woman. We have a customer for you."

Grant heard her coming down the stairs as he changed out of his costume. When he drew the curtain across he saw the old man's wife, a striking lady despite her advancing years.

"May, this gentleman has an important function to go to and he has to look like an, an," the word stuck in his throat, "an Arab."

"Theo," she scolded him, "an Arab?"

The old costumier shrugged his shoulders. "Business is business, can you make him Arab?"

May looked closely at Grant's features, turning his head from side to side.

"He's a better face for a nice Jewish boy, but if he wants Arab….."

CHAPTER 51

The Hotel d'Angleterre on Kongens Nytorv is one of the most expensive hotels in Copenhagen and has played host to several kings and queens and heads of state. The liveried doorman was not surprised when the Arab gentleman alighted from a taxi outside reception. He opened the heavy swing door and Grant stepped into the glittering marble and crystal reception area.

The concierge behind the plush marble reception desk smiled as the figure approached. Arabs were among the best tippers at the hotel.

"Good afternoon sir, welcome to Hotel d'Angleterre."

Grant remained stone faced.

"I am personal secretary to His Royal Highness Sheikh Ali Bin Khan Mohammed who arrives in Copenhagen today for the OPEC summit. In addition to his embassy residence, His Royal Highness requires a suite of rooms which he may or may not use for private meetings. I am here to see if you have anything of a suitable standard."

The concierge moved from behind the desk and came around to where Grant stood.

"I must inform the manager," he said nervously. "I am sure the penthouse would be suitable."

He disappeared into an ante room marked Private and reappeared a few moments later with an impeccably dressed older man in a dark grey pinstripe suite.

"Your Excellency," he fawned. "It is a great honour for our humble hotel to be of service of His Royal Highness. Permit me to show you the penthouse suite."

He ushered Grant towards a bank of lifts off the main reception area.

"The suite is very popular with our VIP guests. How long would his Royal Highness be requiring it?"

The manager took out a key card and swiped it through the control lock. The lift doors opened.

"Two or three days," said Grant.

"You will forgive me for pointing out," stammered the manager, "there is a minimum rental period for the suite…"

Before he finished the sentence Grant waved a hand.

"This is of no consequence. Security is my only concern."

"Of course," agreed the manager as the lift glided to a halt. "We pride ourselves on our security at Hotel d'Angleterre….."

Grant stepped out of the lift in the main lounge of the penthouse suite. It was indeed fit for a king, decorated in sumptuous fabrics, glittering chandeliers, expensive paintings and tapestries.

"Is this the best you have?" Grant asked dismissively.

The manager stammered again.

"Is there something not to your liking, Your Excellency?"

Grant walked around the room trailing his fingers across the back of the Louis XIV settee.

"It may be adequate," said Grant. "How many bedrooms are here?"

"Four," replied the manager, now almost apologetically. "Let me show you the master."

He ushered Grant into a magnificent bedroom with a canopied four poster bed resting on a luxurious three inch pile white sheepskin carpet. Grant grunted, feigning indifference.

"Is there a private entrance?"

The manager smiled.

"If you would like to come this way Your Excellency," he said taking Grant to a corridor which linked two of the other bedrooms and bathrooms and pointed to a plain steel door.

"This is a private lift to the basement car park. There is no need for His Royal Highness to use the hotel reception if he does not wish to do so."

Grant nodded approvingly.

"It will suffice," he said. "My people will contact you shortly and make the arrangements. I assume we will have use of the hotel limousine? You do have a limousine?"

"Of course sir, a Rolls Royce, it is at your disposal."

"Excellent," said Grant. "I will need to check its suitability."

"Will His Royal Highness have any special dietary requirements while he is here," asked the manager. "Our kitchens are amongst the best in Scandinavia. Our reputation…."

Grant silenced him again with a wave of his hand.

"His Royal Highness has his own chefs," he said. "He may not be eating here, however, he may be entertaining special guests. I take it we can count on your upmost discretion."

The manager nodded like a demented donkey.

"Of course, Excellency."

They returned to reception via the main lift. A black Rolls Royce Silver Spur was parked outside.

"Please, with our compliments," said the manager walking Grant to the car. The chauffeur opened the car door and Grant climbed in. When in the driver's seat the chauffeur asked where Grant would like to be taken. "The Taboo Club" said Grant, "on Istergade."

CHAPTER 52

Detective Constable Steve Tanner brought the Ford Orion to a crunching halt on the gravel driveway of Sara's home in Yorkshire. He pulled up ten yards behind an ambulance that was waiting with its back doors open wide. He got out and went across to a uniformed police officer outside the front door. Steve showed him his warrant card.

"What's going on?" he asked.

Two paramedics came out manoeuvring a stretcher. On it lay Liz Mattherson attached to a drip.

"What happened?" asked the detective.

"Looks like a drugs overdose," said one of the paramedics "probably heroin. It looks bad."

Tanner looked at the pale lifeless form of the woman on the stretcher. Shit, he thought. Templeton is not going to like this.

As Liz Mattherson was being rushed into A&E, in the forensic laboratory two floors above, Professor William Klineman was peering into a microscope at a sample of tissue taken from the spleen of her late brother-in-law.

"That's odd," he mumbled, "very odd."

The young assistant who had been helping with the autopsy stood by his side.

"What is it professor?"

The grey haired bespectacled scientist stepped away from the microscope.

"Take a look yourself," he said.

The young man was a great admirer of the professor. He was his mentor. He looked through the scope.

"I see what you mean, sir," he said, "massive tissue damage. What could have caused it?"

The professor scratched his chin and frowned. "I'm not sure yet," he said, "but what is certain is that this man did not die from a gunshot wound."

CHAPTER 53

The doorman at the club looked longingly at the Rolls Royce as it pulled up at the club. Big cars usually meant big tips. When he saw the chauffeur open the door for the Arab in the back he could feel his wallet swell. He stepped forward to greet him.

"Good afternoon sir, welcome to…"

Grant swept past ignoring him. Sara had given him a good description of the club and he had mentally familiarised himself with the layout. The doorman, affronted by the visitor's lack of attention followed him inside.

"Look you can't just barge in here as though you owned the place," he stormed. His raised voice alerted Aziz who was standing by the bar watching the Vietnamese girl on stage engaged in a lesbian show with a woman in her sixties.

Aziz turned to the doorman. "Okay Jan, what is it?"

"This guy pulls up in a Roller and barges in like he owns the place."

It was the reference to Roller that grabbed his attention.

"Leave this to me and go back outside," he commanded.

Grant looked at the scene on stage.

"I am the servant of my master," said Grant.

"And who might your master be?" asked Aziz.

"My master is a man who enjoys many pleasures and who is willing to pay exceedingly well for what he enjoys."

"Do you think he would enjoy the company of those two?" asked Aziz pointing to the stage.

"Whores and dogs! Perhaps I have come to the wrong place." He turned to leave. Aziz caught hold of the sleeve of his robe. Grant glared and he let go quickly.

"I am sorry," apologised Aziz. "Perhaps if you tell me what your master does enjoy, I am sure I can help."

Grant looked back to the stage. The Vietnamese girl was using a large black dildo on the older woman spread beneath her.

"My master prefers younger company," said Grant.

"I have a wonderful 18 year old Dutch girl," began Aziz, but stopped when Grant raised his hand.

"Younger? Something truly special?" said Grant.

Aziz gulped.

"How much younger? I can get you any age you like, for the right price."

Grant remained impassive.

"Money is of no consequence. You must understand in my country a girl is taken for a wife when the flower is in first bud. My master prefers his companions very fresh. For such a prize he would be willing to pay, say £10,000."

Aziz gulped again, "With a bonus of say £5,000 if the girl were to disappear afterwards," added Grant.

Aziz licked his lips at the prospect of the money.

"£15,000?" he said.

"Only for the right girl," said Grant, "young fresh faced, fair haired and a virgin."

The description matched the girl in the club the previous day, the one willing to sell her body for £5,000.

"Do you have such a creature?" asked Grant.

Aziz's smile broadened and the jewelled tooth glinted in the light.

"I have the very girl," he leered.

"There is one condition," said Grant. "If my master is pleased with the girl you will collect the bonus, but if she displeases him you only get the fee."

"Agreed," said Aziz. "Where and when?"

Grant took out a card he had picked up in the reception of the Hotel d'Angleterre and handed it to Aziz.

"Send the girl to this hotel at six o'clock this evening. Tell her to ask for the Penthouse suite. She will be expected. When my master is finished he will send one of our staff down to reception to pay your man. When the girl comes down you will dispose of her as you see fit."

After I have finished with her, thought Aziz. He offered Grant his hand, but Grant turned and walked out before he turned and repeated "six o'clock."

Aziz watched as the Rolls Royce drove away then went back into the club and picked up the telephone. He dialled the number of the hotel. The concierge answered. Aziz said: "I would like to book the Penthouse suite." The clerk smiled.

"I am sorry sir it is already taken for His Highness Ali Bin Kahn Mohammed," he said boastfully.

Aziz put the phone down. In his mind he was already spending the money. He lifted the receiver again and reached into his pocket for the card Sara had given him. He dialled the number of the Richmond.

"Could you put me through to Flick Colby," he asked. The receptionist connected the call. Sara was waiting.

"Hello, Flick Colby," she said. "Who is this?"

Aziz could picture himself running his hands over her naked body.

"Miss Colby, it is Tariq Aziz. I think we may be able to do business together. I have a client who wants to meet you at the Hotel d'Angleterre at 6pm. You are to ask for the penthouse. They will be expecting you."

"What about the money?" Sara asked.

Aziz hesitated, "£5,000 as agreed."

"When do I get the cash?" she asked.

"Afterwards," said Aziz.

"No way shit head," said Sara. "How do I know the pervert will pay me? I want all the money up front or the deal is off."

Aziz could see the money slipping away. Ah, what the fuck he thought, she's never going to live long enough to spend it.

"Very well Miss Colby, one of my men will hand you the money at the hotel's reception. He will also stay there to make sure you keep the appointment and don't abscond with my cash."

Sara put the phone down. The plan was set.

Grant arrived back at the hotel ten minutes later. She flew into his arms.

CHAPTER 54

"Looks like we are getting somewhere at last, Kay Carpenter told Templeton as he swung his feet off the desk when she entered his office. Kay stood in front of him dressed in a neat two piece brown woollen suit and was carrying a clip board. The previous night she had stood in front of him wearing a leather cat-suit, thigh length boots and carried a riding crop.

"We have interviewed the skipper of the cargo ship. He was back in Denmark when the ship sailed from Essex, but a security guard remembers a man matching Campbell's description and a young boy boarding the ship. Although they were checked off the ship he never saw them leave. The chances are they are in Denmark. We have circulated their photographs through Interpol and the Danish police authorities in Copenhagen and they have implemented a search. If they're still there it's only a question of time before we find them."

"What about this Chinese business Cody was talking about?" asked Templeton eyeing the knee length boots the young detective was wearing. "And where's the autopsy report on Alan Mattherson?"

Kay handed him the clipboard. "We're still waiting for the autopsy report. There's been some sort of hold up. We do know that George Travers was until recently a director of Mattherson Industries and died in a car crash nine days ago."

"Did he have shares in the company?" asked Templeton.

Kay shook her head. "No, the majority shareholder was the missing girl's father. After his death..."

"...another car crash," interrupted her boss, "sorry, go on."

Kay continued, "After his death the shares reverted to his wife."

Templeton looked up. "Not his daughter?"

Kay shrugged. Templeton frowned.

"Have we brought the mother in for questioning?" Kay grimaced.

"I thought you were going to ask that. We went to pick her up, but we were too late. She's in Bradford General Hospital with a suspected drugs overdose. Looks like heroin."

Templeton ran his hands though his hair.

"I don't like the smell of this. Book me on the next flight to Copenhagen."

Kay went to leave the office when he called after her.

"And Kay, you had better come with me."

CHAPTER 55

Grant arrived at the Hotel d'Angleterre still dressed in his robes. The front of house manager greeted him enthusiastically.

"We have not heard from your embassy yet, Your Excellency. "I hate to mention it, but …."

Grant took out two 500 krona notes and handed them to him.

"I will telephone from the suite. May I have the key?"

The man handed Grant the VIP key card.

"His Royal Highness will be expecting a guest - a young lady – at six o'clock. Please send her up as soon as she arrives and admit nobody else."

He crossed to the lift inserted the key and went up to the penthouse. He crossed the lounge to the Louis X1V sideboard and poured himself a large glass of Remy Antique. He went to look at his Rolex, but of course, it was missing. The grandfather clock told him he had twenty minutes to remove his make up before Sara arrived.

Sara wore the same modest outfit that she had on at the Taboo Club. The club's doorman was in reception waiting for her. She noticed a smartly dressed businessman in a blue chalk stripe suit sitting on the large leather settee reading a copy of the Herald Tribune. Then she recognised the club doorman. He walked towards her and reached inside his jacket pocket. For a moment Sara's heart froze.

"I hear it's going to be your first time," he whispered in her ear. Sara flinched when he touched her shoulder. "Don't be nervous," he said and handed her a white envelope. Sara looked inside and flicked through the wad of notes.

"You sure better be worth it," said the Dane. "Because Mr Aziz says if he gets any complaints about your performance then it's going to be the last performance you ever give. I'll be waiting." With that he went and sat on a vacant armchair.

Sara crossed to the desk. The concierge looked up.

"I am expected in the penthouse," said Sara.

"This way," he said and escorted her across to the lifts as the doorman watched. He put the key in the lock and the doors opened. Sara walked inside. The Dane watched the doors close. His orders were to wait for the payment and then bring the money and the girl back to the club for Aziz's entertainment. He had already decided he was going to have a little fun with her first.

Grant heard the lift approach and stood to one side of the wall. His heart was pounding. The doors opened.

"Grant?" Sara called. She stepped out of the lift and shrieked when Grant grabbed her.

"Grant, you scared the life out of me," she said.

Relieved she was alone he picked her off her feet and kissed her.

"Are you okay? Did you get the money?"

She reached into the leather shoulder bag and handed him the envelope. He opened it and took out the money fanning it out then he hugged her again.

"You little beauty, you did it"

She flung her arms around him and kissed him hungrily on the mouth.

"We did it, Your Excellency. What now?" Grant let her go and picked up a chair from around the dining table. He opened the lift doors and wedged the chair in the gap to keep them from closing. He took her by the hand.

"Come on," he said. "We've got to go and see a man about a boat."

As he led her past the master bedroom Sara stopped. The door was slightly ajar and she could see the magnificent bed. She pulled him towards the room.

"No, no, no," said Grant resisting temptation. "We're getting out of here, now!"

Sara pulled a grumpy face.

"Shame to waste it," she said impishly.

Grant pulled her past the bedroom into the corridor and to the private lift. He took the key card from his pocket and swiped it. The doors opened and they stepped inside. Grant pressed the button marked B and the couple stood hand in hand as the lift descended silently. It landed with a slight thud. When the doors opened they stepped out into the car park. Minutes later they had joined the throng of Copenhageners and were heading towards the night ferry to Malmo.

CHAPTER 56

Chief Inspector Templeton and WDC Kay Carpenter were greeted at Copenhagen's Kastrup International Airport by inspector Rud Holgett. He drove them to the Central Hotel where his secretary had booked them twin rooms. On the way he updated them on their search for the British fugitives.

"We think they checked in to a hotel on Nyhavn using the name Mr and Mrs Smith," said Holgett.

"Very original," replied Templeton.

"But they have not been back to the hotel in the past 24 hours. Naturally it is being watched."

"Naturally," echoed Templeton.

"We are continuing our inquiries in other hotels, guest houses etc, but you must appreciate at this time of year with so many tourists in the city it is not an easy task. From what you have told me this man Campbell is very resourceful."

Templeton grunted.

"Have you been to Copenhagen before chief inspector?" asked Holgett.

"Never," he replied.

"And you, officer Carpenter?" asked the Dane.

Kay leaned forward from the back seat.

"Me neither," she said.

"In that case," said Holgett, "I would be delighted to take you both on a tour of the city tonight and buy you dinner."

"It's kind of you," said Templeton, "but WDC Carpenter and I will be tied up tonight, perhaps another time."

Kay sunk back in her seat. She knew exactly what her boss meant.

CHAPTER 57

Grant and Sara checked into a small hotel in the downtown area of Malmo. Grant paid cash in advance for the double room and no questions were asked. They dined at a local Italian restaurant and returned to the hotel and went straight to bed and made love.

A few miles away above the Shamrock Bar a pot-bellied Irishman writhed in ecstasy as the woman who sat impaled on his short fat penis lashed him across the face with her pendulous breasts. She had blindfolded him and trying to catch her claw like nipples as they swung past and catching them in his teeth was one of his favourite games. It reminded him of bobbing for apples back in Ireland when he was a boy.

Across the water in a hotel in Copenhagen Kay Carpenter was administering a soap and water enema to her boss. He was handcuffed to the mixer valve in the bathroom and lay in the bath on his side.

Sara slept peacefully in Grant's arms dreaming of a new life in the tropics of Malaya.

Noel Geary heard Inga gasp and smiled broadly to himself at the thought of how one small Irishman could give such a strapping Viking girl so much pleasure. She was still impaled on him, but had stopped moving. He couldn't touch her because his hands were tied behind his back. Noel could feel the sticky warm wetness seeping across his groin.

"By all the saints, sure you are wetter than the Liffey itself down there. Tis like a flood."

Still no reply.

"Inga, will you stop messing with me, shagging is a serious business."

As he tried to raise his head from the pillow the blindfold which had protected him from the bloody horrors which were about to unfold was ripped from his head. There, still sitting astride him with a wide curtain of blood pumping from the gash across her throat was his beloved Inga. Her head was held back by her long black hair by an enormous Chinaman. He went to scream, but was not given the chance. A second man clamped a hand over his mouth making it difficult for him to breathe, the weight of his lifeless lover pinning him to the bed, her sightless eyes forlorn witness to his plight.

The little Irishman's struggles were futile.

"We do not want to kill you, we merely wish to ask you some questions," said the man whose hand was blocking Noel Geary's airwaves. He released the pressure and the bar owner sucked in a lung full of air. The other man holding the hair of his dead partner wrenched her off him and threw her crumpled blood-soaked body to the floor where she lay like a marionette with its strings cut. Noel had never felt more naked, more vulnerable in his life – a life he had convinced himself was about to end.

The Chinaman reached into his jacket pocket and produced two photographs, the first of a pretty teenage girl – Sara.

"Have you seen this girl?"

Noel shook his head.

"What about this man?" said the oriental inquisitor showing him a photo of Grant.

Noel looked hard at the image, his vision hampered by the sweat which drenched his forehead and dripped into his eyes.

"I don't know," he said "maybe."

The other man grabbed Geary's new flaccid penis and testicles and yanked them up with such force it lifted Geary's bottom off the bed. He screamed in pain.

"Look again," said his tormentor.

"He was here. He's trying to get away with the girl."

"Where are they now?"

Geary felt the grip tighten on his genitals.

"Please, please, I don't know. He said he would be back tomorrow lunch time."

"How were you getting them out of the country?" asked the Chinaman.

"A Russian coal ship," stammered Geary. "It leaves tomorrow night for Malaya. I bribed the captain."

"Is he bringing the girl here tomorrow?"

The sweat was now pouring off the Irishman.

"I don't know, he didn't say."

The Chinaman turned to his accomplice.

"We need them both. We can't take any chances." He turned back to Geary. "You will meet him tomorrow, but tell him there has been a change of plan. You will tell him that he and the girl must go to the address I am about to give you. Tell him there they will meet someone from the ship. They must be there by one o'clock. Do not open the bar tomorrow. Do not talk to anyone. My friend will remain here. If anything goes wrong and this man is alerted we will kill you. Do you understand?"

A terrified Geary nodded his head. As one Chinaman left the Irishman started sobbing. He wished he'd never left County Clare.

CHAPTER 58

Templeton and Kay Carpenter were having breakfast in the hotel when Rud Holgett arrived. The chief inspector wiped his mouth with the pink linen napkin to remove any flakes of croissant as the Dane approached.

"Good morning Chief Inspector, I hope you had a comfortable night."

Templeton almost smiled. "We had a shitty night, tied up most of the time, weren't we officer Carpenter?"

"Yes sir," she blushed.

"I'm sorry to hear that," said Holgett. "Perhaps the news I have will cheer you up. One of the crew members on the Malmo ferry has identified your man and the girl. They took the night sailing. We have contacted the Swedish police and they are conducting a search."

"How long will it take us to get there?" asked Templeton.

"We can be there within the hour," replied the Dane. Templeton got up from the table and brushed the crumbs from his grey two piece suit.

"Well, what are we waiting for, let's go."

It was 10am and Grant was up and dressed. Sara was still asleep. It was only a short walk to the Shamrock Bar – no more than 10 minutes. Grant wanted to make sure the Irishman had made all the necessary arrangements. As he opened the room door Sara woke up.

"Grant?"

"He looked across to her, this girl-woman who had turned his world upside down, who had given him such pleasure that had come with such inexorable pain; the desertion of his family, the killing of a man, a transition from successful businessman to fugitive. Yet for all that Grant had no control over the deep feelings he had for this wondrous creature. He crossed and sat on the edge of the bed they had shared. He put a hand on her cheek and she held it there with her own.

"I love you Sara Mattherson. Always remember that. I should be back in half an hour." He bent down and kissed her gently on the lips.

"Be careful," she implored. "I love you."

Grant arrived at Noel's bar to find it closed. He knocked on the glass fronted door. At a table inside sat a dishevelled and unshaven Noel Geary, a shadow of his former self. Concealed in the bar was the Chinaman holding a 9mm Smith and Wesson. He motioned for Geary to go to the door.

Grant knocked again. The Chinaman stepped back into the recess behind the bar so he couldn't be seen. Geary opened the door a few inches.

"It's me," said Grant.

For a split second Geary thought about taking his chances and making a run for it, but knew he would be dead before he got through the door. The sight of Inga with her throat cut so severely her head was almost severed still tormented him.

God forgive me, he thought as he opened the door and let Grant inside.

"Tis a grand fine day that it is," mimicked Grant. "I have your money." He reached into his jacket and produced the envelope Sara had handed him at the hotel.

"£5,000, it's all there."

The Irishman shuffled back to the table where he had been sitting and picked up two passports and false identity papers and handed them to Grant.

"If you don't mind me saying, you look bloody awful. Either Inga's getting on top of you or you should take more water with the Old Paddy."

"There's been a change of plan," he told Grant. "You and the girl have to meet someone from the ship at this address, St Christian's Church just off Lilla Torget at one o'clock. He pushed the piece of paper into the breast pocket of Grant's jacket.

"They will take the photographs needed to complete the passports and seamen union cards."

Grant took his hand and shook it warmly.

"I can't thank you enough, my friend." He noticed the man was now wearing his Rolex watch.

"I hope it keeps good time for you," he said and let himself out.

Noel sat back down at the table, the envelope in his hand. He didn't hear the Chinaman behind him, didn't hear the hushed explosion of air as the 9mm shell left the silencer. The bullet entered the back of the Irishman's cranium piercing the occipital lobe passing through the auditory cortex and exiting through the right eye which popped like an egg in a microwave leaving the optical nerve dangling on his cheek. He slumped forward onto the table. The Chinaman picked up the envelope containing the money and left.

Sara was dressed and ready when Grant got back to the hotel. He threw the passports onto the bed and hugged her.

"A new identity, a new life," he said. "When we get to Malaya we'll disappear and nobody will ever find us."

"As long as we are together," she sighed.

Chief Inspector Templeton, Kay Carpenter and Inspector Rud Holgett were in the Malmo police headquarters when the message came in. Inspector Kurt Amueller took the call. When he had finished he turned to his visitors.

"It seems we may have found your fugitives. The body of a man and a woman have been found in a bar down by the docks. The girl has had her throat cut and the man has been shot through the head so most of his face is missing."

Templeton stood up.

"How do you know it's them?" he asked.

Amueller reached for his coat. "We don't, but the man is wearing a Rolex watch with the name Grant Campbell engraved on the back. Shall we go?"

Grant and Sara could hear the police sirens minutes after they had checked out of the hotel. They turned into the doorway of a jeweller's shop as a car carrying the British detectives raced past. It was 12.50.

"Do you think they are on to us?" asked Sara keeping a tight grip on Grant's arm.

"I doubt it," said Grant reassuringly. "They are probably late for their lunch."

Two armed Swedish police guarded the entrance to the Shamrock bar. Both came to attention when the car pulled up and they recognised Inspector Amueller.

"What have we got?" he asked.

"Two bodies, sir," replied the officer, "the man downstairs in the bar and the girl upstairs. Nothing has been touched."

They entered the bar and were drawn to the limp form of Noel Geary slumped over the table, his head resting in a pool of thick viscous dark blood garnished with pieces of grey membrane and shards of white bone. Some of the blood spilled off the table and dripped onto the tiled floor. Templeton went to pick up the dead man's wrists to look at the watch.

"May I?" he asked. He turned the watch over. Inscribed on the back was the name Grant Campbell. He lifted the dead man's head off the table and looked at what was left of the face. Kay Carpenter wretched and aborted the continental breakfast she had eaten earlier.

"Let's take a look at the girl."

A young policeman led them upstairs to the bedroom where the bloodied body of Inga lay.

"Does that look like a 15-year-old girl to any of you?" asked Templeton. He turned and went back downstairs.

"Is there any other identity on the body?" he asked.

"No, only this, a piece of paper in his shirt pocket," said one of the officers and handed Templeton a piece of paper. On it was a note, St Christian's Church, Lily Torget 1pm. Templeton looked at his watch. It was two minutes past one already.

Grant hadn't needed to look at the piece of paper Noel Geary had tucked into his jacket pocket. He could remember the address. Had he checked the note he would have read the little Irishman's warning that the meeting was a trap.

Grant looked around the 16th century square filled with half-timbered houses adorned with hanging baskets of flowers. In a side road off to the left he saw the church.

"Come on," he said and took Sara by the hand and led her up the stone steps leading to the arched doorway.

"I hate churches," said Sara. "After daddy died I vowed never to go in to a church again."

"Not even to marry me?" said Grant. "Come on."

He squeezed her hand and pushed open the heavy oak door. A rush of cold air greeted them along with an impenetrable silence. The floor was tiled all the way up to the altar, the red and black pattern only broken by the inlaid marble tombstones. At the end of the aisle directly in front of them was a high altar, behind which were two rows of choral pews. The walls were pale cream with gothic stained glass windows on either side. The ceiling was heavily timbered, microphones hung from the rafters on spidery cables.

"It's beautiful," whispered Sara.

Grant and Sara hand in hand took their first steps down the aisle together – their first and their last.

Out of the corner of his eye Grant caught a fleeting glance of a black object hurtling towards him before it struck him to the ground. He tried desperately to cling on to Sara, but she was snatched from his grip. His head hit the floor and the coldness of the tiles numbed his face. In dream-like vision he saw Sara being dragged across the floor by two large oriental looking men. One was punching her in the face, the other ripping her jeans off. Behind as a backcloth to this ethereal nightmare the large gold cross glinted on the altar flanked by two candlesticks.

Grant summoned every ounce of reserve from his body and managed to haul himself onto his hands and knees. With an arm outstretched he began to crawl forward towards Sara. Then the black shape came again and he felt a blow to the back of his head.

The pain was no longer intense. A heavy boot crashed into the side of his face and he could hear bone splinter, it echoed around the empty chamber of his head. One eye was completely closed, his whole head swollen like a ripe melon. Through the half closed slit of the other eye he could make out the form of the attackers. They had turned her onto her front and splayed her legs into a wishbone. The larger of the two men was kneeling on her arms, pressing her head onto the cold tiles. Spade like hands were on her buttocks tearing the flesh apart. The other man, crazed with excitement shifted on his knees to get a better position between her thighs. He sobs were quiet now, more like a child's whimper. Then she screamed a scream so loud as to disturb every tormented soul in Hell as the attacker drove the full length of his member into her. That's when Grant blacked out.

Sara's scream penetrated the 400 year-old oak doors and the police in the patrol cars which pulled up outside instantly drew their weapons – Uzi automatics.

Templeton, Holgett, Amueller and Kay Carpenter arrived seconds later. Amueller drew a 9mm Beretta from his shoulder holster and motioned for his men to move forward. Two armed officers burst through the church doors. The Chinese man pinning Sara down reached for his gun, but was sent reeling backwards by the force of seven bullets to his chest and throat. The man raping Sara too reached for his gun, but was hit by fire from two of the Swedish officers. His gun was sent spinning from his hand by a spray of bullets two of which caught him under the chin and sent pieces of scalp flying into the next five rows of pews.

The cacophony of gunfire ceased and the smell of cordite and the pall of smoke settled on the sacrilegious tableaux.

Sara, whimpering, bleeding, crawled across the aisle to where Grant lay, unashamed by her partial nakedness.

Kay Carpenter took off her coat and rushed over to cover up the teenager. Sara cradled Grant's bloodied grotesque head in her small hands and kissed him gently, her tears streaming onto his lifeless form.

She looked up pathetically at the detectives.

"He tried to save me," she wailed. "He loved me. He really loved me."

Kay lifted the teenager to her feet. Sara turned and looked up the aisle to the altar where the gold cross glinted in the sunlight.

EPILOGUE

It rained the day of the funeral. It was a small family affair held at St Andrew's Church, Hampstead. Jill and the four children all dressed in black stood in solemn silence as the coffin was lowered into the ground. The children wept openly, huddled together bound by their grief. The other mourners included Grant's parents and his partner from the advertising agency. Chief Inspector Doug Templeton and Kay Carpenter also attended. They had helped make the arrangements to have Grant's body flown home. Two hundred miles away in Yorkshire, Liz Mattherson was recovering in a drug rehabilitation centre.

As the funeral cortege left the cemetery a black limo pulled through the gates. The two detectives watched from the shelter of their unmarked car as a heavy set chauffeur opened the rear door. Tom Cody climbed out. He reached back inside and produced a pair of metal crutches. From the other side of the car emerged Sara dressed in black trousers, boots and a black raincoat.

The chauffeur offered her an umbrella which she refused. She took Tom's arm and walked across to the grave.

"It must have been a blow not being able to attend the service," said Kay Carpenter looking out of the rain splattered windscreen of her car.

"Would you have wanted her there at your husband's funeral?" asked Templeton.

"I wonder what will happen to her now?" said the woman detective.

Templeton shifted in his seat.

"She's young she'll build a new life for herself. She's a very wealthy young woman. Her mother confessed to changing the will, which means she will inherit everything."

"Have the drug squad boys come up with anything on the Chinese connection?" asked Kay.

Templeton gave an indignant grunt.

"They recovered £2million of heroin and cocaine from Alan Mattherson's property, but they'll never get anywhere with the Triads. It looks like they were going to use Mattherson Industries to smuggle drugs all over the world using their canning factories and would have done too had the girl's father not stopped them. They will just go somewhere else. It looks as though they finished Alan Mattherson off in the hospital. The autopsy showed a large concentration of opiate poisoning in his system. It's a trademark Triad killing."

Tom bowed his head and gazed at his friend's open grave. Sara knelt in front of him looking at the walnut coffin, tears staining her young face. She turned and looked up at Tom.

"Please can I have a minute alone with him?" she asked. Tom stifled back his own tears. "I'll wait back at the car," he said.

Sara could see part of the gold cross on the coffin lid. She couldn't bear to think of Grant lying there all alone. He would be so cold without her next to him to keep him warm.

"You said you would never leave me." The tears flowed. "I don't know what to do without you. I need you now more than ever." She thought about their brief time together. She remembered the day she first saw him in the hotel swimming pool. She remembered their magical kiss on the beach and the feel of his strong arms around her. She remembered how vulnerable he had been, how he made her laugh, how he had taught her the beauty of lovemaking, how he had saved her from drowning. Now he was dead. He had given up his world for her, but was unable to share the new life he had created inside her. She would not have to cope alone. She was two months pregnant with their child. She only found out when she was taken to hospital after the attack. The doctors had offered her an abortion because of her age, but Sara wouldn't hear of it. She knew they would have a son and he would grow up to be like his father. Soon she would have him back by her side.

THE END

www.ingramcontent.com/pod-product-compliance
Lightning Source LLC
Chambersburg PA
CBHW060605310726
48982CB00008B/1246/J

* 9 7 8 1 8 3 8 4 9 6 7 2 2 *